Supermodel Fabiola Crow is often the center of attention at this spring's crop of weddings, but never the bride. She's always in the company of Ethan Warrick, but says they're just pals. "Just buddies," she insists. "We're neither one of us the marrying kind."

Up in Vancouver, I hear Grace Madison, wedding planner with Engaging Events, has the unique opportunity of planning her *own parents'* remarriage. Mom and Dad are going through with it, despite the efforts of her mother's divorce lawyer, Noah Burnside, who seems to have eyes only for Grace....

And then there's the wedding that didn't happen. Bill Thornton's bride, his secretary, Jessica Warren, had second thoughts just minutes before the ceremony was to begin last week. I hear Jessie took off to parts unknown, and Bill dispatched his best man, and best friend, Liam Malone, to bring her back. Now, that Malone is one handsome devil....

Stella Cameron is the bestselling author of more than fifty books, and possesses the unique talent of being able to switch effortlessly from historical to contemporary fiction. In a one-year period, her titles appeared more than eight times on the *USA Today* bestseller list. This British-born author was working as an editor in London when she met her husband, an officer in the American air force, at a party. He asked her to dance, and they've been together ever since. They now make their home in Seattle, are the parents of three grown children and have recently become grandparents.

Bobby Hutchinson is a multitalented woman who was born in a small town in the interior of British Columbia. Though she is now the successful author of more than thirty-five novels, her past includes stints as a retailer, a seamstress and a day-care worker. Twice married, she now lives alone and is the devoted mother of three and grandmother of four. She runs, swims, does yoga, meditates and likes this quote by Dolly Parton: "Decide who you are, and then do it on purpose."

Sandra Marton wrote her first story when she was seven years old, and began to dream of becoming a writer. Today she is the author of more than thirty novels, the winner of the Holt Medallion for Best Single Title and the *Romantic Times* Reviewer's Choice Award—twice—for Best Harlequin Presents of the Year. The mother of two grown sons, Sandra lives with her husband in a quiet corner of Connecticut, where she alternates between extravagant bouts of gourmet cooking and take-out pizza.

STELLA CAMERON
Bobby Hutchinson
Sandra Marton

MARRIED IN SPRING

TORONTO • NEW YORK • LONDON
AMSTERDAM • PARIS • SYDNEY • HAMBURG
STOCKHOLM • ATHENS • TOKYO • MILAN • MADRID
PRAGUE • WARSAW • BUDAPEST • AUCKLAND

ISBN 0-373-83461-6

MARRIED IN SPRING

Copyright © 2001 by Harlequin Books S.A.

The publisher acknowledges the copyright holders
of the individual titles as follows:

WE DO!
Copyright © 2001 by Stella Cameron

ENGAGING EVENTS
Copyright © 2001 by Bobby Hutchinson

MALONE'S VOW
Copyright © 2001 by Sandra Myles

Visit us at www.eHarlequin.com

Printed in U.S.A.

CONTENTS

WE DO!

Stella Cameron

CHAPTER ONE

January

FABIOLA CROW WAS PLANNING something wrong, something deceptive, and the possibility that she would forever regret it was so high she felt sick with fear. She was also excited to her toes, wobbly, giddy. If she pulled this off...she had to pull it off.

What she wanted wasn't really wrong, just the way she intended to get it. At least, she supposed it was. She wanted the brass ring and it was tough to reach as long as she clung to her safety net. Ethan Warrick was her friend, her rock. If her plan backfired she'd lose him and never so much as touch the brass ring.

Through the glass wall of the master bathroom in her lakefront town house condo, Fab saw a pale sun finally struggle clear of heavy cloud, only to start sinking behind the Olympic Mountains. Winter in the Northwest didn't mean what it did in most places. Here the new year uncurled very slowly and could take until mid-May to pass through a cold spring and into the start of summer.

Fab shivered in her damp cycling gear. The little town of Kirkland was a suburb of Seattle and wet went with the whole territory. Snow covered the mountains. The sun shot a gold profile along peaks and ravines, and sent a slick track of silver across Lake Washington. Almost instantly the track disappeared like faded lightning and any sign of the sun was gone.

She loved this place, and the life she'd carved with few advantages to help her on her way. Fabiola Crow, supermodel. She'd been riding on top of her professional wave for several years and could give it all up tomorrow, never work another day in her life, and never want for anything—except Ethan Warrick.

If there were another way to change the way he thought of her she'd have found it by now. Her twin sister Polly's husband, Nasty—his lifelong nickname—Ferrito, together with Dusty Miller, an older buddy of Nasty's from his navy SEAL days, and Ethan Warrick—also an ex-SEAL—were partners in a marine business. And for two years she'd waited for Ethan to show even a hint that being her best friend wasn't enough for him. She'd waited for him to give her one tiny sign that he thought of her as more than a good pal who could hold her own against him in a tennis game, and keep up with him on a bike, be no more than half a mile behind him when they ran, someone who loved good food and didn't need to fill every silence with words.

Nothing.

Not a thing.

"Fab, you're something," he'd say. "I don't know another guy who's lucky enough to have someone like you. We do everything so well together, but we don't make any demands."

Once she'd abandoned caution and said, "One day you'll marry, Ethan. Maybe sooner rather than later. Things will have to change then."

"No way," he'd said, catching her in a one-armed bear hug that felt so good it made her heart hurt. "I'm never going to change. And neither will you, buddy. You're not the marrying kind, either, or you'd have done it by now."

He wouldn't let her repeat her thanks for having stopped a jealous man from beating her, or for dealing with an attempt on his own life afterward. What happened within weeks of their first meeting had sealed a friendship based on trust, but it had also seemed to close the door on romance.

Already barefoot, Fab faced the windows directly and stripped off her biking tights and top. She reached back to unhook her bra, but for once didn't enjoy the sensation when her breasts were free. Instead she looked down at herself, and kept on looking when she hopped from foot to foot, removing her panties.

She was thirty. Just. Her body hadn't changed

noticeably, but why would it? She worked out every day. And she'd never had a baby....

Darn it, she did feel sorry for herself, and not because she thought she was getting so old she should worry about having a family in a hurry. But she did want babies. She wanted to run along the Kirkland waterfront pushing a stroller, and sit by the lake telling her child about the ducks. And there ought to be a big, shaggy dog that went swimming, then climbed out and shook himself all over them while they laughed.

But Fab Crow had to be picky, she had to limit herself to wanting only one man in the entire universe and he wasn't the marrying kind. Oh, yeah, and she did want to have babies *and* be married. Who'd a'thunk it? Fab the free spirit, object of speculation in every magazine in the U.S. and most other countries, the face on a thousand covers, her name linked with those of a dozen wealthy, successful men, and underneath it all she longed for a husband and children, for home and hearth—and as much anonymity as she could grab.

Why wasn't he the marrying kind? Could she be sure he wasn't? What had been the strongest hint? Probably that Ethan liked to tell her it was wonderful to be around a woman who didn't try to change him, who didn't take anything about him for granted, a woman who didn't *need* him. Pretty good hint there, but being Ms. Perfection was wearing Fab out.

A sharp bang stilled her racing mind. She listened.

She shuddered again and slapped her hands over her ears. The distant tinkling of bells sounded, the one that only came when she was around Ethan. She didn't have time to worry about it. There was no turning back now.

From the shower off the guest room next door came a sound like air thumping in pipes. Or it could be a fist thumping something.

Pipes. Fab knew what she was hearing.

The bells were there again, and the rubbery sensation, but nevertheless she smiled, actually grinned and felt completely wicked, like a kid who had pulled off a prank. That sensation didn't last long. She hadn't pulled off a thing yet. Absolute terror and the instinct to flee followed, to fling on her robe and race through the condo to the kitchen, which was as far from the bedrooms as possible.

Ethan said something in the other bathroom. The soundproofing was too good for Fab to know what it was. Probably a single curse word.

She wrapped herself in a bath sheet and pulled the band from the ponytail she'd worn under her helmet for their long Saturday ride.

This was all going to backfire, or at least come to nothing. Just because she'd convinced herself she knew what he would do when the guest shower wouldn't work didn't mean she was right.

The door to her bathroom swung open.

I was right, I do know the way he thinks.

Fab dropped her towel and turned toward the shower.

Ethan had slammed the door behind him and taken several steps before his irritation at there being no water in the guest shower cleared, and he saw Fabiola staring at him over her shoulder. His expression became one of awareness and indecision.

She glanced from his reddening face to her towel, and back again.

Ethan glanced at a lot of things before he looked at the ceiling—as if that would either put her clothes on or give them both amnesia—and said, "Damn it, Fab, I'm sorry. The other shower isn't working."

He wore a towel around his waist and if the towel tried to join Fab's on the floor it wouldn't make it past the impressive peg Ethan must be unable to ignore. Fab decided silence was her best weapon. After all, wasn't she the one whose privacy had been invaded? She gave his towel another covert peek. Sheesh, it was a wonder there was enough blood still in his head for him to blush with.

And he hadn't left yet....

"You said you were going to put something in the oven before you showered," he told her. Oh, yeah, Ethan did have the manly trait of wanting to make sure blame was properly placed. "And your bedroom door was open. Your clothes aren't on your bed. I didn't hear a thing in here, so I thought I could be in and out before you came.''

It's my fault, Ethan, it really is. Only she wasn't going to tell him she'd hoped this would happen. "Don't worry," she said, clearing her throat as if she'd just unfrozen her tongue. "We're both big people."

With that she reached in to turn on both heads in the huge shower built to her specification. It sloped and needed no doors. With a smile at the gaping Ethan, Fab stepped in. "We're old buddies. Use the other end."

He crossed his arms and bowed his head.

Fab's heart and stomach leaped around in unison. Guilt almost made her confess her sins and tell him...tell him she *loved* him. He was honorable, darn it, and what she was doing wasn't. She didn't need medical training to figure out that his body had already let him know what it wanted, and that he had to be strong willed to remain standing where he was, but she was glad, actually thrilled at what she'd accomplished. Thrilled and scared. She had a history of succumbing to guilt and spilling the beans in the end. If she did so this time, she'd be saying goodbye to the buddy she loved.

She put shampoo on her hair and hoped he didn't sense that she was trembling. She closed her eyes against the lather that ran down her face, her neck and between her breasts. When she'd rinsed, and she opened her eyes again, it was to find Ethan looking directly at her. His expression was something she'd never seen before.

Ethan was angry. He was angry, incredibly aroused, and incredibly confused. Fabiola was a very tall woman, but Ethan was considerably taller and this evening his presence felt overpowering. He was as dark haired and dark eyed as she was blond and blue eyed. Women stared at him, but more because he was striking than handsome. If they saw what Fab was seeing now they'd stare, too.

His towel came off with a snap and he threw it aside. Turning his back to her, he got into the shower and stood under the water. He braced his weight with both hands against gray stone tile.

"I felt sticky," Fab said tentatively. "I decided I had to shower before starting dinner."

"It was my turn to make dinner," he said. "I should have insisted on going to my place."

She forced a laugh. "You tried. I'm headstrong."

"No, you're not. You just aren't a pushover when you want something."

No kidding. Pale against the rest of his skin, he had the best toned buns she recalled seeing. And with Ethan where he was right now, it would be so easy to lean against his back and rest her cheek on his shoulder, wrap her arms around him and touch him in places that ought to make him forget all about being so strong.

That was a move she must not make.

"This was never supposed to happen," Ethan said. "It's scaring the hell out of me."

Fabiola dropped the soap.

"You do know you're incredible, don't you?" He straightened but didn't turn around. "Of course you do. That's why you are who you are."

"What I am," she said quietly. "It's not who I am, Ethan."

"You know what I'm saying. You can't walk along a street without heads turning. Everyone knows who you are. You're the most lovely woman I've ever seen. You're unforgettable. I'm one more man. But I like the way we are with each other. What we've got is special. I like that, too, but to keep it we both know there's a line we don't cross."

"Damn it, no one's making me stay here. I blundered in, I can walk out, can't I?"

"Yes."

He started to turn off his showerhead.

"But you might as well finish. I've splashed soap on you. Anyway, it's a bit late for modesty."

"True," he said, pulling his big shoulders back. "You're absolutely right." And he faced her.

Fab retrieved the soap.

"We've never even kissed," Ethan said. "Not

even in fun. Under-the-mistletoe fun. Know why?''

She shook her head. ''Not really.''

''Because I knew you wouldn't want it, and because I knew I'd want more.'' He ran his hands over his face. ''I'm doing a lousy job of digging myself out of this.''

Fab had to open her mouth to breathe. Was he going to say what she wanted to hear?

''We've never kissed but we're showering together. I'm just a man. And I'm not in control right now. One of us had better get the hell out of here.''

''Turn around,'' Fab said.

''Huh?''

''You think too much. *Turn* around. I'm going to wash your back. And we aren't going to allow a little change in our routine to stand between us.''

Shaking his head, he dropped his arms and Fab did look away then.

She'd fallen in love with the man, with who he was inside. Of course she had liked the way he looked, but being with him like this made her ache with arousal. In time a man and a woman moved into their own intimate world. They got there by way of kissing and petting, of foreplay that led to making love and maybe showering together and finding dozens of ways, spontaneous and designed, to make love again and again. At least, that was the way Fab saw it. What she had engineered tonight was an arrival at the finish line without ever seeing the starting blocks.

His hands framing her face, turning it up toward his, made her jump. The feel of his fingers against her scalp, his palms beneath her cheekbones and across her ears, was one more first. Fab smiled at him and tried to make that smile reassuringly meaningless, as if they were not both aware that whatever did or didn't happen now, they *had* crossed the line Ethan spoke of.

"If I didn't know better," she said with a laugh, "I'd think you were shy."

He looked at her mouth. "I'm not shy."

She just bet he wasn't. "Neither am I. As a model, I can't be."

Something flickered in his expression, tightened as if he were irritated. "Well, why not have my back washed by *the* Fabiola Crow. It'll make quite a story if I ever have anyone I want to tell." He faced the wall again.

The soap was getting mushy. Fab rubbed it over his back and replaced it in the holder. She massaged his shoulders with her fingertips, swept the flats of her hands inward and down his spine, then back to rub his sides. It was Ethan's turn to shudder. Thorough in her job, Fab retraced the path upward to his neck before returning to the level of his waist. He didn't carry any extra poundage on his body and it felt as if the skin had been laid directly over muscle and bone. There was a lot of muscle.

Intensely aware of even the smallest move, she let the heels of her hands skim below his waist while her fingertips rested on his hips. Ethan jerked and bent forward, allowed the water to beat down and rinse his back.

And his derriere collided with Fab's belly.

He made a noise and stumbled immediately out of the shower. Facing away from her, he scrubbed at his hair and eyes with a hand towel. Evidently he'd decided he didn't care if he put clothes on over a layer of soap.

She wouldn't let him see her cry—even out of self-pity. He'd blame himself for that, too, and he'd already suffered too much because she was selfish. "I'm sorry," she muttered, and let water pound on her head.

Minutes passed while Fab kept her eyes lowered.

Ethan didn't leave. She could see his feet—long, well-shaped feet with a smattering of dark hair on top, to match the dark hair on his very tanned legs. It didn't seem to matter whether it was summer or winter, Ethan was tanned. Fab always wore strong sunblock and covered as much of her fair skin as she could without melting.

Even if he'd touched her, Fabiola couldn't have been more aware of his presence. Slowly she looked up. With his right hand curled into a fist, tapping it repeatedly against his mouth, Ethan's eyes seemed to study some part of her legs. The study session was moving upward. Her thighs, her hips. He swallowed hard enough for her to see his throat move.

There was no way to control her response to him. She pressed her thighs together and quivered. A piercing sensation passed through her, sweet and oh, so dangerous in its implications.

Her stomach was now the object of his fascinated stare. He didn't seem to have as much as an inkling that she was observing him. If he slowed his progression even more, Fabiola might sink to her knees and pass out. Already she felt lightheaded. Didn't he sense that she'd been under the water long enough to turn her into a white prune? Cute. That should be a really appealing picture.

Ethan had reached her ribs, which meant...yes, now he was staring fixedly at her breasts. She guessed it was one thing to all but see something in a deliberately posed shot in a magazine and quite something else to look at the flesh itself. For an instant, while she considered how photographs were supposed to vastly improve on nature, she smiled and wondered if she was coming up short in his eyes.

Then she saw him take a deep, shaky breath and figured she had her answer, and if anything he was even more erect—difficult to imagine.

Their eyes met.

No man should feel so much longing mixed with such haunted indecision.

Enough, Fab thought. She looked away and reached to turn off the faucet.

"Don't do that." Ethan's harsh order shocked her into stillness. He stepped back in the shower. "Unless you tell me to get out of here, I'm not going anywhere."

There were no words at all, none that she had any hope of actually speaking aloud.

With a hand beneath each of her arms, he pushed her back against the tile. Her nipples were already erect, but feeling his intimate touch made them tingle and turn hard.

"Talk to me, Fab. Do I stay, or do I go?"

She couldn't talk to him, but she managed to smile, knowing he would take it for the response he wanted. Closing his eyes, he rested his forehead on hers and the faint softening of his features made her want to cry, yet again. Perhaps this was only about sex. Of course that's what it was. But that didn't mean there couldn't be a way to lead him through wanting her this way to wanting her in every way—all the time. That had been the gamble she took.

Ethan dipped his head and kissed her. The mouth that could look so harshly made met hers gently, brushed, with skin barely meeting skin, slowly from side to side.

Fabiola only had one repeating thought—*I love*

you. A moment more and even that blurred. She wound her arms around his neck. He played his fingers over her shoulder blades and settled his thumbs on the sides of her breasts, and the kiss went on and on, and deeper and deeper. They were breathless, gasping, and still they kissed, twisting the angles of their faces, finding every sweet, erotic contact.

At last Ethan paused long enough to look at her and he seemed changed: fevered, driven, possessive. They kissed again and this time his thumbs came together at her waist with his hands spread wide, and moved to settle beneath her breasts, then to cover them.

"Fab," she heard him say, and he repeated her name several times, leaning against her, his hardness pressing her stomach. His skin, the textures of him, fascinated her and she sought every inch she could reach. This was her friend, the man she'd known so well for two years, yet had not known at all as he was now. Inside she trembled.

Making a sodden rope of her shoulder-length hair, he used it to pull her head back. The kisses he placed along the length of her neck were short and firm. When he kissed her breasts, it was with tender urgency. Urgency alone described his touch between her legs. Her cry of release came almost instantly.

Dark hair glistened on the back of his still-bowed head. Fabiola urged herself even closer to him, plucking at his shoulders, trying to make him understand that she wanted him inside her without having to say the words.

Ethan raised his head and searched her face and said yet again, "Fab?" But the question was definitely there this time. She bit her lip and nodded.

For an instant he paused and seemed about to draw back. Fab understood and managed to smile. "It's okay," she said. "Pills."

His expression became inscrutable. He held her thighs and lifted her as if she were a small woman, something she'd never been. Fab clung to him, watched when her breasts were level with his face and he pressed his lips to them again. But at the same time he found what he sought and lowered her until she knew they were completely joined, and she had, once again, to fight tears.

Without prompting, she wrapped her legs around him and crossed her ankles on his solid butt.

How could something so wonderful be sad as well as sweet?

They moved together as naturally as if they had been together like this a thousand times. Ethan pushed her face into his neck and kept his forearms between her and the tile. Even now he worried about hurting her.

"Ah. Oh, Fab." His head fell back, revealing clenched teeth, and pulsing veins at his temples.

Imagining the strength it had to take to hold the weight of them both, to expend such sexual energy without falling to his knees, overwhelmed her. Her own legs felt like water, or maybe rubber, soft rubber.

The rush of his climax brought her unbelievable joy. He was too often uptight and right now, before her eyes, she watched him relax, smile faintly before he nuzzled her face.

Very carefully, he lowered her until her toes touched the bottom of the shower, but when he started to step back, she began to slip downward and he held her up. And that was when the other expression gradually took over. A frightening, intense darkness. His lips parted as if he would say something, but he remained silent while he watched her—all wariness and concern.

"It's still hot," he said at last, testing the water, and placing her squarely beneath the jet. He handed her a bar of soap and said, "You are generous, unbelievably generous. And you're more than beautiful."

"Ethan?" He looked at her, but she found she didn't remember what she'd intended to say. She began to wash, again, while he turned the other showerhead back on and did the same thing—very rapidly.

He cranked his water off, slicked back his hair and stepped quickly out.

"Ethan?"

His ears were assaulted by a furious rubbing

with a towel. He didn't show any sign that he'd heard her.

Dread speeded Fab's heart. "Gathering of the clan at Dusty's tomorrow," she said, as lightly as she could. It sounded out of place, foolish. "Should be fun to be with Polly and Nasty's kids."

He was distracted as if the perfunctory toweling he gave himself took concentration. "Uh-huh."

"Shall we bike over?"

"I'll let you know." He took a dry bath sheet and wrapped it around him. She noticed a short but very deep scar just beneath his ribs but this wasn't the time to ask about it.

Fab said, "Fine," although the word nearly choked her. "If you've got something else on, Dusty won't mind. He's easy about those things, thank goodness."

"Yeah. I'd better go and get dressed."

"Sure." She turned off her own showerhead. "And I'd better get out to the kitchen before I burn something."

Seconds passed in which he visibly fought with himself over what to say. Then, abruptly, he told her, "I just remembered something," and struck his brow with the heel of a hand. "I've got an appointment, damn it. I have to run if I'm going to make it. Forgive me, please, but I won't stay for dinner. Bye, Fab. See you."

She was left clinging to the faucet to stop herself from falling. And the bells did far more than tinkle.

THE FIRST THING ETHAN NOTICED when he walked through the door of Dusty Miller's yellow house and into its yellow interior, to the big room off the kitchen, was that Fabiola wasn't there.

"Hey, Ethan," Nasty Ferrito called, coming to slap palms and apply a bone-crushing grip. Nasty grinned but never stopped chewing his gum. "We were getting worried about you two."

You two. "I got hung up. Guess who stopped by. The guy who thinks we should give him a quantity discount if he buys two of anything. *Sunday,* and he stopped by my home."

Polly and Nasty's boy, Bobby—Nasty had adopted Polly's son after their marriage—slammed in from the side yard where the dock into the lake started. At ten, he was entering the stringbean phase, all arms and legs. "We gotta have some of those Jet Skis, Nasty," he said, and went to his side. "They are so cool."

"Don't fit my image," Nasty said. "We're the guys in the black wet suits and the black Zodiacs, remember?"

"Yeah, yeah," Bobby said, no longer impressed. "IBS, right? Inflatable boat small. I'm gonna be a SEAL when I grow up."

"No, you're not," Polly said sharply.

Bobby knew when to hold his tongue. When he

noticed Ethan, he looked around. "Where's Aunt Fab?"

"You know women," Ethan said, having decided since the previous evening that he knew absolutely nothing about them—or about himself.

His comment hung out there while his friends narrowed their eyes and waited for him to finish whatever he intended to say. Ethan had nothing else to say. "Will you look at you, Venus?" he said to Polly and Fab's mother. "Terrific. How do you do it?"

That got him a scowl from Venus of the curly red hair, magnificent makeup and ever more outrageous wardrobe. "You mean how do I manage to look as if I'm still breathing when I'm such an old bag I ought to be in a nursing home—or six feet under?" she asked. "Easy. I've got to *do it* or lose this man of mine." She put a hand under Dusty's arm. "He's a fast one. I have to run to keep up, I can tell you." Venus taught belly dancing at a center in nearby Bellevue and the clothes were appropriate.

Dusty, mid-sixties, wiry and white haired, only had eyes for Venus.

"You know I didn't mean that," Ethan said, rolling his eyes. He sat on the couch. "Sometimes a man can't win."

"I heard you arrive, Ethan," Polly Ferrito said, coming from the kitchen with her face flushed from heat. "Where's Fab?"

Ethan had an urge to shout, *Leave me alone, damn it. I don't know where she is and I'm worried out of my mind.* Instead he said, "I had to rush away without making final plans yesterday. I rang her bell on my way here but she didn't answer so I thought I'd better come ahead on my own." He wondered if that sounded as weak to them as it did to him.

The front doorbell rang.

"There she is," Nasty said. "I'll go." He left the room and Ethan didn't miss the way his wife watched him. He'd like a woman to look at him like that. Oh, shove it and tell the truth—he'd like Fabiola to look at him like that, as if she could hardly wait to get his clothes off.

"That's not Fab," Dusty said. "She doesn't ring the bell, she comes in."

Ethan saw Polly's frown but pretended not to. "Where's that beautiful baby Anne? I feel like a cuddle." Did he ever, and much as he loved the Ferritos' eighteen-month-old angel, the hug he needed was from Fab—if she ever came within arm's reach of him again.

"Anne's sleeping," Dusty said shortly. He wore a frown as deep as a crevasse and sat down beside Ethan. He dropped his voice. "What the hell's going on here? You and Fab always come to these things together. You two have a dustup?"

"No. Of course we didn't. Fab and I have never had an argument."

"Arguments are healthy if they're handled right. No two people agree all the time. And she's never failed to show up when she's said she's coming," Dusty said. "So excuse me if I'm off balance and suspicious. That girl has a heart of gold. Venus couldn't have had a kid who didn't. And you look like hell. Total hell. Did you sleep last night? Don't answer that. I can see you didn't. Fess up. What the—petunia did you do? Make a clumsy move on her and scare her? It's time you quit just drinking coffee with her, or whatever you do, time you took a good look and really saw each other. But if you made her unhappy, I'll beat you senseless."

Ethan was tired. He didn't point out that Dusty would put up a good fight for a man closer to seventy than sixty, but he wouldn't win—not that Ethan was about to fight with his old friend. "I don't think I'm cut out for civilian life. Maybe I'll reup for active duty," he said. "I've got some good years in me yet and I don't think being in is as dangerous to the health as being out."

"Sure. Sign up and leave Fab behind. Look at me." When Ethan didn't, Dusty said, "I said *look* at me, you big oaf. You and Fab are good together."

"Do you think I don't know that?" Ethan wondered how Dusty would feel about yesterday's unexpected bonus. Probably be thrilled. Hell, Ethan was thrilled. He couldn't keep his mind on anything except how much he wanted to be with Fab again. But those things could go wrong and they'd built a firm foundation for something really special. Occasionally she still tried to give him a laurel wreath for tearing that crazy man off her a couple of years back. She didn't even know he'd then had to follow the guy while he dogged her, just to make sure she didn't get hurt. But she had known about the attempt on Ethan's life. And he knew she made a habit of clearing her social plate almost entirely for him. When she wasn't working, she put him first. No woman had ever done that. Hell, no one had ever done that, period. But she had the kind of career most people only imagined and it was Number One in her life. He couldn't fight that, but he would fight the prospect of losing her altogether.

He slid deeper into the couch. Of course she was on the pill. She would never risk a pregnancy when it could change her body. He had no right to feel angry about that, yet he did. Maybe the anger stemmed from the fact that she obviously wasn't on the pill because she'd expected something sexual to develop between them.

"I'll have some fast talking to do if you blab about me saying this, but we all care about you— not that you deserve it." Dusty rushed his words. "And we care about Fab. We haven't had a wedding around here in too long."

Ethan looked sideways at Dusty.

Dusty frowned at his knobby, laced hands.

"Stay out of my business," Ethan said quietly and with as much control as he could muster. "Thanks for the friendship, but stay out of the personal stuff. What you're getting close to is way out of line, even for you. Didn't I tell you that the last time you raised the subject?"

Dusty fidgeted beside him. "You're a disrespectful pain in the ass, know that? Remember who trained you out of diapers when you came into the platoon. I could whup you then, and I can whup you now. I know a few tricks I don't teach anyone—just in case I need a little element of surprise."

"Language," Ethan said.

"All I said was pain in the ass."

"Can it for now," Ethan told him.

Nasty, whose frequently silent presence could take over any room, returned, ushering a sleek brunette before him. She was dressed in a red gingham shirt, tight corduroy pants and low, brown suede boots that matched the jacket nestled on her shoulders. Cindy York needed no introduction. She was Fab's personal assistant and, as far as Ethan was concerned, nice enough but just a little too overconfident.

"Hi, Cindy," the chorus went up.

Venus came forward and said, "I met this child this morning and she said she didn't have a thing to do tonight so I invited her to join us if she felt like it. We're trying to catch up with Fabiola, Cindy. You should be our best source for that.''

Ethan felt himself being watched and caught Nasty's curiously pale brown eyes, pale brown in a lightly tanned face with sharp, Nordic lines and blond hair to go with it. Despite a limp from a not-so-little skirmish in Bogota, the sometimes ominous impression wasn't hurt by the man's size and whipcord fitness. As usual, Nasty chewed gum rhythmically, a habit Polly hadn't given up on squelching.

Raised eyebrows suggested Cindy's surprise. "Fabiola isn't here?" she said, each word clearly enunciated. "I wrote the event in her daybook. She gave me the weekend off so I haven't seen her since Friday." The woman's eyes returned to Ethan frequently.

"Crumb, what's the matter with you people?" Polly snapped, sounding completely unlike herself. "Are all the phones out of order, or what?" She went to the closest phone and dialed. After much too long, she said, "Hi Fab, it's Polly trying to hunt you down. Sorry you aren't there because we're worried about you. We're all here at Dusty's. Where are you? You promised we'd get to talk this evening. When you pick up this message, get right over here. Dusty's built the biggest fire and it's wonderfully cozy and yellow in here.''

Everyone laughed.

"If…" She looked at the receiver and said, "Time ran out," as she hung up.

Nasty took Cindy's coat and she promptly sat on Ethan's other side. "It is cozy in here," she said, raising her chin. Reddish light showed in her hair and flickered on her eyelashes. Her mouth was soft, her profile perfect. "But it's also very yellow."

"A long time ago Dusty was married," Ethan said. "His wife died in an accident. Her favorite color was yellow and, ever since, it's been Dusty's. Venus won't hear of him changing even an inch to something else."

Cindy chuckled. "Smart woman."

"Loving woman," he told her. "Dusty worships Venus."

Damn, he couldn't sit here like this, wondering. This was his careless fault. Despite the confident, come-on public face that millions stared at, Fabiola was insecure in her way, and a lot of her saunter and hair-tossing posing was to shore up the public image and boost the private woman. She was like iridescent glass and he'd known it from the day they'd met. Despite the hopes of their mutual friends, he'd also known he could never truly be in the running for anything more than a friendship. But whenever she needed a strong shoulder to lean on, he was there.

But he'd ruined it. He wanted to beat on something. Last night he had, not that it had helped.

And he'd spent the night sweating and recreating the scene in the shower. He'd been thinking of Fab almost nonstop for months. Now he'd gone too far, probably turned her off forever, and didn't know if he could even dream about getting over her.

The side door opened again and Fabiola came in. She wore black tights and a big, puffy red parka. Her cheeks looked windburned and her eyes watered. She pushed back her hood and allowed her hair to escape—and Ethan saw the aura once more. He gazed at the golden haze that had begun to surround her head almost every time he looked at her, and decided not to fight it. Something had happened to him and it was called Fabiola. She rubbed her hands together and said, "Brrr. It's so chilly out there. Hi, everyone, sorry I'm late. Rode the old mountain bike over and got a flat on the way."

And he should have been with her to fix it.

"You should have been there," Dusty said into Ethan's ear. "I'm going to let it go for now if I can, but we've got things to finish later on, boyo. Meantime, get your ass over there."

Ethan looked at him straight on and gave a brief nod.

"Something's going on between you two, isn't it?" Cindy murmured, leaning toward his other ear and resting a hand on his forearm. "Something different. She's great, but you and I know what's most important to her, and it'll never be anything but her work until she decides to quit. I shouldn't be saying a word of this, and I'll deny it if you say I did anyway.''

''And your point is?'' Ethan asked.

''Fabiola is accustomed to getting her own way. Men take one look and fall at her feet. I believe she craves a man who will not be as easy to control as her many other men have been. If you want to sleep with her, and of course you do, domination is the answer. I've only been with her a year but I'm skeptical about this platonic relationship. Who could look at you two and not be skeptical? Fine, but don't expect to keep her even if you do sleep with her.''

''Thank you,'' he said, scarcely listening. Fab smiled at him, but he saw uncertainty and worry in her eyes. He also saw that she probably hadn't slept more than he had, which was almost not at all. He started to get up, but Cindy made furrows in his arm with her fingernails and if he broke free it would be obvious. Fab took off her parka and hung it on a hook inside the door. Her long-sleeved top was also black and close fitting. The cold air made her hair stand out wildly. She was incredible to look at but, more important, she was incredible to love.

''Damn you to—petunias.'' Dusty hissed the words into Ethan's right ear. ''Now you've done it. Why did you ignore her like that? Better start choosing your weapon, ass—petunia.''

Ethan registered the word, "love" and narrowed his eyes, too muddled to make sense of his feelings. He looked at his knees and concentrated on the man beside him. "Petunia" had become Dusty's alternative to the foul words he used to pepper through his language before there were kids around almost all the time. Unfortunately the way he said that word had turned it into something even Bobby had learned to spit out with venom.

"Don't rush to her," Cindy said. "And don't crowd her."

But that was what he wanted to do—rush to her. "I appreciate the advice," he said. "No offence, but would you dig your nails out of my arm?"

She rubbed the back of his hand instead and turned so that only he saw her face. "I'm important to her, to her career. Don't forget that. I have influence. Better not to get snarky with me."

"I thanked you for the advice."

Across the room, Polly and Fab were hugging. Dusty had gone to hug Fab, too, as had Venus. Then Dusty and Venus had moved on to the kitchen. Bobby was outside again. And Cindy still leaned in front of Ethan.

"Does Cindy know Ethan well?" Polly asked.

"Well enough," Fab said. She longed to leave. She hadn't wanted to come at all. "They see each other at my place."

"She's telling him something and trying to be sneaky about it."

Fabiola closed her eyes, horrified at the thought that Ethan might be hearing any of this conversation. "I doubt it. Cindy's intense. She talks one-on-one exclusively."

"Well," Polly said, "let her talk one-on-one to someone else."

"Keep your voice down, Polly, love," Nasty said quietly. "You're getting upset, and you're upsetting Fab. Can I help?"

"No," Polly told him in a fierce whisper. "Men are the cause of these things and they're no good at putting them right."

Fabiola opened her eyes to be confronted with Nasty's considerable chest. He'd placed himself where she and Polly wouldn't have a clear view of the couch.

"Do you think I haven't figured out you're in love with Ethan?" Polly's face was a less flamboyant copy of Fab's own, her eyes as strikingly shaped but more bright than deep blue. Right now her skin was much too pale. "I've waited and waited for the two of you to make some sort of announcement. *Platonic.* Ha. Vibrant, sexy men and women with no reason not to screw their brains out, *do it.*"

Nasty choked on his gum. "Where did you hear a thing like that? You, the woman who's forgotten how to say anything more X-rated than *crumb* because of your squeaky-clean image?" Polly had her own children's TV show called *Polly's Place,* and was beloved by young schoolchildren across the country.

"I don't know." A brilliant blush stained Polly's face. "I must have read it somewhere. But why don't you do it? Make a commitment, I mean. You're thirty and he's no baby anymore. And you've known each other two years. What are you waiting for?"

"Polly," Nasty said. "Maybe we should butt out."

"You never butted in."

Fab had never seen Polly so mad or so visibly torn. Nasty pulled her against him and rested a cheek on top of her head. He hushed her and raised his brows to Fab.

"We haven't had that kind of relationship," Fab told them. "Ethan's a tough, independent man. You know the type." Fab eyed Nasty and thought of Roman Wilde, another ex-SEAL and comrade of the group who lived with his wife, Phoenix, and their children in Montana now.

Polly muttered, "Weird. Tennis, bikes, running. Anything you can do together and still pretend each of you is alone. Someone should lock the pair of you in a room with nothing but a billiard table in it. Then we'd see how long it took for you to sleep together. These may be tough men, but when they fall, they fall hard."

Nasty raised his brows again and said, "Flat on our faces. I'm not even going to argue."

Polly reached up to kiss his neck. "No point in arguing. And I think Ethan's fallen for Fab." She sounded stubborn again.

Fabiola didn't comment.

"Let me get you a drink?" Dusty arrived and hooked an arm around Fab's shoulders. "You want Ethan—I mean a gin and tonic."

"You know she doesn't drink hard liquor," Nasty said, making no attempt to hide a rare grin. "White wine, right, Fab?"

"All of you are watching us," she said. "You're all making assumptions. And you're wrong. Ethan and I have never—"

"Been in each other's pants," Dusty said, completely serious. "Ever consider there's something real strange about that?"

"Oh, Nasty," Polly said in a thin wail.

"Yeah," Nasty said, rocking his wife, whose mouth was quivering suspiciously. "Forget Dusty's crudeness. You two never did get together that way, Fab. So you already told us. I've got to talk with that boy. Should have done it a long time ago. How was I to know he was sexually arrested?"

"He's *not* sexually arrested."

The two men cleared their throats and Dusty took off to find wine at once. Fab was left with Polly and Nasty staring at her and wearing smug expressions.

"It's not what you think," Fab said.

In the kitchen Dusty pulled white wine from the refrigerator and took a glass from a rack above the sink. Venus watched him and he thought how wonderful she looked framed by the window and with the lake and trees behind her. He was a lucky old dog. "Marry me," he said.

"Okay."

"Yeah, that was proposal number forty-seven and I ain't givin' up until…what did you say?"

"I said I'm going to marry you, but before you go leaping in there making an old fool of yourself, we've got trouble to deal with first."

Dusty angled his head toward the other room, but set down the glass and hugged the second love of his life tight. "I never expected to get another chance with a great woman. Then you came along. I am one lucky man."

"And I'm one lucky woman." The little copper dragons edging her bronze-and-rust-colored skirts and the bottoms of her sleeves tinkled faintly. Underneath her multilayered skirts she wore her signature animal-print tights. "I haven't said much about Fab and Ethan, but they've worried me for a long time. What's wrong? Whatever it is is blowing up right now. I feel it, and as you know, I have special insight into such things."

Venus had second sight. She'd forecast all kinds of things that came true. And she never failed to point out how accurate her predictions were.

"You think they're in love?" Dusty said.

"I think they've been in love a long time. What I can't decide is why they've pretended not to know it."

"She didn't go to him when she arrived."

"He didn't go to her." Venus frowned and opened the oven to check on several quiches. "And why should she go to him first?"

"Why not?"

"My Fab smiled at him but he didn't smile back."

"Now you're making things up." He filled Fab's glass to the top. "I'm gonna make her sit by him with this."

"Don't interfere."

Dusty had left the refrigerator door open. He slammed it shut now.

"It's going to get harder to find harvest-gold appliances," Venus said, but her face was pinched.

"I'll keep fixing these. Or paint new ones." He left and marched to take Fab by the hand. "You aren't lookin' so hot, my girl. Come and sit down. Put your feet up."

"I'm fine here."

"Humor me. I got some bits of fabric for you to look at—for new curtains all through. You got the best taste around." He led her toward the couch, but she balked.

Ethan saw her coming and had a sensation as if tight bands were starting to let go inside his chest. He wanted her near him. That was before he saw

her expression clearly. She was making sure their
eyes didn't meet.

"Cindy," Dusty said, "Venus wants to show
you the view from a few places around the house.
Polly and Nasty's little one will be awake soon.
Then it'll be too late. She's a scene stealer."

The woman beside Ethan took her hand from
his wrist. She turned her face up to Fabiola's and
looked surprised. "Fab! Good grief, I was so engrossed I didn't even see you come in. You won't
forget you've got a camera crew coming tomorrow, will you? One of the local affiliates. You'll
be on WNYW, New York. The *Good Morning*
show. Live and very early."

"I had forgotten," Fab said. "But those are the
things I know you do so well. Thank you, Cindy."

"Venus is waiting," Dusty growled with his
customary subtlety.

Cindy got up and went to the kitchen while Fab
allowed Dusty to push her down onto the sofa and
slide an ottoman under her feet. He handed her the
wine, then pulled a large manila envelope from a
table drawer and emptied the contents over both
her lap, and Ethan's. Dozens of fabric swatches,
every one of them predominantly yellow. "Pick
out what you like, you two. Think about this room
first, and the kitchen. Venus thinks they should be
the same. I don't know."

"Same," Ethan and Fab said in unison, and
Dusty grinned while he walked away.

Fab picked up one piece of fabric after another.

Ethan took what she discarded and made a pile of them.

"Do you like Cindy?" Ethan asked.

Fab considered. "She's efficient and knowledgeable. She's worked for me for a year now and she hasn't given me a reason not to like her."

"She's ambitious."

Fab smoothed a field of yellow roses on satin finished cotton. "Yes. So am I. But you don't think that's a good thing in women, do you?"

"I didn't say that."

"I think it's what you're hinting at," she told him.

He made a move as if to hold her hand, but replaced his own on his knee. He said, "Close your eyes and open them a slit. This house looks like something you'd see when you had a hangover— or maybe it's straight out of *Little House on the Prairie*."

"You ever see *Little House on the Prairie?*"

"Nope."

"Didn't think so," Fab said. "I find this house way-out, wonderful, a place that invites you to snuggle down in front of the fire."

"I think I know what you mean." He wasn't just looking at her, he was staring at her. "I came by and rang your bell."

"I heard you." There had been enough deceit.

"And you decided you didn't want to answer. You knew it was me?"

"Yes. And, yes. I didn't know what to say to you. I still don't."

"Then we're even. Are we going to get past this, Fab?" Damn, it hurt to ask when he knew only one answer could make him happy. He wanted to be with her again, just as they had been last night. He wanted everything with her.

"Do we have to?" she said. "I mean, why get past it rather than ignore it and pretend you never even came to my condo last night."

Ethan's head lowered as if it were too heavy. "Because I did and I don't want to forget it. Not the way you mean." The last was added hurriedly. "We need to deal with the issue here, not pretend. Once a man and woman have been intimate, it never goes away. But we can make peace with a reckless decision and move on."

"Then we've lost what we had, haven't we? You're never going to want to be my friend again—and you're going to feel unsure how to act every time you're near me."

"Garbage!" He glanced around, met too many eyes and lowered his voice. "Garbage, Fab. Where else am I going to find someone I can beat at most of the things that matter to me." Except making love, and she held her own very well in that department. He glanced up, skimmed his eyes over her breasts, then her mouth, and settled on her eyes. "You just don't run as fast as I do."

"I'm going to train harder." Fab wanted to feel relieved. She didn't. What he'd said was true. They could never erase facts.

Ethan stared at the yellow carpet until it blurred. He'd done it. He'd reassured her enough to get past the setback and give them a chance to rebuild her trust. He'd have to find peace doing without the rest of what he wanted. For a very long time he'd managed fairly well.

"They look comfortable together again," Nasty told Polly and Dusty.

Fab was holding Ethan's arm with both hands. "They look awkward to me, like they're trying to look comfortable," Polly said.

Just like a woman to see pebbles where there were eggs. "Polly, my love—"

"What?"

"Can we give optimism a try?" He loved this woman of his so much. "I think they look comfortable. You think they look awkward. Maybe they look somewhere in between and this is a good place for them to be. Among friends. Safe while they work things out."

"I wish Venus hadn't invited Cindy. There's something about her. I don't know why, but I think she's a bad influence on Fab."

"Your mother does what she thinks is right and usually makes the right decisions," Dusty said.

"Not this time." Polly didn't feel like being mollified. "I don't like Cindy, never have. So she's efficient. There are other efficient people in the world. I think she's afraid Fab might get distracted. That could mean Cindy's job wouldn't be such a plum anymore."

Nasty groaned and said, "Only women think that way."

"Fab and Ethan seem miserable," Polly said, trying not to stare.

Dusty sniffed, sorted through his pockets for a tissue and said, "Probably having a lovers' tiff. But what do I know?"

"Nothing," Nasty and Polly said together.

Ethan couldn't take it anymore. Three sets of eyes were pretending not to stare while they kept obvious watch over the couch, and feeling Fabiola beside him and so electrically unhappy turned him inside out. He got up and looked down at her. "I'm really behind with paperwork, Fab. Will you forgive me if I get to it?"

She didn't raise her eyes from his midsection. "Of course I will. I'll have to leave in an hour myself. You go ahead."

"I'll call you, okay?"

"Yes, absolutely."

"Maybe tomorrow?"

"Maybe tomorrow."

CHAPTER TWO

February

PLAYING TENNIS INDOORS wasn't Ethan's preference, but the rain that drummed on the green bubble enclosing the country club courts meant there was no choice but to play inside.

He'd finished stretching and warming up, and dropped to sit on his haunches while he waited for Fab. Each meeting was strained now. Not that there'd been many meetings. In the five weeks since The Shower, as he'd come to think of the best night in his life to date, Fab had been away on location for two separate weeks, but during the three when she'd been at home in Kirkland they'd been together—alone—only seven times. He knew because he could replay every minute of each one of them and did so frequently when he looked for revealing things either of them might or might not have said.

Mostly they hadn't said anything meaningful.

This time was going to be different. This time

he'd loosen up because he had a hunch that if he did, so would she.

She pushed through the air-lock doors into the bubble.

He yelled, "Hey, Fab," and waved. "Hope you drove."

From a distance he saw her smile and she looked like the old Fab. A man's heart shouldn't double its beat over a smile.

The haze of gold was there again, outlining her whole body this time. He had to stop being a fool and get his eyes checked.

He didn't see gold halos around anyone else, though.

At the back of their court, she unzipped and shed her warm-ups, then jogged toward him in white shorts and polo shirt. Her ponytail swished each time she alternated the jog with a squat, or stopped to pull a knee to her chest. She was elegant in every move she made.

"It's awful out there," she said when she drew close enough for him to hear. "I hate to give in, but I did get the car out." And she'd noted with more than a little satisfaction that Ethan's bike was outside, chained to a rack under cover of an awning.

She expected him to gloat about the inability of the rain to dictate what he did. He didn't gloat. He did keep on smiling and she smiled back, but the smile wasn't in his eyes. In fact, he appeared to be staring and smiling, but not seeing her at all.

Then the distracted gaze faded. "Maybe there's some sort of sidewalk hydroplaning we can take up," he said. "Why hasn't anyone around here thought of that? There's standing water for enough of the year to qualify it as a year-round sport."

Fab chuckled and pumped her legs fast in place. "You and your water sports. Why don't you design something? A prototype. We'll get lots of coverage for the trials."

His smile became more forced. "You'd get lots of coverage even if the thing didn't work."

Pretending to tighten a shoelace, Fab bought thinking time. When she stood up again, she went to the net. "A kind of short ski? Is that what you're thinking?"

"Kind of."

"If you could make something work—or if you ever wanted a spokesperson for the business even, I'd do it, Ethan. You do know that, don't you?"

"Serve or receive," he said.

"I asked you a question."

"We're doing real well, but not Fabiola Crow well."

"How well do you have to do to buy some short regional spots? I'm sort of a member of the family, so I'm free. I'd like to do something meaningful for you."

Sort of a member of the family. She was threaded through every piece of his life now, and with each tugging apart that had happened in recent weeks, he'd felt more damaged.

He shook his head and reached to give her a familiar good-buddy pat on the arm. "Thanks, I'll keep the offer with all the other terrific things I know about you. Why don't you serve?"

If he had his way, Ethan thought, he'd rather she wasn't a face everyone recognized. He didn't want to lock her away all of the time, just most of the time. But she'd just shown, yet again, that although she knew the power she had, she wasn't obsessed by it. She wasn't even impressed by it.

Fab's first serve went wide. Way wide. She never did that, but he didn't say anything. Her second ball was a weak lob that dropped softly right where he could kill it anywhere on her side of the net. With a lot less power than he might have used, Ethan returned the shot to take the point and crossed to the backhand side, checking his racquet strings as if he sensed nothing different.

"Ready for my next ace?" she called.

"Don't think I can take it," he said loudly, and tumbled to lie flat on his back. Would this charade get much more difficult before it got better? He'd made up his mind a long time ago that he didn't want to get married—ever—so the sooner he worked his way through this infatuation, the better. That's what it was, an infatuation, nothing more. He wanted them to be friends, really good friends who spent a lot of time together. An affair might be nice and solve some pressing problems, but that would only end up ruining the friendship.

Her serve barely missed him and he jumped up in time to see her crossing over. "Hey, that's not fair. You can't serve to a man who's down."

"I waited, but you didn't move. Are you hurt?"

Wiggling everything that would wiggle, he said, "Nope."

"Sick?"

He felt his forehead. "Nope."

"Then that was a service ace. It's against the rules to take a nap on the court while play is in progress." She did a little war dance and made circles with her hips.

Growling, Ethan got into position. Maybe they were going to be okay after all—as long as she didn't swing her hips around him too much. Twirling his racquet, he got into position.

Two more serves and Fab was going down in the first game. Ethan hitched the legs of his shorts higher up his thighs, pretended to get ready and twirled the handle of his racquet some more.

The toss was the familiar high one this time and he stood up to run backward. She sent the ball, a bomb, to the adored spot every strong backhand player dreamed about. He returned it full force—and hit Fab square under the nose.

She cried out.

Ethan threw his racquet aside and ran. He vaulted the net and grabbed her. Tears streamed from paralyzed ducts, joined by blood from her nose. The upper lip was already swelling.

The pain overwhelmed Fabiola. There was nothing she could do about the water pouring from her eyes, or the blood mixing with it to drip onto her white shirt and shorts. She felt stupid, would feel more stupid if she didn't hurt so much.

Ethan had come at her in a rush. She knew the speed he was capable of reaching but had never been at the receiving end of his going-into-action mode. Swept from her feet, she grabbed at his shirt and realized she'd also grabbed hair, but his expression didn't change from controlled anger.

As much pain as she was in, a problem became solved there and then. While she looked at him, the mystical bell sound started and if he put her down she was certain she'd stumble all over the place. Those things were her reaction to feeling his annoyance. She couldn't take tension. End of mystery. "Put me down, Ethan. I'm too heavy."

His dark eyes were very close. "Sure you are. I think I can do this. Ice first." He pushed her head back as he ran. "Damn, damn, damn. I ought to have better control than that."

"I ought to know better than give you the ball on your backhand that way, then just stand there. I'm playing a lousy game. Maybe you've woken me up and I'll improve."

"The game's over."

"Nuts," she said, looking up at him while her surroundings swished by in a green blur—and the tinkling grew louder. She was grateful they were the only players around. "I don't want you to have to quit because of me. A little bang doesn't mean we stop. Happens all the time."

"No more tennis tonight. I'm getting ice, pain-killers, checking the bone in your nose and taking you home. I'll use your bike rack and drive while you keep your head back. Fab!" He paused. "What if I've blacked your eyes?"

It would cause a wrinkle or two in her schedule, but she wasn't about to tell him. "There's nothing that can't be postponed. Maybe I'll get to do a guest appearance for *ER*."

"Maybe." She was always thinking and there was always an alternative opportunity for Fabiola Crow.

"It'd be a hoot. Ow, Ethan. I'm trying with the bravery, but I hurt."

"I know, sweetheart. My brother hit me there with a baseball bat when we were growing up. I cried for twenty-four hours, and I still don't know why he didn't break my teeth and nose."

Ethan had called her "sweetheart." Just a re-flex, she thought. Fab stuck a finger in her mouth to feel her teeth all around, then squeezed her eyes tightly shut.

"You're going to the hospital and I'm calling in a plastic surgeon."

"Ice and knockout drops, please. I'm still breathing so I'll probably survive."

In the club office she got plenty of TLC from a woman in turquoise tennis gear smattered with yellow daisies. Despite the torrent and lack of sun, a matching visor supported her curly salt-and-pepper bangs. "You sit her down there right now. Ice coming up." The woman's skin resembled draped mahogany leather and her fuchsia lipstick bled into crevices that fanned from her mouth, but she exuded a good heart and good hearts were what Fab needed in abundance at the moment.

"I'm Mrs. Wexford," she said, and tossed a small bag to Ethan. "With those hands, mushing this up should be easy," she said and smiled.

Duly Ethan "mushed up" the ice, wrapped it in a piece of thin flannel and applied it gently to Fab's upper lip and beneath her nose. "You could juggle plates with this lip," he told her, peering closely. "It's turning transparent and purple with a sac of blood at the biggest bit. And your eyes are going to be black. Maybe only a little bit black."

"Thank you for the report, Ethan." Fab winced.

"Hang in there, lady. It'll get numb."

Mrs. Wexford said, "I never saw anyone in such a mess who looked so beautiful."

"That's what I was thinking," Ethan said.

"And there ought to be a law against men who look like you," the unsinkable Mrs. Wexford said.

"I used to tell my husband that. Still do sometimes, just to see the pleasure it brings him."

Oh, yes, Fab decided, Mrs. Wexford was one of
the good ones. Still not numb, the pain she suffered
was unbearable. She caught her breath and held it
and everything went out of focus. Someone spoke,
and someone else, she was no longer sure who,
and she felt consciousness slipping.

She did sense when they went outside and she
was buckled carefully in a car. Must be her car.
Must be Ethan. Next she heard an engine and felt
movement. She closed her eyes and drifted. She
was in the car, and Ethan was driving and mutter-
ing. Even through the haze she felt his anger.

The bell in her head rang in muted cascades.

NASTY FERRITO WATCHED Ethan Warrick from a
distance and used a freestanding screen as cam-
ouflage. So far Nasty hadn't revealed his presence
in the Overlake Hospital Emergency Department
to a staff member, but he had managed a few
words with Ethan.

Ethan sat beside Fabiola, holding her hand and
leaning close as if watching her every flicker of
expression were essential to recovery. Curtains
were pulled on each side of the bed but left open
at the end. Polly and Venus were in downtown
Seattle shopping, and since Venus didn't believe
in cell phones, Nasty had been unable to reach ei-

ther of them. It could be hours before they came back.

Fabiola was awake with a bandage around her nose and head to keep the ice pack in place. She looked only at Ethan. Nasty moved his gum from one side of his mouth to the other. Courting Polly had been hard, but Ethan was having a hell of a time. In fact there wasn't any concrete evidence they were courting at all.

Rapid footsteps approached from behind and started to pass Nasty. Cindy York to the rescue. Without having to leave his spot, Nasty stopped her progress and pulled her back where she wouldn't be seen. "Evening," he said, thinking how much he didn't like the particular kind of determination she obviously had. "No more visitors till Polly and Venus get here. That's why I'm out here." A lie. He hadn't asked to go in.

"I was told I could visit. We've got business to discuss."

"Fab's full of painkillers and she's badly swollen. They've said she's got to take it easy for a couple of days."

"Take it easy?" She snickered nervously. "My God, do you have any idea what kind of a schedule she has? Taking it easy isn't even an option."

"No choice," Nasty said. "Her nose doesn't seem to be broken, but she's going to have black eyes and her lip is huge."

"Then it's time for damage control. I'm the one

who should be with her, not her tennis buddy. I do
everything for her, do you understand! I'm her
right hand. Who do I talk to?''

That's what Cindy was all about, protecting the
job that had already been pretty good to her.

Doctors and nurses shuffled constantly in and
out of cubicles. Nasty chose the doctor who had
apparently been particularly uncooperative with
Ethan at first, and flagged him down. ''This is
your guy,'' he said, and went back to chewing his
gum.

''I'm Cindy York, Dr....'' She peered at his
name tag. ''Dr. Root. I'm Ms. Crow's assistant and
I need to discuss her schedule with her.''

Dr. Root looked from Cindy York to Fabiola,
who was awake but definitely groggy. ''She seems
to be resting quietly and getting comfort from the
man who brought her in.''

''She's a model. Her schedule—''

''I know who she is. And a surprisingly nice and
unaffected woman she is, too. But her schedule
will have to be rearranged. Obviously. Her face
looks worse than it is, but she won't want to be in
front of any cameras for a week or so, more likely
two or three weeks to be honest. The good news
is that there are no broken bones, but she is
shocky.''

''Ethan Warrick shouldn't be in there. I
should.''

''Why?'' Dr. Root asked. ''Are you a relative?''

She opened her mouth and Nasty saw her form a "yes," but she looked at him and said, "No, but he's a busy man and doesn't need to hang around for nothing. I'm employed by Ms. Crow."

"If you want to wait here, I can't stop you," the doctor told her, "but I see no reason to upset the patient and her sensibly supportive visitor at this point. Be warned that you are not to enter that room." He glanced at Nasty, who nodded briefly, acknowledging that he absolutely agreed.

"Well, damn his pointy little ass," Cindy said as the doctor walked away. "Keep a lookout for me. I'm going to spring Ethan. He's got to be fed up with this. Once I've got him out, you go in. If the doc asks, say Ethan had to leave."

"An answer for everything," Nasty said, studying her while she powdered her nose and reapplied lipstick. "Are you afraid Ethan might make Fab less dedicated to her work?"

He'd give her full marks for cool. There was nothing hurried about the way she returned the lipstick and compact to her purse, or the way she drew the flap over the top of her bag. But when her eyes met his he could only think about his close encounters with snakes. "No, she'll never do that, but someone could make it more difficult for her. Fabiola Crow is a very famous, very vulnerable woman who needs a keeper. That's all, and that's me. I look after her. That's what I want to do because I'm good at it. And in case you continue to have your theories about my reasons, Fabiola gave me a job that would take me places when I couldn't get a job like this anywhere else. I owe her. But she's been spending too much time with him.'' She indicated Ethan. ''What am I supposed to make of that for a press release? I've been finding ways to link her with important men for too long—it's getting old. My job at this point is to make sure she *is* linked to someone on the media 'A' list. I want her with someone the talk show hosts want to interview on his own. I want an idol no woman has managed to catch. Now, don't let Ethan see you while I get him out. We'll figure out how I'll replace you afterward.''

''Ethan is no slouch and no woman has caught him yet. Go in there and I'll yell for help.''

''You wouldn't.'' She tossed her hair and looked completely disbelieving.

''Want to try me?'' He kept a smile on his face while, from the corner of his eye, he saw Ethan draw the curtains across the bottom of Fab's narrow metal bed.

''YOU SURE YOU'RE READY TO GO?'' Ethan said, offering Fabiola a hand, which she held.

If Fab heard, she didn't make any acknowledgment. ''What time is it?''

''Around seven-thirty. You only snoozed for about forty-five minutes. Whatever they gave you

calmed you down and sent you to la-la land for a
bit. Oh, hell, your poor nose and lip.''

"So what?" she said, searching around until she
saw the plastic bag that contained her belongings.
"The only thing that matters is having people who
care about you, and I do. My family loves me no
matter what I look like. But I've got a pot roast in
the oven. Fortunately it's in stoneware so it'll cook
forever without burning, but there's a point when
it isn't so good anymore.''

Well, he wasn't a member of her family but he
chose to think she included him in there somewhere. Fab could very well be telling him, in a
roundabout way, that she loved him. She was one
sweet thing, and in a not too roundabout way, he
might be discovering that what he felt for her
wasn't infatuation, but much more. It could have
been much more for a long time.

"I'm going to hurry and get out of here," she
said, swinging her feet to the floor. But she seemed
more wobbly and occasionally pressed one ear or
the other.

"You ought to wait for the doc to take another
look at you.''

"I'll take my first real look at him on the way
out. Only fair I get my turn. From what I did see
he was pretty cute," she said, and hiked the big
bag onto the bed.

"I'll wait outside," he said, making to leave.

Fab shook her head. "No need. If I see ap-

proaching feet I'll send you out to tell 'em they've
got the wrong cubicle.''

Resigned to live through the agony of listening
to her dress, he turned his back.

''Face me,'' she ordered, ''so you can see if I
signal for you to head off the advancing armies.''

Once more he did as he was told. Fab unwrapped the ice and set it on the bed. Looking at
her battered face made him furious with himself.

''Don't worry, Ethan. The gown will cover
me. I'm not going to do a striptease.'' Standing
on one foot, she pulled a panty leg up to her
knee, then balanced precariously while she repeated the exercise on the other side. The shorts
followed and she dug around to find very wet
shoes. ''I'm not putting sodden socks on inside
these.'' The shoes went on and her feet made
squelching sounds.

A bloodstained white bra emerged and she wriggled into it under the drape of her hospital gown,
which she then tossed aside. Ethan fixed his eyes
on her face and prayed his body wouldn't notice
he was getting excited.

Some hope.

She frowned at the filthy polo shirt and took it
to a recessed sink where, with her back to him, she
attempted to sponge away some of the worst
marks. In the light over the sink her hair turned to
spun gold and glowed. ''Watch for feet,'' she or-

dered, and Ethan realized she'd caught him staring too closely.

OUTSIDE THE ROOM Nasty was having a hard time restraining Cindy. "This is a hospital," he told her. "Nobody thinks anything of showing a little skin around here."

"She undressed right in front of him. They were facing each other. If I don't stop what's been going on it'll be the end of her career. I know his type. He's already jealous. I've seen the way he looks at her. Next it'll be marriage and children. She's got some more good years, but not if she ruins her figure carrying kids. I'm not having everything I'm working for go down the drain because of some hick who makes sails."

Nasty didn't feel like setting her straight about what Ethan did, or what he had done—the decorations he'd been awarded for valor, his reputation among other SEALs. He did say, "Sails aren't a big item for us."

Cindy ignored him and said, "Are you putting a stop to this or am I?"

"You and I are going to butt out, Cindy. Didn't anyone tell you how pushing people one way usually means they go another? It's true. I've seen it happen."

She returned to staring at Ethan and Fabiola's feet.

Nasty made sure he looked passive enough, but she'd never make it as far as the cubicle.

ETHAN REALIZED Fab was weak. She tried to wring
out the shirt but didn't get far. He went to her side,
took the shirt himself and removed as much water
as possible. "That was smart," he said. "You
can't put this on now."

"Oh." She frowned, gripping the edge of the
sink. "I suppose I can't."

He'd never understand why the sight of a
woman in a simple white bra was such a turn-on.
Maybe it wasn't to anyone else, but he doubted
that. The valley between her breasts was deep, the
flesh that rose softly above half cups, creamy. He'd
seen her more or less like this so many times when
they'd gone swimming. He'd seen her naked. This
was different. This was even more personal, the
hidden stuff.

He had to stop thinking about the two of them
in her shower.

She seemed confused again, and vulnerable, and
very young. He took off his jacket and pulled his
own shirt over his head. "Put this on and wear
your sweats. You'll be warm enough and I'll take
you right home."

When she only stared at the shirt, he took it from
her and pulled it over her head. He threaded her
arms into the short sleeves, which nevertheless
reached her forearms, held her warm-up pants for
her, then tucked in the shirt. "Feel better?" He
wished he did.

"Fine. I'm sorry to be a pest, but I feel light-headed again."

Immediately he lifted her and stretched her out on the bed. "Should I ring for a nurse?"

She rolled her head from side to side.

Ethan sat on the bed, leaned over her and propped his feet on the bed rail. "There's nothing to worry about."

"Where's Polly?"

"Shopping downtown. She'll be back. So will Venus."

Her deep blue eyes studied him and the sadness he saw there confused him.

NASTY WAS PRAYING for Polly's arrival. In future, whether Venus liked it or not, his wife would carry a cell phone.

"For God's sake," Cindy said. "They're in bed together. Right here in an open emergency unit. What are they? Rabbits? If this gets out the press won't be good. 'Fabiola Crow to change her name to Fabiola Bunny after a wild night in ER with a robust navy SEAL. Sources say they closed the curtains but no one could get a moment's sleep.' Oh, my God."

The urge to laugh almost destroyed Nasty's composure, but his friend wouldn't be amused if it did. "Let's go out and get some fresh air," he told Cindy, taking a firm hold on her arm and walking her rapidly out into the cold darkness.

FAB'S FACE WAS A CHALKY WHITE. The swelling showed up, bright purple, and tiny red hemorrhages covered her nose. But she was taking deep breaths and showing signs of collecting herself.

"Don't forget the ice," Ethan told her. "I'll guide you so you don't trip."

"This is so dumb," she said, retying the bandage that had held the ice in place, then trying to see where they were going. "I feel *stupid*."

Ethan brushed back her hair and smiled at her. "They said you were probably more shocked than you should be and you could spend the night. Do you want to do that?"

"No. I want to go home and I don't want any more fuss. Please, Ethan, don't leave me—"

"Okay, okay. Settle down. I happen to think you're exhausted from working too hard and the injury put you over the top. I'm getting you checked out and taking you home. Then I'll make sure you're looked after."

She'd been going to say, "Please don't leave me alone," but was glad he'd stopped her from making a fool of herself again. *Looked after*. He'd make sure Polly and Venus traded off looking after her. The men and the children would pop in and occasionally he might come and stay a few awkward moments. It wouldn't have been like that before...not before they made love. Now he was determined never to let anything like it happen again because he didn't want it.

But she wanted everything with him and they were moving further and further apart.

FABIOLA WAS STILL IN BED and withdrawn from the world a week later when Polly and Venus decided to take Anne and keep each other company on one of the visits that were so stilted as to be hard to bear.

"Now, Mom," Polly said, drawing the embarrassing lime-green Hummer Nasty had bought her into a spare space under Fabiola's building. If Nasty Ferrito's family couldn't drive around in a tank, they'd have the next best thing. "We need to talk about how we're going to handle things this time."

"We are going to tell her that she must rise and face a new day, a new life," Venus said in the lofty tones she used when in her guru mode.

"No, no, don't even start that," Polly said. "She's wounded."

"We all know she was hit in the face with a tennis ball, but that was a week ago and that Cindy York told me on the telephone—how I detest those things—she told me that Fabiola was improving every day."

In the back seat Anne made herself heard. She loved coming to Fabiola's where she had her own things and was thoroughly spoiled.

Polly allowed her mother to finish before she said, "I was referring to her wounded heart, not her wounded face. Her face isn't nearly ready for the camera yet, either.''

''Regardless, she's not behaving like the Fabiola we know. Oh, look at that, we must be very, very careful. Look. You must see that darkening. The black clouds gathering.''

''It's going to rain,'' Polly said. ''Again.''

''It's a warning. If we are not vigilant, something dreadful will happen to Fabiola. Disaster will overtake us all.''

In Polly's opinion her twin was dragging her convalescence on a bit long. Certainly she was into the blue, green, yellow phase of bruising, but she shouldn't be spending so much time in bed. However, Polly wasn't about to support her mother's flights of fancy. ''We're going in now. You will not mention how withdrawn she's become, or say you know Cindy is in New York to beg for more convalescent time.''

''I wasn't going to.''

Whenever Venus's greenish eyes took on an innocent expression, Polly's peace of mind reached new lows. ''And you will not mention Ethan unless she does.''

''I'm cold,'' Venus said, opening her door. ''Let's hurry in and get warm. Anne's cold, too, aren't you, Granny's little coochie, poochie angel? I've got something special for you and you shall have it at Aunty Fab's.''

Polly looked at the sky but didn't say a word.

"And we need to make sure that girl is eating enough, Polly. Dusty came by and said she looks like a skeleton dressed by Victoria's Secret. Did you notice she's losing weight? I can't understand it. Gorgeous but much too thin."

"Mom," Polly said in warning tones, but Venus had collected her casserole from the floor in the back seat, slammed the doors and was on her way to the door from the garage into the town house. Each of them had a key.

Polly went into action. Anne pounded her car seat with fists covered in soggy, smashed hard biscuit. The baby was, as Venus said, deeply in touch with tactile elements and loved being smothered with gook. She smiled and sucked between her fingers. "You're a mess, babe," Polly said, giving up on trying to clean her in the garage. "We'll have to ask to use Aunty Fab's bathroom."

Carrying Anne under one arm and a bag of bread and fruit in the opposite hand while she juggled a bunch of flowers, Polly followed Venus. She would have gone directly to the mudroom sink if she hadn't heard Venus's raised voice, from two floors up, punctuated by short, sharp sentences from Fab.

Polly left the bag and flowers in the mudroom and struggled in the direction of the noise until she ended up in Fab's bedroom. Fab lay under a white matelassé spread and white eyelet sheets with fluffy white pillows behind her. And Venus was

right, she had gotten thinner. Polly ought to have
noticed. Fab hardly made a bump under the bed-
clothes.

Venus pirouetted around the room in her elegant
green-and-orange caftan, her graceful arms wafting
and her hips undulating. Polly looked at Fab. Their
mother was a remarkable woman, but sometimes a
little went a long way.

"May I wash Anne's hands and face in your
bathroom?" Polly said.

Fab offered her a wan smile and said, "Of
course you can. Go and wash up in Aunty Fab's
bathroom, babycakes."

"Mom," Polly said as she began to enter the
bathroom. "What are you supposed to be doing?"

"I am encouraging a certain determined presence to go on its way and I am dancing a dance
of peace and fulfillment for your sister," Venus
said, far from dismissed by Polly's disapproval.

"We were afraid we might not find you in,"
Polly said, smiling brightly while she sponged and
dried Anne's hands and face. "Ethan said he came
to visit you and you said you'd be returning to
work today. But Dusty thought you would be
here."

Fab turned her face away. "Ethan brought the
roses," she said. "It's not his fault he thinks I'm
not here today. I told him I'd be out."

Anne struggled and reached to be placed on
Fab's bed. Polly put the little girl down on the bed

and she promptly crawled beneath the covers and on top of her aunt. Quite suddenly, Venus's expression became pinched. She sat on the very edge of a chair and was silent. Polly strolled to a pale wooden cabinet near French windows that opened onto the upper terrace.

"What beautiful flowers." She turned the vase this way and that, careful not to touch the thorns.

"No thorns," Fab said. "Ethan stood there and took them all off."

"Sweet," Polly said.

"I think he was preoccupied," Fab responded. "And figuring out how quickly he could leave without letting me know he was in a hurry."

Suddenly Venus threw up her hands and her full sleeves fell back over her arms. With her eyes closed, she wound her arms about each other, then stood and continued as if reaching for the ceiling.

Fab's eyes filled with tears. Anne put a pudgy hand on each side of her head, sighed hugely and scrambled up to place one of her drooly kisses on Fab's mouth. Fab took her in her arms and squeezed hard. "Thank you, baby Anne," she said. "You know how to make your aunt feel so much better."

With a shaky sigh, Venus pushed her hands into the slit pockets of her caftan. "I am so troubled I can't concentrate. There are great problems here. I am convinced they can be solved, but only with considerable giving by two people. And by honesty."

"Please don't worry, Mama," Fabiola said, and her mother burst into tears.

Fab looked at Polly and shrugged helplessly. "Now we're all going to blubber."

"You never call me Mama anymore. Not unless you're very upset. I—I want to help you."

"There isn't anything wrong," Fab said in a voice that grew smaller and tighter by the instant.

The vista from the slightly open window became intensely interesting to Polly. She stood, silently watching the sheer draperies lift and fall over the view of the lake. "There's nothing wrong?" she said. "Is that why you reveal—even if it's only by inference—that you're really unhappy? You want someone to tell you what to do? I don't blame you. We all want that sometimes. And you can't turn to Cindy about this."

"She's more ambitious for my career than I am. Understandable. Her star is hitched to mine. But I'll make sure she's all right."

"You told Ethan you'd be out today because you can't cope with being near him. That's it, isn't it? So you lied. Do you have any idea the power you have over that man? He's never been close to a woman before and he worries about you."

"Because he takes duty seriously and he thinks he has a duty to look after me. And he feels responsible for this." She touched her nose and winced. Fab sighed again and Anne settled down with a thumb in her mouth and her head under Fab's chin.

Polly couldn't be diplomatic anymore. On the one hand she had Ethan, a crazy SEAL who had spent his adult life proving he didn't need anyone but the men he'd trusted with his life when on active duty. On the other was Fab, wonder girl, who also didn't need anyone. And they needed each other. Her head felt as if it would explode.

This was it. "I think you're in love with Ethan."

Fab looked like a wild animal about to flee. "I am not."

Beside the bed was an overturned basket of used tissues. Fab didn't have the sniffles, or a cough. Polly felt her brow and it was cool. "You don't seem to have a cold or fever."

"I don't. I'm a bit under the weather, that's all. I keep wondering if I shouldn't get checked out for mono."

"Under the weather," Venus said, getting up and going to the CD player. She put on a disk and crooned, "'And a nightingale sang in Berkeley Square.' Isn't that a sweet song? A girl smiled at a man and he heard a bird sing. They were in love and such strange feelings come when you're in love."

Like hearing noises in your head? Fab chewed the inside of her cheek.

Venus slipped in a Robson and Jerome disk and was instantly lost in dance again.

"You told him you'd be out today because you want him to stay away. You're not up to running around yet, and putting distance between you that way, so you'd just have to face him and really talk. He might say, 'I love you.' Then it would be up to you and you might just be off balance enough to say, 'I love you, too, Ethan.'"

Fabiola hid her face in Anne's hair.

"Oh, yeah," Venus mouthed silently and did a series of bumps with her hips.

"I'm going to get some ice in case he comes back. Your eyes are all red where you've been crying."

"I haven't."

"You have," Polly insisted on her way out. "That's what all the tissues were used for."

"You used to be such a truthful little girl," Venus commented.

Carrying an ice bag, a brush and comb, makeup and perfume, Polly returned and homed in on Fab. She wiped her face with a cool cloth, pushed her onto her pillows and applied ice.

The white peignoir set she wore was truly beautiful, almost bridal, in fact. "When Ethan comes back, the best thing to do is tell him just what you want from your relationship."

"I want what we've had," Fab said promptly. "If more men and woman had wonderful friendships with each other, the gaps between the sexes would be forgotten.''

"But you can't be best friends, and lovers?''

"I thought it might be possible. But, no. No, it doesn't work.''

Venus and Polly exchanged a look that telegraphed they'd figured out what Fab had meant.

"You're in love with him,'' Venus said.

"No, I'm not,'' Fab said with vehemence. "Leave me alone. You're making me feel sick.''

"Your face is really getting better,'' Venus said in conciliatory tones. "What's left could be covered with makeup if it had to be.''

"I don't believe you, Fab,'' Polly said, and ignored her mother. "Your feelings are written all over you.''

"You need to buy some glasses, then,'' Fab said.

"You are so stubborn, sis.''

"And you're not?'' Anne had fallen asleep on Fabiola's chest, exhausted from her busy day.

"I don't have a thing on you,'' Polly told Fab. "When I was beaten, I gave in and married Nasty. I should have done it earlier instead of behaving like an ass.''

"Sometimes it isn't that clear.''

"And it isn't that clear between you and Ethan?'' Polly crossed her arms and Venus followed suit. "Is that what you're saying? That you're having a hard time with Ethan? Something has happened between you—I can feel it. But perhaps he hasn't told you he loves you so you're holding back.''

"That's not it.''

Venus leaned over Fabiola. "He *has* told you he loves you but you're not sure how to answer?''

"No! That's absolutely not the way it is and you're driving me mad.''

"Fab,'' Polly asked in a soft voice, "*are* you in love with Ethan?''

"We mustn't meddle, dear,'' Venus said quietly, earning herself a scowl from Polly.

"I could be,'' Fab admitted.

Polly let out the breath she'd been holding. "Then tell him, darling. Just tell him.''

"He'd laugh.''

Venus held her face and paced. "You don't know that.''

Tears clung to Fab's lower lids now. "No, I don't, and I don't intend to find out. So I'm putting it behind me. In fact I'm already less sure I ever loved him at all. Proximity can make you feel those things.''

"I brought a casserole,'' Venus said. "There's enough for several meals—even enough to serve some to Ethan. And there's bread and fresh fruit from Polly. Shall we fix you a plate?''

"No, thank you.'' Fab stroked Anne's fair curls. "When I get upset I can't eat. Anyway, after I was so rotten to Ethan, he won't be coming back.''

"Rotten," Polly and Venus said. Polly added, "Rotten how?"

"I made sure he understands there can't be anything romantic between us. Certainly not in the near future."

Venus let out a loud breath and said, "I see," before carefully lifting Anne from the bed.

The little toddler's toes tangled with Fab's coverlet, pulling it back, and a pile of photographs cascaded to the floor. Fab made to leap from bed but Polly stopped her. "You're queasy. Stay put and I'll pick them up for you."

"It's a good thing this one didn't make it to the floor." She lifted the photo in a silver frame from the bed and piled the rest of the photos on top.

Venus came to lean over Polly's shoulder while she looked through the snapshots. They remarked together how lovely Fab looked, how you could see the devilish side of her under the angelic outside, and how Ethan was what they called a "stud"—and wasn't he wonderful with all that character in his face that showed he'd lived a lot, but also that he was a thoughtful man. And then they came to the portrait in the silver frame, and fell absolutely silent.

"What's wrong?" Fabiola asked at last, and Polly noted how her feet bobbed beneath the covers. Fab's feet always bobbed when she was impatient, or anxious.

"I've never seen this picture before."

"Neither have I," Venus said, frowning.

"That's because it's mine and I don't display it."

Polly squinted at her. "I'm kind of surprised he gave it to you."

Fab looked anywhere but at her sister.

"Did he give you this?"

"No, he *didn't*. I took it and framed it. There, now are you satisfied. I stole it because I wanted it and he's not the kind of man who spends time looking at pictures of himself. I bet that's something he detests about me, the way my looks are so tied up with who I'm supposed to be."

Polly's heart beat fast. "I doubt it. He knows that's just part of your job. Where was this taken?"

"I'm not sure. But that's a jungle, isn't it? And some horrible murky river. He's wet and covered with mud. And he's smoking. Ethan doesn't smoke."

"If you don't like it, why do you want it?"

"I *do* want it. That's Ethan. Who he really is. He's in pain but there's a kind of peace in him. He's stoic. Whatever has happened is because it was part of his duty and he gets some sort of satisfaction out of that. I think he was stabbed in the abdomen. That's what it looks like. And he's fabulous, isn't he? An almost civilized warrior. A little while before that was taken he was probably fighting for his life, but he's already slipping back into being a civilized man. You won't tell him I've got it, will you?"

Polly made a disbelieving face. "No, Fab, we won't tell him. Now we've got to get this little lady home and down for a nap."

Goodbyes and false cheer smoothed the parting.

When Venus and Polly stood beside the Hummer again, Polly said, "She really does love him, Mom. A lot."

"I know."

They eyed each other.

"We mustn't meddle," Polly said.

Venus shook her head slowly, and Anne copied her. "Absolutely not," Venus said.

CHAPTER THREE

March

MAD MARCH WINDS. Ethan sat in his car in the public lot at Marina Park. The surface of the lake pirouetted, a billion wind-driven wavelets. Boats jostled together in the nearby marina. Hardy walkers leaned to keep their balance, or sat on benches watching winter's grip loosen. Even the coats of dogs turned upside down, and tree branches whipped to and fro.

He had just left Room Below, the dive and water-sports shop Dusty still maintained, and was gathering courage to start the battered black Jeep and head for Fabiola's town house.

He turned the key in the ignition.

Not calling ahead had been the right decision. His trusty co-conspirators, Polly and Venus, were sure Fab was home from her last shoot. They were also sure that she was becoming increasingly unhappy, listless even. She was exactly what she needed to be when she was working, but when she got back to Kirkland, she seemed to fall apart. Often she insisted she had a lingering flu and went to bed. Even Cindy York was concerned enough to be kind.

A knot tightened in Ethan's stomach. He was worried about Fabiola, and about the part he might have played in what was happening. They'd played one game of tennis in a month. He'd done his best to hold back without appearing to do so but he needn't have bothered because Fabiola played as if she were in a trance and could hardly wait to go home. She'd refused to run with him at all and on the two occasions when they'd ridden bikes, he'd been forced to ride slowly or risk losing track of her.

At Kirkland Avenue and Lake Street, Ethan turned right onto Lake and traveled the several blocks to Fab's place. His own condo looked down on Central Avenue, only blocks west of Fab's. Usually they walked in either direction but today he had a cargo to transport—and there'd been stock to deliver to Dusty.

He parked next to Fab's Toyota Camry, pulled his various bags out and locked the Jeep.

Fab had a key to his place, as he did to hers. He considered ringing the bell, but used the key instead. As he went in he yelled, "Fab, it's Ethan."

The town house was the left side of a duplex. A short passageway led from the garage, through a mudroom to an open space furnished with large, comfortable furniture. The television was there.

Ethan called her name again and climbed to the main floor and the living room, dining room and kitchen. She wasn't there. He went to the windows to check the lower terrace and the dock that angled out but where there were no boats. A little sun lightened the sky and played on miniature whitecaps.

After setting down his bags, he took a few hesitant steps up the stairs. "Fab?"

"Hello."

"It's Ethan." The knot pulled harder inside him. "Fab, it's Ethan."

More time passed before she said, "Hi. I'm being lazy."

"May I come up?"

Again the silence.

"I shouldn't have come without calling."

"Don't be silly. When did you have to call first? Come on up."

His stomach relaxed a little. "Be right there," he said, and sprinted back down the stairs to retrieve a gift-wrapped box from one of his bags before retracing his steps.

Her door stood ajar and he pushed it lightly. "Coming in."

When he saw her, he stopped. "Hey," he said. "You okay, buddy?"

She said, "Sure," but pressed a hand to her right ear and squinted.

Oh, boy, did she do things to him. But in the ten days since he'd last seen her, she'd lost more weight, or so it seemed to him. Her hair was brushed back at the sides and secured with gold combs. At least, he thought they were gold. The aura was there and more intense than it had ever been before, but he would not look away, could not look away. If his eyesight was going and Fabiola was to be the last thing he remembered seeing, so be it. There was nothing and no one else he'd rather remember.

"You're angry, Ethan. What is it? Have I done something?"

"You've never done anything to make me angry." Except to start shutting him out of her life. "But I think I may be making things harder for you. Between—well, we're mature enough to mention that something happened between us. An animal thing. Best forgotten. Between that and the not-so-little fact that I nearly knocked your head off with a tennis ball, yeah, I'd say I've made your life harder."

Continuing to deny the obvious was pointless. He loved her so much he couldn't think straight anymore.

Fabiola found she couldn't lie there looking at him, knowing she'd been the one to start what he called her "harder life." If she did, she'd blurt everything out. She could have done that at the time, or even shortly afterward. Now it was too late. "You planned nothing," she told him. "Now, please sit down. I'm getting up. I want to be by the windows. It's so beautiful out there—one of my favorite times of year."

"Yes, ma'am." He shrugged off his old leather bomber jacket and draped it over the end of the bed, then went to one of two ivory tub chairs flanking a low, round cherry table. The chair was too small for him, but he sat down and stretched his legs way out in front of him, crossed his ankles and appeared more relaxed than when he'd come into the room.

"Is it cold?" she asked him, and pulled on the pale lavender robe that matched her nightgown.

"Chilly," Ethan said, his face averted to the window. He found the cord and pulled open the sheer draperies.

The buttons on the robe were small and covered with satin that slipped around as she worked them through the holes. Once she'd managed all of them she got up and went, barefoot, to look outside. "Silvercaps!"

"What? Oh, yeah, yeah, exactly. I couldn't think how to describe the water when the sun came out, but that's it." The next breath he took was deep and raised his chest. "You always know the right words. Something else I envy you. But you're—

well, you're a special woman, buddy, and special things come from you.''

If she told him that it had been the sense of who he was inside that drew her to him, that and discovering he was honorable to his soul, he'd only shrug off the compliments. So instead she said, ''Thank you. What a nice thing to say. Careers in the beauty biz aren't good for the spirit. You have to fight to hang on to even a shred of yourself. It's too easy for many girls and women to get so tied up with the way they look, the fawning, the glamour, that they forget it's all going to go away. Whew, that's a lot of philosophy. I'm hot. Mind if I crack the window?''

He wanted to say, ''How did you get to be so smart?'' but swallowed the words she might or might not accept. Leaning down, he opened the bolt on one of the French windows and pushed it outward. ''Maybe I'd better make sure the wind doesn't throw it open and break the glass.''

''I'm just going outside to take some breaths. Don't worry about securing it.''

Any attempt to protest would only make her more determined to go. ''I'll come with you.''

''No. Thanks, but no. I'll only be a minute. Just long enough to untangle my wind sock.''

Ethan plastered on a smile. Her sleeves ended in tight bands at the elbows, showing the rest of her very slim arms. Up close, the skin on her face and neck had a transparency and her eyes glowed. Then

there was the golden haze that seemed determined
to surround her at all times now. She stepped outside, immediately closing the French window behind her. Her gown and robe were made of an
opaque fabric that shone slightly. They reached her
ankles, where the wind behaved as if she were
dressed in the finest lavender sand and twirled the
hems around her ankles, then her calves, her
thighs.

Her back was to him. Standing on her bare
toes—he shook his head at the sight of them—
standing there, she pulled on her pink pig wind
sock, freed it from the eaves and made certain the
streamers that had replaced its little curly tail could
enjoy the play.

"Okay," Ethan said aloud, starting to get up,
"back in with you. You are really going to be sick
if you keep this up."

Holding handfuls of her robe and gown, Fab
seemed to be thinking, or rather struggling with
something in her mind. He saw a comb whip from
her hair and skitter off into the water. Fab didn't
show she'd noticed her loss.

If he had to look at her like this for much longer,
he'd just have to leave.

She came toward him then, still tugging the robe
into Grecian folds between her breasts. He got up
to pull her inside. "You aren't dressed to be out
there," he said, closing the French window again.

"You're right."

"Almost forgot." The package was in his jacket pocket and he got it. "I tried to remember if I'd ever given you a gift. Not for your birthday or any particular reason, but just because I wanted to. I never have." He pointed to the other chair, and when she sat, he handed her the box.

"There's always got to be a reason," she said. "Just because what?"

"Because you're something else," he said, and knew it was a lame response. "Open up."

What she needed most, Fab decided, was a tissue. Silly woman, she cried so easily these days. The ribbon and big bow were white gauze edged with silver. Silver stars scattered white paper. She laughed as she tore them away and opened a gray velvet box.

"I don't even know if women wear them these days," he said. "Do they? Do you, I should say? If you don't, we'll change it for something else."

His anxious smile, the way he watched for her response, turned her heart over. "It's so lovely." Inside the box a gold charm bracelet glistened on white satin.

"You would have had it sooner, but all the charms had to be made."

"A tennis ball." Fab wiggled her nose. "You've got a nerve." There was a racquet, a tiny bike, athletic shoes. "What's this one?"

"An ice bag."

"You're pushing your luck, Ethan." She pointed to another charm.

"That's the ski for riding sidewalk puddles." He knelt beside her and said, "And a plane, a boat and a train because you travel away—you're away a lot. The shaggy dog you've talked about getting from the pound. A globe because you're a globe trotter. See all the tiny diamonds in the places I know you've been? And a baby because you're the best aunt and baby-sitter around."

That was it. If she didn't burst into tears, she'd deserve a medal.

His wrist, sun darkened and lightly covered with black hair, rested on the arm of her chair. The diver's watch he wore looked very right against the corded muscle and vein there. His wide, long-fingered hand hung, almost relaxed, but for the forefinger, which settled on the back of Fab's hand. Beside him, she seemed fragile. She almost laughed aloud. Fragile was something she'd never had a chance to be and she didn't want to start now.

"The bracelet is the most lovely thing I've ever had. Put it on for me."

The way he fumbled with the clasp suggested he hadn't had much practice with such things. When it was undone, he wrapped it around her wrist and employed the same frowning concentration while he fastened the clasp and the safety.

Bells, the faintest sound of bells confused Fab,

until he looked at her again and said, "There, it looks as if it was made for you, and it was." No more bells. "Honey, it's that time, you know. We can't put it off anymore. We've got to come clean with each other. There's too much we could lose otherwise. Are you ready for that?"

"I don't know." She looked into his face and he was much too close. Light faded outside and the pupils of his eyes were almost obscured. Was everything about to come out? He'd given her a beautiful gift, but he wasn't happy with her.

Oh, please turn off the bells.

"Thank you for thinking of me and giving me a gift." She got up and returned to stare into the approaching night. He'd called her "honey," that was new, too.

"You're welcome." Ethan had known this would be one of the hardest things he'd ever done, but maybe even that had been optimistic on his part. He got to his feet and stood a short distance behind her. "The shower, what we did, was a fluke. A chance caused it and it won't happen again."

With her right hand and wrist, she lifted the heavy hair from her neck as if she were hot. Several curls remained. How slender and vulnerable that neck was.

"We've disproved the myth that a man and a woman can't be best buddies without falling into bed with each other. Except for a single infraction, which we've recovered from.''

Fab could feel herself sinking. "Oh, yes, of course we have.'' What planet had he been on for the past three months?

"Maybe this isn't the time for this, Fab. You really don't seem well. You should go back to bed.''

"It's been several weeks, but I haven't been able to get all the way back to normal. I seem to catch every bug that flits by. But I'm starting to feel much stronger.'' Feeling stronger, she thought? She might not die, but she could very well wish she had before long.

"How about a game of tennis?'' He was being facetious but he didn't know how to deal with this.

"I'm not feeling that much stronger yet.''

"In bed with you, then. Let me coddle you—I like that idea. You'll be under my power.'' He gave her a toothy grin. "I'll heat the chicken soup I brought and make some tea. Green tea?''

"You made soup?''

He felt himself flush. "It's in cans but it's supposed to be great.''

"It will be. But I'm not hungry right now. Are you?''

He shook his head. "At least sit on the bed.''

She did, and looked at him with close attention.

"I'm not sure I'm up to this, after all,'' he said. "Ethan Warrick, the toughest of the tough, the one who would never fall for a woman. I can't believe it may have happened to me. And I do think it's happened.''

Once more Fabiola fought tears. Breathing took too much effort.

"But what happens if the feeling passes, Fab? If I believe in it then it goes away, we'll never recover from the disaster. I can't stand the thought of not being able to turn to you." He'd thought this was a good way to give her a chance to speak her mind. Now he felt like a total heel.

"I absolutely agree," Fab said, the thumping of her heart so loud she scarcely heard her own words. "I'm in a waiting mode, too, so we're lucky again. We're always lucky. I wouldn't want to make a mistake, either. But I am in a bit of a muddle." She looked at him and smiled behind her fingertips. "You're going to know just how much of a flake I am, but you know what they say about confession and how good it is for you? Ethan, I sense when you're unhappy and I hear bells, little bells in my head."

He put his hands on his knees and bent to look into her face. He felt her head. "You don't seem to have a fever."

"That's not all. My legs get wobbly."

He smoothed her hair back. He'd never know how she struggled not to hold his hands.

"Okay, I can come clean, too," Ethan said. "I look at you and you seem to turn gold. Not always, but more and more. Mostly around your head. It used to scare me, now I sit back and enjoy it.''

She completely covered her mouth and snorted. They both burst into laughter. Ethan sat beside her on the edge of the bed and they laughed together.

"Nuts," Fab said, leaning against him and feeling better. "We'll be okay, won't we? We'll get over it all and carry on."

"You bet, but are you sure the bells in your head have anything to do with me?"

She punched his arm. "We're being absolutely honest, right?"

"Absolutely."

"I hate that you called our lovemaking 'animal.' It demeans it. Animal's heads and hearts aren't involved in these things."

He settled a hand on her thigh. There was nothing animal about the excitement he felt, or the strong sexual urge. "I think women want to believe men think the way women do. They don't really, Fab. The urge for sex is stronger in a man."

"Says who?" Her glare shocked him. She was absolutely furious. "Now there's a myth. We are very sexual. We talk as much if not more about men and about sex. We probably think a whole lot more about men because we aren't as goal oriented. We like to think of all the juicy stops along the way. Would you turn down the offer if I wanted to tie you to the bed and do things to you for hours before we actually got to what you think of as the *goal!*"

He felt himself pale. "Fab," he said weakly.

"Fab, what? You would like it, or you wouldn't?"

"I guess it would be pretty cool."

Fab bent her neck forward to hide her face, and she closed her eyes. "Right answer. And the thought turns me on, too. It's called foreplay and women think about it a lot. But I don't think there are too many animals who plan that way. Oompa, the sexpot elephant, walks by and Big Ears, the stud elephant, sends her a signal. She stops, presents the appropriate parts. He moseys up, and voila. They walk on. That's animal."

"My choice of words was poor," Ethan said.

"Very poor." An unbelievable apathy swept over her. "I don't want to admit this, but I feel weak."

"Get into the bed. You've got to see a doctor again, but right now you need food."

"Not now. Maybe later."

So much for progress, Ethan thought, having no choice but to move away from the bed while she got in.

"Thanks for everything," she said, her voice muffled.

"Why don't I stick around while you sleep, in case you wake up and need something."

"I'm okay. Please lock up on your way out."

He felt like breaking something. "Okay, okay. If that's the way you want it. You've got it."

"Yes." And to his confusion she pulled the covers over her head and curled into a ball beneath them.

"Fab? Maybe we should just get married."

"Goodbye, Ethan."

He cast his eyes heavenward. His timing was lousy. Fab was crying quietly.

WITHIN TEN MINUTES of Ethan's departure, Fab's phone rang. She considered not answering, but it could be a member of her family so she picked it up. "Don't hang up," Ethan said. "I am such a clumsy idiot. I can't believe I sprang that on you like that."

"Forget it," she told him. "We're handicapped, just think of it that way. We haven't had a lot of experience at this."

"You have."

"No, I haven't. The men I meet don't ask me to marry them, they ask me to sleep with them, offer me expensive gifts and want me to be publicly photographed with them. That's it."

"Give me a list of names. They're dead meat."

She plucked at her gown. "Look, I've been a bit teary eyed lately. Too emotional, I guess. But I don't want to cry anymore tonight so I'm going to sleep. We'll talk again very soon." She hung up.

Five more minutes and she called him back.

There was no answer at the condo so she left a message, then tried his cell phone. She'd never known him to decide to go on a bender but there was always a first time.

"Ethan Warrick here," he said shortly.

"It's Fab. Forgive me for being a pill tonight. Thank you for caring about me."

"I do, buddy. Very much."

"Thank you."

"You're the best," Ethan said. "Men who never know a woman as a real friend—"

"I know. They miss out. Ditto for women. Good night, Ethan—my friend."

IN THEIR HOUSE in the hills above the lake, Nasty nestled Polly against his naked chest and kissed her hair—when he wasn't taking advantage of her being on the phone to slide a hand inside her nightgown and stroke her breasts.

She wiggled, but only in anticipation. "So what are the two of you waiting for?" she said into the mouthpiece, growing testy. "You're mad about him, he's said he doesn't want to lose you. End of story."

Fab repeated parts of her story yet again while Polly waggled her head. "So you've already told me. Ethan came bearing gifts and chicken soup and lots of attention and you told him to get lost."

On her end Fab had descended to being maudlin. "Some things are really wrong, Polly."

"True."

"Like a little girl growing up with a name kids laughed at but which pleased mom because she's always had to be free spirited, no matter who she hurt. I used to pretend I didn't care about the teasing, y'know, but I did."

"I know. I was there, remember. I took my share of knocks." She looked up at Nasty, whose face she never tired of seeing. Right now he looked deeply troubled.

"I know you did, Pualani. Can you believe you got that because Venus was on a Hawaiian kick?"

"I believe it. I've accepted it. What I detested was the way she pretended our father was away at sea all the time. When the kids laughed and said he had to be a fossil by now, they scared me." Polly got a lump in her throat. "Even now she doesn't admit they were never really together."

"I think I'm losing it. It's as if I'm looking for reasons to be miserable." Fab lowered her voice and said, "Don't tell Nasty, but I really love Ethan."

"Okay, sis. Now, please, get some sleep and I'll be there in the morning."

Polly hung up the phone and turned to kiss her husband. "Fabiola really loves Ethan."

ETHAN HADN'T LEFT FAB'S. He couldn't in case she needed him. Instead he stretched out on the comfortable couch in the basement and turned the television on with no sound.

Phoenix Wilde. The name just popped into his mind. Now there was one sensible woman. She had taken and tamed Roman Wilde after a bizarre meeting at a so-called social club where they were both trying to infiltrate deep enough to locate a missing woman. And another self-reliant SEAL who had vowed never to love had bitten the dust in Phoenix's arms.

Just in case Fab decided to make a call, Ethan used his cell phone and was grateful when Phoenix was the one who picked up the phone on their Montana ranch. Roman the rancher. That still made Ethan smile.

"Phoenix, babe, can you spare a few minutes?"

"Well, I do believe I hear the dulcet tones of Ethan Warrick. And I may be pleased to talk to him when he apologizes for calling me *babe*. Really, Ethan."

"Sorry, ma'am. Mrs. Wilde." He launched into the long tale that sounded horrible in his ears. "I blew it at every turn. We care about each other. More than care about each other. Unfortunately, I want more than we've had up to now." He gritted his teeth and told her about the golden auras and how Fab had told him about bells in her head.

The utter silence on the other end of the line embarrassed him. "Forget I told you that, please."

"I'm honored you trusted me. I think you two are deeply in love."

"Thanks, Phoenix. Give my best to Roman and I'd appreciate it if you'd save my reputation by not mentioning the auras."

"You've got it, but don't hang up. I'm going to tell you what you want to hear. After all, that's the only reason you called. Tell her you're getting married. Just do it. Then call us back when it's done so we can make arrangements to be there."

"OH, ROMAN, I'm sorry to interrupt you," Fabiola said. "I expected Phoenix to pick up."

"She just got off another line and has gone to check on the kids." He sounded funny. "Will I do?"

The idea of talking to Roman, although she knew him well, embarrassed her. "No. Sorry to bother you. I'll call back later."

"I think you're upset. You sound upset. Spill it. We're both grown-ups."

Fab visualized the big, rugged man who was a tad war torn and the more electrifying for it.

"Let's have it, Fab, or I'll call Ethan to see what's going on."

"You are so underhanded," she said. "But you're lovable." She told her long, boring story. She started at the beginning and ended with the mortifying admission that she looked at Ethan and heard noises if she thought he was unhappy.

After the briefest of pauses Roman said, "I thought you had a real problem. This is easy. Marry the guy and make sure he's always happy."

"He hasn't asked me. Not really."

"So ask him. Then maybe he'll quit seeing halos over your head."

They got off the phone and Fabiola fumed. How many other people had Ethan discussed her with?

ETHAN DIDN'T WAIT too long before starting to climb the stairs slowly. In the kitchen he used the instant boiling water dispenser to make two cups of green tea and fished out the bag of fortune cookies he'd bought. Fab liked to pull out all the fortunes while he ate the cookies. He set the soup cans on the counter. The champagne and the wonderful cake from Park Place were already in the refrigerator.

Up he went with the tea and cookies on a tray. Fab's light was on.

"It's me again, Fab. Ethan. I come bearing tea and cookies."

She didn't answer at once, then said, "You left."

"I'm back." No point in talking with a door between them.

"I'm a fright. You can't come in."

"Are you decent?"

"Yes."

"I'm coming in." And, naturally, she looked

terrific although she'd taken a shower and her hair was in a damp knot on top of her head. Her gown was of thin white stuff with panels of lace. She sat in one of the barrel chairs near the windows.

"Tea," he said, sliding the tray onto the table beside her and putting the bag of fortune cookies in her lap. He sat down and removed the tea bag, putting it into a spare saucer before passing her a cup of tea.

She took a sip and said, "How's my halo?"

He felt his mouth fall open. He hadn't mentioned halos to Fab—a golden glow, yes, but not *halos*. Wait till he got his hands on his dear old friends. "It's great. Hearing any bells? If you are, it isn't because I'm unhappy, it's because I'm *mad*. Friendship means you keep confidences, doesn't it?"

"I think so. You know I do."

"I've got to do this now. Fabiola, will you marry me?"

She took a great breath and let it out, and looked at him. "You're asking because you think I need to be rescued from myself. I don't. I've had some difficult weeks with my health. Maybe I'm overworked. That's all it is."

"You don't need rescuing. I asked because I love you."

She set her tea and cookies aside and sat with her hands in her lap. His cup joined hers while he tried to decide where to go from here. Easy. The guy kissed the girl. He left his chair and bent over her. Angling his head, he did just that, softly, pushing her face up with his thumbs beneath her chin. Too soon the soft kiss wasn't enough and his eyes closed tightly while he put into that kiss all the longing, the wanting, the frustration of too much waiting.

Fab caught at his arms and felt a sense of heaven, of everything being right. She stood up and held him.

"So," he whispered, "will you marry me?"

"It feels so strange to hear you say that."

Ethan said, "It feels great."

"I'm afraid it might not work."

He stroked her shoulders. Panels of lace revealed her nipples while the thin, almost gauzy stuff of the rest of the gown turned to the color of her skin where it touched her. Yes, he lusted for her and felt no shame. He also loved her.

"Are you afraid?" she asked.

"It's already too late to turn back. But what do you think could make us a bad idea?" he asked her. "We've shared everything, except the kind of sex that takes the whole night and means we wake up together in the morning. Is that what you're afraid of, bad sex?"

Fabiola pushed hard on his chest. "I don't want to talk to you. Why do men always think sex is the most important part of—whatever?"

Ethan stung, from what he'd said and from her reaction. "Of marriage?" he asked.

"That, too, I suppose."

"So is it the fear of unsatisfactory sex that turns you off saying you'll marry me?" They'd settle down and come through as winners, they had to.

"Sex can ruin things."

Muscles between his shoulders cramped. "So that's what the story is. You want more proof that it works for us, first."

"I—yes." She massaged her temples and said in a small voice, "No, Ethan, it's not. I'm sorry I keep messing up."

"We both keep messing up," he said, and wrapped her tightly to him again.

Fab shuddered. There were things she had to say.

Ethan could hardly swallow. "You're too gentle. You need to fight back when I come on too strong."

Obviously forgetting the revealing gown, she wrenched away from him and settled her hands on her hips. "I'm going to fight back and I'm going to fight dirty. When we made love, I planned it. I turned off the water in the guest bath and hid the shutoff key. It might not have, but it all worked and everything was great until you started to feel guilty."

Caught between shock and a desire to laugh, he looked away, buying time to find the right reaction.

"Please say something," Fabiola said.

Wait a bit longer, Ethan, don't be too quick. She sorta said sex was an issue. "I think you're the one with more to say."

"I loved it—being with you. But I deceived you and now I'm pregnant. We were together shortly before my period was due in January and I was taking pills. The pills failed. Now the doctor says everything looks great for me to have a healthy baby."

A sensation resembling a punch to the belly stole Ethan's breath. "A baby?"

"What else would I have but a baby?"

Fabiola was pregnant. *They* were expecting a baby.

"I am having the baby and keeping her."

"Him." He was light-headed and stared at her stomach where he saw nothing different.

"Her or him," Fabiola said. "It doesn't matter. I apologize for what I've done to you. That sounds so weak, but I don't know what else to say."

"I don't believe this," he said, catching her up in his arms. "What you've done *to* me? It's what you've done for me." His smile was wide, thrilled. "Will you marry me?"

She believed he wanted this as much as she did. "Yes, Ethan."

Very slowly, he rotated with her. Different shades of light from the bedside lamp and the glow from the bathroom passed over her face. She relaxed and became heavier in his arms. Looking into his eyes, she kicked her feet and the gauze gown fluttered like some sort of antique wedding gown, Victorian, maybe. What did he know about those things?

"You're going to get dizzy," she said.

He stood still and swung her back and forth. "I can't bear to stop holding you. I truly never expected such happiness to come my way." He frowned at her stomach. "How long before it's obvious?"

There came the bells, like carillons this time. "A couple of months. It's there even now. Round and firm. Will you be embarrassed when it really shows?"

"Are you kidding? I want everyone to see. Fab..." He peered closely at her and inhaled sharply. "No, surely I can't hear your bells."

"Well, I can see that gold stuff in your eyes."

"We'd better not talk about this again—not to other people," he said. "I'm going to set you down, but I'm not leaving."

"Now you're going to be masterful?"

"You'll need that sometimes." Throwing back the covers, he settled her, straightened her legs and made sure her gown was pulled down. He felt her tummy from different directions and grinned. "Your tummy's so tight my baby's going to have to punch his way around to make room."

"He'll manage."

Next he sat beside her again and put his ear where his hand had been. "Ethan Junior, you're going to be an Olympic swimmer. And we're going white-water rafting and sailing and diving."

"You won't make all the decisions about what our children get to do," Fab told him. She opened his shirt and tweaked his nipples until he caught her wrists and stopped her. "You're killing me. Do you know how that feels?"

"Nope."

"Too good. Keep still." Promptly he slid her gown upward and over her hips. She wore a skimpy white thong but apparently even that was too much for Ethan. He took it off and squeezed lotion from a bottle at Fab's bedside. With this he massaged her belly, smiling with every gentle stroke over her womb. The massage continued down her lean hips, to her thighs. He worked the lotion into the length of her legs, making sure he found the most responsive place on her body with each pass. Each time he touched her there, her hips lifted and she pressed her palms into the mattress.

An aching pull built languorously. Because of the way Ethan teased, she kept expecting the sensation to go away. He stretched out beside her and the teasing was gone—and in seconds she looked at him with soundless satisfaction while he smiled. But his face and eyes were darker, more intense.

She felt air on her breasts as he raised her gown higher, then once again the stimulating ministra-

tion of Ethan's hand covered with lotion. Fab
rolled from side to side beneath his hand, holding
her breath, wishing she could ask for all she
wanted.

Fabiola undid his dark gray shirt to the waist,
struggled with his belt and made enough room to
stroke his belly and chest. "You make me want to
spend the rest of my life in bed," she said. "Forget
I said that. I want to be running around with you
again as soon as possible, and I will be. But I do
want to lie with you, Ethan. I want to know we'll
be together like this whenever we want to be."

He laughed, and lowered his head to kiss her
breasts. He reared his head to look, and he concentrated, considering them from one angle, then
another.

"Don't do that," Fabiola cried. "You're embarrassing me."

"Just a survey. They're larger. And I'm not
sure, but I don't think the veins were so obvious.
Beautiful. I think it would be better if you didn't
wear clothes until the baby's born. Then I won't
miss anything that happens."

"Mad," she said, "completely mad. This gown
doesn't feel comfortable under my arms like this."

"No problem." He helped her take it off and
she immediately burrowed against him and shot a
hand down inside his jeans. "D'you need a
shower?"

"Fabiola!"

"I hope you're not going to keep saying that in the same tone of voice."

"We can't say sexy things, or make sexy suggestions. Not right now. We have a child to consider."

"She won't mind." This was what she had never had, this intimacy that was electric but so natural.

Fab pushed deeper. "I want that giant chili pepper."

Ethan sputtered, and howled when she reached her goal. He turned onto his back and panted.

"And your sumptuous figs. And I'll also want you on your stomach so I can check out your honeydews."

"You've gone to the dogs," Ethan said. "How could I not have noticed what was happening? I can't believe your mouth, madam. Chili pepper?"

"This is code. We know babies hear in the womb. You just told me to be careful what I say in front of her, so I'm being careful. This way she won't guess what I'm talking about. Please finish taking off your clothes."

He stood up and did so and she realized this was the first time they'd ever taken off their clothes in front of each other. Dropping towels was different. Things were going rather well. After retrieving the lotion, she knelt and patted the bed.

Ethan looked at the lotion and she saw him swallow. While he stood there, she took advantage of the opportunity to study him without feeling nervous. The puckered puncture scar beneath the left side of his ribs folded in on itself and looked evil. "Mmm, I do like looking at you. That's quite a scar."

"It's nothing."

And he wasn't about to talk about it, so she wouldn't push him. "Kindly lie down so I may practice the ancient arts I've learned. On your back, first."

There wasn't even an attempt at hesitation. He all but flopped onto the mattress, folded his hands beneath his head, closed his eyes while a gentle smile turned up the corners of his mouth, and wiggled his toes.

Well, two could play his games.

Rather than put the lotion on her hands first, she held the tube high and drizzled a thin line over his torso. His eyes flew open at once and he moved to take his arms down but the lotion hit one underarm then the other and he held still. Fab made sure her expression was serene and distant.

Drizzling on, she made small circles around his nipples, his navel, and a wider one on his abdomen. He flinched at the cold.

Fab considered the rest of him while she knew he watched her with some alarm. A single thick bead the length of his legs would do the trick.

She sat back on her heels and considered the remaining part.

"Better start rubbing that in before it gets all over the sheets," Ethan said.

"It'll get all over the sheets anyway. I don't care. Let me think here."

He squirmed and rocked his pelvis—with a predictably erotic effect.

She nodded, held the bottle, and while Ethan yelled, "No, Fab!" she put a steadying hand on him and squeezed the tube, producing an artful, free-form design on his groin that brought his hips off the bed.

Fab massaged every inch of the man. He had more hyperreflexes than she'd ever seen—or maybe he was more tense than she'd realized.

He arched his neck and closed his eyes. "My fabulous Fab," he murmured. "You are so beautiful and so sexy."

"I won't always be beautiful."

"Ah," he said as she ran her thumbs up and down him. "But you will always be sexy and you will always be mine. I've changed my mind about that baby on your bracelet. It's our baby, okay?"

"I knew it as soon as I saw it."

He didn't guess her intention until she sat on his calves and bent over him. He smiled, but only for a second before she began the sweetest torture of his life. "Fab," he panted. "Fab, I can't take it."

"Sure you can. We're going to want lots of babies. I've got to take good care of things here." Taking good care consisted of squeezing and strok-

ing him in a way that threatened to make him climax instantly.

"Kiss me," he said on a long breath. "Kiss me,
love."

She took him into her mouth and kissed.

Ethan shuddered, gripped her beneath the arms
and pulled her over him. "I meant my mouth," he
said, and they kissed. They kissed and Ethan
guided himself into her.

At first they rocked together, his feet beneath
hers, supporting them. Fab pulled up her knees,
kept on kissing him, and fell into a beautiful
rhythm that jarred his breath under his ribs. Slowly
at first, but with increasing desperation, the dance
as old as all time carried them.

When he rode on the tide of his own release,
Fab rode with him until they fell into a heap together. Obviously depleted, Ethan reached for a
sheet and covered them. He rested on one elbow
to look at her, gave her a long, long, deep kiss,
then fell instantly asleep.

Fab watched him as long as she could before
she, too, succumbed.

SHE AWOKE ALONE to a cool room. Holding very
still, she peered around, trying to make out shapes.
Then she saw him. Ethan sat by the round table,
his head turned in her direction. He appeared to be
waiting.

"Ethan?"

"At last. It's about time. I was afraid you'd sleep all the way until morning and I couldn't have stood that. I'd have had to get you up."

She scooted to turn on a lamp. "What's the matter? What's happened?"

"Me. That's what happened. My memory goes on the fritz when I'm on edge."

"Did it do that when you were on active service?"

He looked bemused. "Why would it? I wasn't on edge, or not this type of edge."

"I see. So what's going on?"

"This. I almost forgot it. Champagne. Actually yours is some of the sparkling cider you had in the refrigerator."

"Is yours champagne?"

He checked his glass. "Yes. I'm celebrating because I'm having a baby."

"So am I."

"Pregnant women don't drink alcohol."

"I knew that," she said, feeling like a dummy for forgetting, even momentarily. "I was just testing you."

He placed her glass on the bedside table and gave her a plate bearing a vast piece of spectacular cake with a raspberry mousse filling. "From Park Place," he said. "And I got you a marzipan pig because you like marzipan."

"Oh, yum," she said. "It isn't going to take long for me to resemble a pig. Come closer, I want to kiss you under your chin. I keep looking at that spot.''

He pretended to drag his feet, but bent over her and raised his jaw. She licked him there and gave him a short, sharp nip, and tweaked between his legs before he leaped away again. "Love that chili," she said, thoroughly thrilled with her own sense of humor.

"Please," he said. "I'm begging you, Fab. Don't let anyone hear you talk like that."

"Wouldn't dream of it. You're naked, Mr. Warrick."

"So are you, Ms. Crow."

"What do you think we should do about that?" Fab asked.

"Not a thing. Here." He took the glass to her lips and she swallowed a mouthful. This he followed with a forkful of the cake that was so light it made her close her eyes.

And while her eyes were closed, Ethan slipped the ring he'd bought onto her finger and her eyes flew open again. Her cheeks were puffed out with cake, there was more cake on her lips and on her hands, and crumbs had fallen on her chest. Her hair had dried into a shaggy mass of curls. He tried to see her as other than delightful and failed.

"Mmm, mmm," she said, swallowing as fast as she could.

"I took a chance and picked it out two weeks ago." He handed her more cider and she managed to clear her mouth. He wiped her mouth himself before taking her plate away, licked the crumbs from her breasts, then cleaned off her left hand. "What do you think?"

She tried to behave as if the ring weren't slipping around her finger.

"If you like it, we'll have it sized by my friend on Lake Street. He made it but I couldn't get my hands on anything to use for sizing."

"It's too much," she said, and her mouth didn't fully close . "You can't afford this."

"Hey, you. I can too afford it. I've never had anything or anyone to spend money on, and I've made a fair amount. Now I want to spend it on you."

Fab studied the emerald-cut diamond from every direction and fell in love all over again. "I never thought I cared about diamonds, but I do now." The stone was incredible.

"These are the earrings to go with it," he said, producing another box. "You'll need them for the wedding, of course."

"Of course. When's the wedding?"

He raised an eyebrow. "Was that sarcasm?"

"Oh, no. After all, you know everything that's going to happen. It only makes sense you know about that."

He gave her a sideways leer. "Glad you understand." He strode around the room, obviously very comfortable in his own skin. Fab had begun to jump around inside hers.

He found his wallet and took out a card. "We need a wedding coordinator. This woman comes highly recommended. Her outfit is called Exquisite Detail. Only exquisite will do for us. Will you call or shall I?"

She rubbed her forehead. In truth she felt shell-shocked and wished he would come back to bed.

"I will," he said. "You take it easy. Just tell me when you want to do it."

"April second," she told him promptly. "That isn't long. Do you think it can be arranged?"

"I've been told this lady can handle anything. But why so sure of the date?"

"Well, I've always wanted to be married in April because I sort of feel spring's on its way, even if it isn't. And I'm not getting married on April Fools' Day.

April second

To DUSTY'S ANNOYANCE, Fabiola and Ethan were to be married on Ethan's terrace rather than at Dusty's house. Venus also made no secret of her displeasure at the decision, but the couple turned off their ire in time for the wedding. Sun favored the day, so the ceremony was outside.

The minister was an ex-service chaplain Ethan knew. Roman and Nasty would stand up for Ethan.

Polly and Phoenix would flank Fabiola with Venus and Dusty standing by to give her away.

A jazz quartet played in a subdued manner in advance of the ceremony, but promised the lid would come off afterward and people would dance in the streets of Kirkland.

Waiting for his bride, Ethan was irresistibly suave in his black tux and tie. But Fab stole the show. In white satin-banded chiffon, she didn't seem to touch the ground when she walked onto the terrace. A halter neck left her smooth shoulders bare, and her train was long in a way that only Fab would wear so well. When Dusty and Venus had done their part and retired, with Venus sniffing loudly, Fab and Ethan stood before an amazing display of flowers. Vases of pale cream orchids with shiny green ti leaves, bird-of-paradise blooms—orange and dashing red—ginger, and pink bromeliad covered specially erected risers. The condo itself was filled with arrangements of the same flowers. Fabiola's unfashionably large bouquet was of pink and white roses and the most delicate of trailing ferns. She had insisted she wanted the kind of bouquet she'd dreamed of as a girl and this was it.

Of the children, only April Wilde was dressed as a flower girl, but she was a serious little girl who, at three and a half, wore the importance of her position with a determined expression that charmed everyone.

The terrace was crammed with people. Cindy York was there with a photographer in tow and she whispered to Polly, "Don't they look wonderful? This'll be everywhere tomorrow."

Polly smiled politely but said, "Be vague about the address, will you?"

"Of course," Cindy said, as if offended that anyone might expect her to do otherwise. Apparently she'd decided to believe Fab when she'd assured her assistant that her job wouldn't end today.

The doors to the inside were open and more people crowded as close as they could get.

At last the pianist broke into a spellbinding rendition of "Ave Maria." The sound of the musician's gravelly voice singing with touching reverence brought Fab close to those wretched tears again. She looked sideways at Ethan and could have sworn his eyes were moist. He held her hand tightly and their fingers shook.

They had discussed their vows carefully, and when the time came, the minister said, "Do you, Ethan and Fabiola, take each other in—"

"We do," they said together, not waiting for him to finish.

He smiled, but repeated the vow and this time they got it right.

There was laughter.

"Will you, Ethan and Fabiola..." The minister finished his question and Ethan and Fabiola said, "We will."

Ethan leaned close to Fab's ear and said in what was supposed to be for their ears only, "We do and we will. Often."

Unfortunately, those closest heard and a ripple of chuckles started there and gradually rose throughout the gathering.

When the ceremony was over, they posed for pictures, the gang creating crazy poses among the unforgettable ones of Ethan and Fabiola. All the little children were let loose.

"Dishonesty shouldn't pay off this well," Fab told Ethan in a quiet moment.

He grinned and said, "Don't worry, I'm going to make you pay. Oh, the things you'll have to do for me—to me, actually. And the things you'll have to put up with me doing to you. It may be some time before I allow you out of the house at all. I've got a present for you."

"Another one? You've already given me way too much."

"I've been waiting for an opportunity to give you this. Come see."

She went with him to his office where he waved her onto the chaise and sat in his desk chair. "Isn't this great? You and me. Married. I feel so great."

"Great," she agreed. "We've got a lot of guests out there."

"True. Meet Scoundrel."

Produced from a small crate beneath Ethan's desk, Scoundrel probably weighed in at around fourteen pounds, had eyes like shiny pebbles, and black-and-tan fur that had no idea what it was supposed to do.

"Look at him," Fabiola crooned. "What a perfect sweetie. Where did you get him?"

"At the pound, of course. He's seven years old, and a bit quiet. Apparently he's been left behind in a couple of apartments. They didn't think they could find another home for him. I told them his home was waiting for him, it always has been."

Scoundrel went directly to Fab, sat down and studied her. He lifted one paw and she shook it. Then he stood up and pressed against her legs. Promptly she lifted him up.

"Watch your dress," Ethan said mildly.

"He's very clean," she said, standing and cuddling the plain little dog close. The lick she got cinched it. "He's perfect. He's going to be my friend. Oh, thank you, Ethan."

"Think nothing of it. Whatever you want, you shall have. Hey, Scoundrel, happy now?"

The dog turned his bright eyes on Ethan, drew back his lips and growled.

Ethan rolled his eyes. "Figures. Ungrateful hound."

"It's a lot to take in," Fab told him. "Come on, or some smart aleck will start getting the wrong idea about where we are."

"We could make it the right idea."

She dragged him from the office to the kitchen,

where food was being assembled and disappearing rapidly.

Ethan, with Fabiola holding Scoundrel, went out onto the terrace and they were instantly surrounded. Scoundrel outdid himself by charming everyone.

When it was time to cut the cake, Fab set the dog down, flipped her train over her arm and sashayed to the table.

When Ethan didn't arrive immediately, she looked around for him. He stood as if he couldn't move, watching Scoundrel pee on his shoes.

ENGAGING EVENTS

Bobby Hutchinson

CHAPTER ONE

"GOOD AFTERNOON, all you listeners out there in radio land. This is Diana Kelly, and welcome to *Woman Talk*." The announcer with the slept-in mound of tomato-red hair and the anorexic, leather-clad body managed to sound hysterically enthusiastic while looking terminally bored.

Grace, feeling older than her twenty-eight years and rather like the before picture in a diet ad, sucked in her tummy and smoothed her perspiring hands down the legs of her navy linen trousers. She reminded herself that this was radio. Nobody could see her except the bald man in the control booth outside the studio window, and he wasn't looking.

Neither was Diana, for that matter.

Grace shoved a strand of tawny hair behind her ear and tried not to breathe audibly into the mike in front of her.

"April's here, the daffodils are sprouting, spring is in the air," Diana enthused, "and since spring is a favorite time for weddings, that's what we're going to talk about today.'' She kept her eyes focused on the paper she was holding, and Grace noticed that one of her artificial nails had fallen off. The real nail was bitten to the quick.

''We're fortunate to have Grace Madison here in the studio with us. Grace is the owner and imaginative genius behind Engaging Events, the business which is fast becoming Vancouver's most popular resource for brides-to-be planning an unusual wedding. Hi, Grace. Welcome to the show.'' Diana didn't even glance at her.

''Hi, Diana, nice to be here,'' Grace lied. Her stomach suddenly gave an embarrassingly loud gurgle, and she had to swallow hard against the awful dryness in her throat. Being interviewed on *Woman Talk* might be good advertising, but she was so nervous she was certain her voice was going to wobble while her brain went dead.

Why hadn't she made Priscilla do this interview? Wasn't that what an employee was for, to take the stress out of the boss's life? Unflappable Priscilla would have found a way to shake up this snotty announcer, too. But they'd talked it over, and Grace had reluctantly agreed that this was one of those times when delegating wasn't an option. Engaging Events was her business. She was the one who should talk about it.

''Tell me, Grace, how did you get into this

theme thing with weddings, anyhow? Could it have been a wedding of your own that got you interested?'' Diana made it sound as if they were two girlfriends having a delightful little chat, but in truth the interviewer still hadn't once looked straight at Grace. Diana was reading from the sheet of typed notes on the table and now she smothered a yawn behind her palm.

"My own wedding did it, all right.'' It was hard to sound chipper while talking to someone who didn't bother to even look at you. Grace soldiered on, however. She was painfully aware that Priscilla and Wayne would have their ears pressed to the radio at the store. And Grace's mother, Lucille, would also be listening, unless, of course, Lucille had found a sale she couldn't resist.

"My mother and I planned my wedding. It was in the backyard of my parent's house, under the massive oak tree where my brothers and I had played when we were little.''

"Sounds idyllic.'' Diana studied her broken fingernail and shook her head in disgust.

"It should have been, but everything that could have gone wrong did.'' Which maybe should have given Grace a hint that the marriage wasn't going to do so well either.

"My high heels sank into the grass during the ceremony, and I fell to my knees when I tried to move. A bird in the oak tree above us messed all over the minister's cassock. A neighbor's dog barked throughout. Hornets attacked the guests and one of them had an allergic reaction. We had to call 911. Afterward, I realized how many things there were to consider about weddings, and how much more enjoyable the entire thing could have been if someone neutral and sane was in charge.'' Too late, she realized that sounded very much like an insult to Lucille.

Hang it all, this was tough. Grace began to talk faster, to get the whole thing over with as soon as possible. ''So within a few months of my wedding, I started Engaging Events. That was four years ago, and the business has really taken off since then.''

So had the man she'd married under that oak tree. He had disappeared from her life, hand in hand with Grace's bridesmaid and lifelong best friend, Melanie.

''Your husband must be very proud of your success.''

Grace was certain she'd told the production assistant she was single. Diana was either vicious or stupid.

''We're no longer married.''

She'd lost a partner and a lawyer, as well as a husband and best friend. Grace's ex-husband,

Lloyd Madison, was a lawyer, and had been the legal advisor for Engaging Events. Melanie had been Grace's partner. The whole happy triangle collapsed the night Grace went to Lloyd's office with a pizza and found Melanie naked on his brown tweed sofa. The divorce had been final fourteen months ago.

Fortunately, Diane didn't pursue the divorce issue.

"Grace, let's say I've *just* gotten engaged to the man of my dreams." Diana rolled her eyes and pulled a face that indicated that was the most ludicrous scenario she could possibly imagine. "I want the wedding to be *spectacular* and *unusual,* so *of course* I come to you. What would you suggest?"

A different bride for the poor sucker? Grace had the distinct impression Diana was a first-class ball breaker. She'd actually called Grace *dear,* in an utterly condescending tone, an instant before they'd gone on the air. It had made Grace want to call her *sweetie,* in a matching saccharine voice.

She shoved the nasty thought out of her mind and concentrated on the question. "First, I'd ask what you planned to spend, Diana, keeping in mind that we use imagination and ingenuity at Engaging Events, at either end of the financial scale." Grace was horrified to hear that her voice had somehow taken on Diana's upbeat, almost manic tempo. "Then, I'd find out what special interests you and your groom share, or what favorite fantasy either of you would like to play out on your wedding day."

"Oohh, fantasies. Well, I'm *sure* we all have some of *those* tucked away," Diana said, leering at her guest. "What sort of fantasy are we *talking* about here, Grace? Keeping in mind that this is a family show, or course." Diana waggled a cautionary finger, and too late Grace realized her remark could be misconstrued. She felt herself blushing and couldn't think what to say.

Diana raised an inquiring eyebrow and tapped her wristwatch. *Can't have dead air time—dear.*

Damn the woman. "I was thinking of something, um, like the masquerade ball we did for a Christmas wedding, or the Halloween wedding we organized last fall," Grace heard herself babbling. "Couples often have a particular date and theme in mind beforehand, but if they don't, the staff and I at Engaging Events thoroughly enjoy finding one that's fun and fitting and unique."

The staff and I? What was wrong with her? Now she was sounding like the president of Wal-Mart, for heaven's sake.

Her heart sank as Diana instantly sensed a weak spot and zeroed in.

CHAPTER TWO

"WE ALL KNOW how much work goes into arranging a dinner party, never mind a wedding. You must have a sizable staff at Engaging Events to assist you, Grace."

Grace swallowed hard and hoped the mike hadn't picked up the sound. "Not really. Two besides myself. Priscilla Philips and Wayne Day work with me full-time. Priscilla's the artistic genius and Wayne works in the shop. He's brilliant at either finding or making the right gown for any occasion. Of course I have a sizable part-time staff available to help out with large weddings."

Right, idiot. And that would be your two hapless younger brothers, and whatever scruffy sober friends they might have hanging around. And, God help her, there was her mother, but to give herself credit, she only called on Lucille when things were truly, horribly, irretrievably desperate.

She should have more staff, Grace knew that. But the simple truth was she couldn't afford them, and that was something she'd really rather not tell the entire Lower Mainland listening audience.

She was digging a deep hole here, one that Diana would undoubtedly enjoy filling in with her in it. Grace waited miserably for the next probing question about employees or ex-husbands or mothers, but Diana missed her cue.

"Okay, let's get back to *my* imaginary wedding, Grace," she said with a dramatic roll of her eyes. "Let's say, just for fun, that the guy I was marrying was a professor of Greek, and we wanted an ancient Greek wedding. Describe it for me."

"Greek. Okay, let's see." She hadn't done an ancient Greek wedding, and Grace prayed desperately for an idea, any idea. If Diana was trying to make a fool of her, catch her without an answer, she was close to succeeding.

"What comes to mind are the gods and goddesses on Mount Olympus," she blurted, surprising herself. "So hopefully it would be in the summer, and we'd do something with lots of feasting and plenty of wine, and we'd set up columns in the style of the Parthenon, and follow ancient Greek wedding rituals." *Whatever the hell they might be.*

She raced on before Diana could ask.

"We'd have traditional Greek food, and maybe

keep the dresses simple and classic.'' With a sense of foreboding, Grace waited for Diana to ask a question she couldn't answer, but the other woman was distracted by the bald man in the control booth. He was pointing at the clock and making windup gestures.

"How delightful. It sounds like just the sort of wedding I've always dreamed of,'' Diana cooed, barely suppressing another yawn. "And I'll certainly call Engaging Events as soon as I locate the professor,'' she added with a laugh that sounded sincere, although it looked phony as hell.

How did she *do* that? Grace again wiped her sweaty palms down her linen slacks, which felt as limp and wrinkled as they probably looked. She should have worn chain mail.

"And now it's time to wind up our show for today, and thank our guest, Grace Madison of Engaging Events, for talking with us. And remember, listeners, if you have a wedding dilemma that needs solving, you know who to call. You can reach Grace at 555-9514, and her shop is at 3547 West Broadway. Until tomorrow, this is Diana Kelly, wishing you a cheerful and productive Monday.''

Grace felt utterly drained. Diana was already on the phone, frowning and talking in a low, intense tone to someone called Louie. She appeared not to even see Grace get to her feet and hurry out of the room.

Her legs felt as if she'd jogged ten miles too far. In the outer office, Tracey, the enthusiastic young production assistant who'd contacted Grace to set up the interview, and who'd undoubtedly provided Diana with the typed questions, gave her a wide freckle-faced grin and a thumbs-up.

"You were absolutely great. You've got a perfect voice for radio," Tracy enthused. "Three people have already called the switchboard. I bet you'll get tons of new customers."

Grace smiled weakly and gabbled a thank-you to Tracy before bolting out the door.

It was a perfect April afternoon, unusually warm for Vancouver in the early spring. The sunshine hurt her eyes, and Grace fumbled in her purse for her sunglasses. She wished she could take off the long-sleeved linen jacket that matched her pants, but since she only had a black lace bra underneath, that wasn't such a great idea. Instead, she climbed in her pickup and turned the air-conditioning on full. It took a few stoplights for her to realize that it wasn't working, and she swore under her breath and rolled the windows down.

She'd have to get her father to take a look at

it. Hugo Gamonski was a genius with motors. Lucille had said countless times she wished Hugo was as attentive to her as he was to his plumbing business and his car.

Grace had always adored her father. She figured maybe her mother had unreal expectations.

Maybe she was like her father in that regard, Grace mused. Maybe she, too, was unromantic and too focused on business. She wasn't exactly beating guys off with a broom. The last date she'd had was at Christmas, with the son of one of her mother's friends. It had been such a disaster she'd told her mother point-blank that she'd never again go out with anyone that Lucille suggested. Not ever, so don't even try.

Which might just mean she'd never go out again at all, Grace thought ruefully, as she reached the storefront that housed Engaging Events and parked the truck. Weddings should be a great place to meet single guys, but even if that was so, she was always too frantically busy to even notice them.

She slid out of the truck, aware that she was way beyond perspiration and into plain old sweat. She felt as if she'd spent the morning working out and then skipped a shower. As well as being hot, her muscles ached and she felt drained.

Inside the store, Wayne was flanked on either

side by an unhappy looking bride-to-be and her two older companions, women who resembled Cinderella's sisters. Wayne's prematurely white hair shone like a peace symbol in the midst of their darkness. They were flipping impatiently through catalogues, making disparaging remarks while Wayne patiently listened and pointed out yet another design. Grace hurried past them, grateful it was him instead of her dealing with them.

"Gracie, congrats, you were *brilliant*. Priscilla's on the phone in your office," Wayne called sotto voce as she ducked through the door behind the counter into the cramped warehouse space that housed the supplies the business had amassed over its four-year lifespan. Grace wound her way to her cubbyhole of an office past stacks of folding chairs and tables, bunches of silk flowers carefully wrapped in plastic, playbills from a theatrical wedding she'd organized for a pair of theater buffs, boxes of snowy linen tablecloths and napkins she'd bought at auction when an upscale restaurant went bankrupt, and a collection of candelabra she'd unearthed from various secondhand stores.

Priscilla was sitting behind the battered oak table Grace used as a desk, her size-eleven western boots propped on the tabletop.

The phone was clamped to her ear, and Priscilla was nodding and quietly saying, "Yes, of course, I fully understand." She said it three times in succession. She scribbled on the sketch pad she was holding in her lap and turned it so Grace could see.

Frank Stubbs. *Not* a happy camper.

Grace pointed a finger at her own chest and shook her head violently from side to side. Mr. Stubbs was the last person she felt like speaking to at this moment.

"I'll certainly give her that message, Mr. Stubbs. Yes, I understand. Absolutely. You're entitled to your feelings. I'll tell her, and I know she'll call you back very soon." Priscilla held the receiver away from her ear and waited patiently as a barrage of indecipherable, furious sounds came pouring out. When they subsided, Priscilla calmly said, "I must go now, Mr. Stubbs. Yes, I heard you loud and clear, and I'm sorry you feel that way. Goodbye now." She hung up gently, swung her feet down and aimed her calm, gentle smile at Grace.

"I heard the interview. You managed to get all the major points we talked about across in spite of that brain-dead announcer. You did good, boss." Priscilla unwound her six-foot one-inch frame from the chair and stretched. Her large hands touched the ceiling, her blond braid touched her waist, and the small office seemed to shrink even further as she moved out from behind the desk.

"I came back here to take Stubbs's call because he's got a loud voice and I didn't want the other customers to hear him raving." The office was Grace's sanctuary.

"I'm glad you did. Having somebody screeching about a disastrous wedding isn't exactly what I want other customers overhearing," Grace sighed. "What's the latest with him?"

"He's suing us. He says the horse bite on his arm got infected and Letitia, the bridesmaid who got thrown off the other horse, figures she's got whiplash and a back injury. And Mrs. Stubbs is still under sedation for hysteria."

It had been a very western wedding.

CHAPTER THREE

THE BRIDE AND GROOM wanted the ceremony performed with the entire wedding party and the minister on horseback. It had been a major challenge to find a minister willing and able to ride, and then find a ranch that agreed to supply the setting and the horses, but Grace and Priscilla had pulled it off, with a little help from Grace's brother, Barney. He had a friend whose parents owned a ranch, and they'd kindly agreed to have the wedding there.

"Stubbs is suing, huh? Well, I've got insurance, and I know the ranch owners are insured. I double-checked on that. And I can't see it was anyone's fault that the bridesmaid's horse went berserk," Grace grumbled. "If Stubbs hadn't decided to play the Sundance Kid and yank at the poor thing's bridle the way he did, he probably wouldn't have gotten bitten, either."

Priscilla nodded sympathetically, but Grace could tell she was biting her cheek to stop herself from bursting into giggles. She met Grace's eyes and, with a stifled snort, lost the battle. "Sorry. I k-keep remembering that poor bridesmaid hanging upside down from the stirrup with her dress up over her head. I swear it was those black thong panties that freaked out the other horses."

"You can bet that's what freaked out old Stubbs as well," Grace said, unable to stifle her own laughter. "He was yanking on the horse's bridle and staring at that girl's bare butt with his eyes popping out of their sockets. And I ask you, who the heck wears black thong panties under a yellow dress, anyway?"

"Not me. Mind you, they probably don't make thongs in any color big enough to fit my butt."

"Cut it out," Grace warned. She'd been giving Priscilla pep talks about self-esteem. The younger woman was large, but decidedly not fat. Priscilla just had the tall, muscular build of an Amazon. "I've told you I'd kill for legs like yours."

"And I'd trade my red Harley to be five-seven and a hundred twenty pounds like you," Priscilla replied.

"A hundred twenty-*seven,* and climbing," Grace corrected with a rueful grimace. "After seeing that radio announcer, I'm ready to lose a couple of pounds. Although she's in danger of going down the drain with the bathwater, she's so skinny. As for me, having Waldo's bakery move in next door isn't doing my figure any favors, not when he keeps bringing over those crème scones for you.''

Priscilla flushed deep magenta. Waldo White was a gentle giant of a man, and although he was at least twelve years older than Priscilla's twenty-four, Grace couldn't help but notice the electricity between the two.

''If he didn't have three little kids and a crazy ex I'd ask him to go for a ride on my bike,'' Priscilla confessed. ''But changing diapers and dealing with that nutty Gina isn't my idea of a good time.''

They'd witnessed Gina throwing rocks at Waldo's front window right after he'd moved in.

''The kids are cute, though.'' There'd been a time not so long ago when Grace had dreamed of changing diapers for the babies she and Lloyd would have, but not anymore. The divorce had been painful, and she didn't ever want to feel such agony again. The way to avoid it was to concentrate on her business and avoid relationships with men. Not hard to do, since there wasn't any Waldo on her horizon bringing crème scones.

''Speaking of crazy people, did my mother call?''

Priscilla smacked her forehead with her palm.

"Oh, jeez, I'm sorry, she did, and she wanted you to call her as soon as you got back. Stubbs and his ranting drove it right out of my head."

"Was it about the radio show?" Grace remembered saying something that could make Lucille mad.

"Nope. It was about her new lawyer. She didn't go into details with me."

"Double lucky you." Lucille was in the process of divorcing Grace's father, Hugo, for the second time, and she'd just changed lawyers for the third time. Lucille wanted the best representation in the city. According to her, that was Noah Burnside, apparently highly sought after because of his killer instincts and his reputation for getting his clients good settlements.

"My mother's making a career out of divorcing my dad," Grace sighed to Priscilla. "She's moved out of the house into an apartment, but she still wants to know if my dad and brothers are keeping the bathrooms clean." Grace shook her head. "Go figure. Why should she care?"

"How old were you when they divorced the first time?"

"Seventeen. Barney was thirteen, Theo eleven. They were divorced for two years, and then they got back together again, remarried, and spent the next six months in their bedroom with the door locked. They have what I'd call a volatile relationship."

"At least you have interesting parents," Priscilla said. "The most exciting thing mine do is buy a new kind of aphid spray for the roses."

"My father's interested in growing roses, but my mother's only interested in getting them, the long-stemmed kind, preferably by the dozen."

"Better call her. She'll think I didn't give you the message."

Priscilla left and Grace slumped down in her chair and reluctantly dialed her mother's number.

"Gracie, thank *God* it's you. Gracie, have you seen the boys today?"

As usual, Lucille's voice implied there was a dire emergency, but Grace was used to her mother's theatrics.

"Nope, not since last Sunday. What's up, Mom?"

Both in their early twenties, Barney and Theo weren't technically boys any longer, although their high-spirited behavior didn't always qualify them as men either. Neither had married yet. Both still lived at home and were partners with Hugo in the family plumbing business.

"They're being absolutely *hateful* to me, that's what's up," Lucille said in a quavering, woebegone tone. "Just because Noah is protecting my rights and asking for what's legally mine in the divorce settlement, they've sided totally with your father.''

Grace stifled a sigh. She was trying hard to stay impartial during her parent's separation, but when it came to money, she, too, was on her father's side. Anyone who knew Lucille longer than fifteen minutes understood that she wasn't capable of managing money. She was a spendaholic, if there was such a thing. Whatever she received as her share of the divorce settlement would be gone within days.

''What's this hotshot lawyer of yours proposing, exactly?''

''Only what's legally mine. Your tightwad of a father wants to keep me tied to him financially. He wants to give me a share in the business, so much each month, an allowance, as if I was a child.''

Lucille was outraged. Knowing her mother as she did, Hugo's offer made perfect sense to Grace.

''Naturally,'' Lucille went on, ''Noah has insisted that I get a cash settlement, so I can be independent financially.''

Grace rolled her eyes and shook her head. Lucille would burn through her settlement like an acetylene torch through a block of ice. Good old

Noah needed a crash course in common sense. Couldn't he tell Lucille was hopeless with money, that Hugo's suggestion made perfect sense?

"How much are you paying this legal giant, Mom?"

"Gracie, I take issue with the way you speak about Noah." Sounding on the verge of tears, Lucille managed to choke out, "I'd never have believed you'd be like your brothers. They asked me exactly the same thing. And I'll tell you just what I told them. Noah Burnside would be a bargain at twice the price."

Grace suspected that meant Lucille had never bothered to even ask Burnside's fee. She was any lawyer's dream client.

"Mom, listen." She knew it would be fruitless, but she had to try, for her father, for her brothers, for herself. "If Daddy has to come up with half the cash value of the business, he'll have to go heavily in debt to raise it. That could mean there won't be enough revenue to service the debt or even to keep Barney and Theo as partners. The business could go under. You don't want that to happen, right?"

"Oh, phooey, don't be silly, Gracie. The business makes plenty of money." Lucille sounded as if she was speaking to a challenged five-year-old. "Your father is just being cheap and controlling."

Grace managed not to holler that Hugo was neither. He *was* a workaholic, he might be quiet and a little staid, but he'd always been generous with his family, particularly with Lucille. She could bankrupt Bill Gates, given the opportunity. And while she was doing it, she'd convince him he was having the time of his life. Lucille was a people magnet, fun loving, giddy, childlike in her enthusiasm, delightful to be around.

Grace had realized long ago that self-centeredness and impracticality were the flip sides of her mother's magnetic personality.

"Try and make the boys see my side of this, Gracie, please. It hurts my heart when my own sons turn against me. And if you met Noah, you'd see what a fine man he is. Why, he even *looks* like a hero. Tall, a full head of dark brown hair, such kind chocolate eyes. And one of those dimple things in his chin. Honestly, Gracie, if you didn't have such a thing about lawyers—"

"Mom," Grace said warningly. "Remember George at Christmas? You promised never again. Besides, if this Noah's that hot, *you* date him. You're single now."

Lucille squealed and giggled. "Don't be silly. He's way too young for me. He's probably not even forty yet."

"It's all the rage now, older women, younger

men,'' Grace encouraged. The thought of her
mother dating anybody but her father gave Grace
a stomachache, but at least it had gotten Lucille
off the subject of money. ''If you're gonna be
single, you'll have to get with the program.''

Lucille remembered to say that she'd listened
to part of the radio show and that Gracie had
sounded good.

They agreed to meet for dinner on Sunday, and
Grace finally hung up the phone, feeling as
though a doomsday cloud was settling in right
over her head.

If her mother's prince of a lawyer succeeded in
getting a cash settlement for the value of half of
Gamonski Plumbing, it wasn't only Barney and
Theo who might be out of a job.

Grace's own divorce had been financially dev-
astating. Melanie had been an equal partner in Engaging Events, and Grace had been forced to buy
out her interest at market value or agree to sell.
She had to take out a loan, and the bank was
reluctant: the fledgling business didn't qualify for
the amount required.

Her father had come to the rescue: He'd loaned
Grace what she needed, and although she was
paying him back as quickly as possible, she still
owed him a sizable amount. She'd insisted the

loan be businesslike, so she'd given Hugo a promissory note.

When Burnside started digging into the assets of Gamonski Plumbing, he'd find out about it. Could he call in the full amount if Hugo didn't have enough to pay Lucille out? Grace wasn't sure, but it sounded plausible. If that happened, she wasn't at all sure *her* business could survive, never mind Gamonski Plumbing.

Hugo's money problems with Lucille could have a fatal impact on Engaging Events, and on Grace's life.

CHAPTER FOUR

OVER THE NEXT SEVERAL DAYS, Grace did her best to put her concerns about money out of her mind. She was busy, which helped. As usual, there was a wedding planned for Saturday, and the final details needed attention.

Stirling Cadder and Monica DeVries had asked Grace to arrange every detail of an outdoor medieval ceremony and celebration, to be held in a grassy field in Stanley Park.

Grace reminded them that April weather in Vancouver could be wonderful, or it could be awful. She suggested having the celebration inside, in a hall, but Stirling and Monica were determined. They'd met in Stanley Park during a medieval festival, and that's what they wanted for their wedding. And it had to be April; they were moving to England. They'd take their chances with the weather.

Grace would take tents and umbrellas.

Early on the Saturday morning of the wedding,

however, it seemed the weather gods were smiling. For the past week, the sun had bathed the city in warmth. The park was spectacular. Snowy swans floated on a sizable green pond, flowering bushes dropped pink and yellow petals on the closely mowed grass, and hundreds of birds trilled a musical chorus.

As usual at outdoor weddings, Grace had corralled her brothers early that morning and supervised the erection of the huge central tent and several smaller ones. She'd also filled a large wicker basket with umbrellas, praying she wouldn't need them.

She and Priscilla had been on-site since dawn, wrapping the tent poles with ivy, hanging the impressive shields the bride's brother had concocted out of plywood and paint. They'd set up the tables in a horseshoe pattern so that the jousting and mock sword fights would have a central stage visible to all the guests.

Priscilla had even managed to borrow a suit of heavy armor from somewhere. It stood just behind the seats the bride and groom would occupy, as if on guard for them, and Grace had to admit the whole scene was impressive, as long as— She squinted suspiciously up at the sky.

"Think it's gonna rain, Priscilla?"

"The forecast said there might be afternoon

showers." Priscilla was spreading the last of the burgundy and forest-green table runners, and Grace was putting wooden plates and pomanders—oranges she'd tied with ribbon and studded with cloves—at each place setting. All the food was designed to be eaten with the fingers, as forks hadn't existed in medieval times.

"A few showers won't matter." Priscilla glanced over at the bandstand where the ceremony would take place. "Do you think we should have a mike for the minister?"

Grace shook her head. "It's Margaret Smith. She's got that wonderful voice, and she's going to get everybody to gather in a circle around the bandstand." They'd decorated it with ribbons and garlands, and Priscilla had denuded some of her father's early roses for petals she could spread in a path for the bride to walk on.

"It's going to be perfect," Priscilla declared.

The first indication Grace had that Priscilla might be a tad too optimistic came when ominous clouds began gathering just as the first guests arrived at noon, all dutifully dressed in imaginative versions of medieval finery.

Grace noted that some distrustful Vancouverites also had modern raincoats with them. They needed them. By twelve-thirty, a light rain was falling, and when it came time for the wedding ceremony at one, the drizzle had become a downpour.

"Hear ye, hear ye." Reverend Smith's stentorian tones rang out to the guests huddled under cover in the tents. "The wedding ceremony is about to begin. Gather round, all ye witnesses."

Umbrellas hoisted, everyone formed a circle around the covered bandstand. Priscilla scattered rose petals in a path for the bride, but the rising wind blew them away.

A series of violent thunderclaps drowned out most of the ceremony, defeating even Margaret's booming voice. When the bride and groom made their way to the head table, everyone scurried gratefully back under cover.

At Grace's urging, the catering staff served liberal quantities of mead, which lifted everyone's spirits, and the sun came out again just in time for the tournament for the bride's garter.

"That grass is as slippery as a bowling lane. I hope nobody gets killed with those poles," Priscilla muttered to Grace. They watched with growing apprehension as the young men in the groom's party, jousting with long wooden staffs, spent more time on their backs in the muddy grass than they did on their feet.

No one was hurt, however, and Grace relaxed

a little. Maybe things were going to go all right in spite of the weather.

The events were staged between courses, and as soon as everyone had enjoyed more mead and an assortment of "knave sandwiches," the next event was announced, a sword fight between Stirling, the groom, and his brother, Rodney, the best man.

Grace had been a little apprehensive about this idea, but the men had insisted that it was traditional, and she'd given in. They'd rented swords from a theatrical supply house, and she'd been surprised at how realistic and heavy they were.

The sword fight began with much posturing, and the guests clapped and hollered encouragement. The sound of steel clashing against steel resounded throughout the clearing, and excitement rose high.

At least everyone was enjoying themselves. Grace glanced around at the smiling faces and excited chatter of the assembly, and a feeling of satisfaction came over her.

She and her staff were good at this. Even under difficult circumstances, things were going well.

A cry of pain, and a scream from the bride, changed her mind.

"He slipped on that damned grass. The sword

caught his wrist,'' Priscilla groaned, taking off at a run.

Grace ran after her, and one glance at the groom's hand told her his wrist was probably broken. Stirling was on the ground, clutching his arm and moaning. The best man knelt at his side, mumbling apologies. One of the guests was a doctor, and he examined the groom and confirmed the wrist was fractured.

Monica was crying, crouched in the mud beside her new husband, and the guests were milling about, not sure what to do. It started to rain again. There'd been a slight breeze all day, but now it turned into a brisk wind. The tents began to billow, and some of the streamers went sailing off across the field and into the pond.

"I don't believe this. It's the western wedding all over again,'' Grace moaned to Priscilla as the bride clambered into a van with her injured husband and the vehicle drove off to the hospital. "We're jinxed! This has all the makings of another full-scale disaster.''

Priscilla's cell phone rang, and she pulled it out of the leather holster she wore on her hip. "It's for you,'' she said after listening for a moment. "It's your mother. She says she's been trying to get you for the past two hours.''

"I can't talk now. Tell her I'll call when I can."

Priscilla shook her head and handed over the phone. "You talk, I'll go calm things down. She sounds pretty upset."

"*She's* upset?" Grace snatched the phone, clamping the tiny cell to her ear, and hollered an impatient hello at her mother. The wind was still rising, making it tough to hear.

"The boys did *what?*"

Priscilla was right. Lucille was in hysterics, sobbing out something indecipherable. "Stop crying and speak up, Mom, or so help me, I'm hanging up." Grace apprehensively watched one of the tents trying to turn inside out. "We're having what looks like a tornado down here. Oh, damn and blast, there go the pomanders." They were flying off the tables, tumbling across the grass.

Grace was glad she was wearing her black silk pantsuit. Other women were battling with the skirts of their long dresses.

"*They beat your lawyer up?*" Her mother's sobbing message was enough to distract Grace momentarily from the scene around her.

Lucille didn't have all the details, but she babbled out what she knew. Incensed by Burnside's monetary demands on their father, Barney and Theo had apparently tracked the lawyer down several hours ago. They went to the gym where he worked out, and in the resulting altercation, Burnside had ended up with a broken foot, for which he was blaming Barney and Theo.

Lucille had rushed to the hospital and tried to apologize to him, but he was bringing criminal charges against Grace's brothers.

Visions of visiting her brothers in Kent penitentiary, to say nothing of a lawsuit that would ruin her entire family, flashed through Grace's mind, but there was no time to dwell on it.

Screams and panicked shouts were now coming from the main tent. The wind had blown over the suit of armor, which tumbled majestically forward and fell onto the central table, demolishing the caterer's culinary masterpiece, a wedding cake that was a four-tier reconstruction of a medieval castle. The good news was that the armor hadn't hit anyone. But as Grace watched in horror, the entire table buckled and slowly collapsed. Guests scrambled to get out of the way of spilled mead, flying icing and wooden plates that became airborne as the ferocious wind caught them.

"Ohmigod. Gotta go, Mom, I'll talk to you later."

Grace could see Priscilla, her long skirt molded against her, saying something to the bride's father, who was gesticulating and shaking a finger under her nose. Undoubtedly he was threatening Engaging Events with yet another lawsuit.

Grace considered having a dose of her mother's hysterics and decided that in the chaos no one would even notice. Instead, she headed over to rescue Priscilla and tell the bride's irate father that if was going to sue Engaging Events, he'd simply have to get in line.

CHAPTER FIVE

NOAH BURNSIDE HAD NEVER given much thought to his right foot before, but at this moment it was the only thing he *could* think about. The two big-league pain pills he'd just swallowed weren't doing a thing so far to diminish the white-hot agony shooting up his leg.

"Okay, Burnside, tell me again how this all came down, and I'll take notes so we're clear if it should come to a lawsuit."

Noah's friend and fellow lawyer, Jaimie Horvatch, had been summoned to St. Joseph's Hospital Emergency Department to drive him home. Jaimie was now slumped in the big reclining armchair in Noah's living room with a bottle of beer in one hand and a notepad in the other.

Noah knew he should have been on the recliner. Instead, Jaimie had dumped him on the matching sofa and taken the most comfortable chair for himself. Noah's right foot with its two fractured metatarsal bones and three crushed toes was encased in a fiberglass walking cast and propped awkwardly and uncomfortably on the coffee table.

Noah wished to God Jaimie would just go away and leave him to suffer in peace. As a friend and legal co-worker, Jaimie was fine, but as a care-giver he was hopeless. As well as taking the chair, he'd nearly tripped Noah coming into the apart-ment, and now he'd forgotten about the bottled water from the fridge, although he'd found the beer readily enough. And Jaimie's lightheartedness in the face of Noah's agony was bringing out buried homicidal tendencies.

"Get me a goddamned bottle of water, *please*. I'm dying of thirst here." He felt so horrible Noah wondered if maybe he was developing a fever, getting an infection or something. Could it set in this fast?

Jaimie reluctantly uncoiled his ungainly length and ambled into the kitchen. Noah heard the fridge open. "Got any chips to go with this salsa?"

"Water," Noah roared, losing it. "What the hell does a guy have to do to get a drink in his own home?"

"Keep your shirt on, it's coming." Jaimie re-appeared, shoved a cold bottle at Noah and settled into the armchair again as if he planned on spending the rest of the afternoon, the evening—maybe even the night?

Not possible, Noah consoled himself. Jaimie had a wife. Noah felt sorry for her.

He loosened the water cap and drank, then gingerly stretched out full-length on the sofa. Hot needles were traveling up and down his leg muscles.

"Walk me through this one more time because I still don't get it," Jaimie was saying. "Who were these goons who assaulted you again, and why didn't you get the ambulance guys to call the cops and arrest them?"

Noah knew that Jaimie's legal technique consisted of just this sort of bulldog tenacity, and he sighed, belched up an undissolved pain pill and gave in. Maybe if he went over it, Jaimie would go home.

"They're the sons of a client," he gritted out between clenched teeth. Just thinking about the Gamonski goons put him in a killer rage. On one level, he knew the accident was at least partly his fault, but he wasn't about to admit it. "I was getting set to bench-press when they barged into the gym, came over to me and started mouthing off about the settlement I'm negotiating for their mother. They figure I'm fleecing their father. In the middle of this, a teenage kid on the bench next to mine suddenly gets pinned under his bar. You're supposed to have a spotter but he's being a hero, lifting way beyond his capacity. It's on his chest and he's turning blue. I race over to help him. I grab one end of the kid's barbell and lift it off his chest and the Gamonski goons grab the other, but they lift it way too high. Three black forty-five-pound weights slide off on my end and one lands on my foot.''

Jaimie nodded thoughtfully and swallowed his beer in long, deep drafts. "So it wasn't an actual assault, then. Was there intent, d'you figure?''

Noah longed to say yes, but innate honesty forbade it. At the hospital, he'd been determined to sue the asses off the Gamonskis, but now the painkillers were beginning to work, and as weariness and bearable pain began to overcome rage and outright agony, he reluctantly admitted he had no case.

He felt badly now about the threats he'd made to Lucille Gamonski, who'd appeared at the doors to the ER just as he was hobbling out on those cursed crutches. He'd been in no mood to listen to her frantic explanations and apologies. In fact, he'd lost his temper and hollered at her, he remembered with a twinge of shame. After all, it wasn't all her fault her sons were cretins.

"They're steamed because they're partners

with their father in Gamonski Plumbing, and they're gonna feel it when Hugo Gamonski pays my client her settlement," he mumbled. "And it's gonna give me great satisfaction to get Lucille Gamonski every last red cent coming to her. You'd think those idiots would be thanking me for getting their mother a fair share of the family wealth."

"Strange how people just don't appreciate lawyers," Jaimie said with a wry grin. He got to his feet. "I've gotta get home. Molly has tickets for that show at the Playhouse. You gonna be okay, or should I call that redhead I saw you with last week, ask her to come over and stroke your brow or something?"

"Mimi's not so hot at brows." She was superb at stroking other things, but Noah wasn't in the mood. He knew he was slurring his words. He wanted to sleep, but he remembered something important. "Damn it, Jaimie, my car's still in the parking lot at the gym."

"No problem. I'll drive it home for you after the concert if you give me the keys."

Noah fished them out of his pocket. "The clicker for the garage is in the car. Slot number thirty-two."

"Gotcha. I guess you won't be driving for a while, and obviously you won't be in on Monday, either. I'll spread the word. Agnes can give you a call in the morning."

"Just tell her to cancel my appointments. I'll call her when I wake up." Noah was drifting off. It was a relief to hear the door close behind Jaimie.

He thought about hoisting himself up on the crutches the hospital had supplied. His bed would be more comfortable, but the effort didn't seem to warrant the reward. His last coherent thought concerned the Gamonski family; he heartily wished he'd never laid eyes on any of them.

"MR. BURNSIDE'S NOT ACCEPTING new clients. Would you like to speak to one of our other attorneys?" Wayne had set the phone down, and was mimicking for Grace the starchy tones of a prim, efficient secretary. "I said, no, thank you very much."

"Damn and blast." She'd tried to confer with her brothers, but didn't like what she heard, so she'd had a restless and sleepless night. But after a creative powwow with Wayne and Priscilla early Monday morning, Grace figured that together they'd arrived at the perfect solution to keeping her brothers out of the arms of the law.

Much as she despised the very thought, Engaging Events needed a lawyer; the medieval wedding fiasco had convinced her that having an attorney to fend off possible lawsuits and deal with raging clients was becoming urgent. What if the armor had brained somebody? The very thought gave her the horrors.

So she'd retain Burnside—damn his hide—to represent her business, without immediately explaining to him that she was a sister to the notorious Gamonski gang. Once he'd agreed to take her on as a client, it seemed unlikely that he'd sue her brothers. After all, he'd be making an exorbitant amount from the female portion of the family, and who knew lawyers better than Grace, who'd been married to one? Money, she assured Wayne and Priscilla, was their main motivation, right up there with illicit sex.

"Well," Wayne said with a shrug, "let's proceed to Plan B."

"Which is?" Lack of sleep was making her thickheaded.

"Research," he hissed. "We'll find out everything we can about Burnside. There's bound to be a chink in his armor. Oops, sorry, forgot."

Grace and Priscilla both groaned at the word *armor*. The man Priscilla had borrowed the cursed iron suit from was not happy with the huge dent in the headgear. And although nobody had arrived yet with a summons from the DeVries family over their medieval fiasco, Grace had the feeling that silence wasn't exactly golden.

"You two have a nice cup of herbal tea and run the front for me for an hour, and I'll wander down to Rosenkrantz and Maclellan and dig up the skeletons in Burnside's icebox," Wayne declared, twirling an invisible mustache. "I didn't read all those Agatha Christie novels for nothing, my pretties."

True to his word, just over an hour later Wayne was back with information and an idea.

"Martinet Agnes wouldn't say a word about Burnside except that he's not in the office today and isn't expected back for the remainder of the week, but Cindy, the sweet girl at the switchboard, was much more forthcoming. It seems Mrs. Burnside's little boy is a bit of a womanizer. A call came while I was chatting with her from a lady named Mimi worrying about his health, and ten minutes later, in walked another one, Annie this time, looking for our friend."

"That figures," Grace snorted. "Typical philandering lawyer."

"He's single. The guy's got a right," Wayne defended. "But we do, too. We can use his weak places to get what we want. I studied Annie. If she's representative of his choice in women, the operative look here is in-your-face trashy. So here's what we do."

CHAPTER SIX

THE BLACK LEATHER SKIRT was short and snug, the strappy sandals had crippling high heels, and the lacy top of the thigh-high silk hose showed an inch beneath the skirt's hem. Altogether, the costume made Grace very nervous, but both Wayne and Priscilla had insisted it was necessary. The white georgette blouse was almost see-through, but not quite, and the push-up bra Priscilla produced from somewhere created cleavage Grace had never imagined she had.

The fluffy little apple-green chenille jacket was her own, but way too hot for the sunny morning. Grace endured it—there was far too much of her bare, except for her face.

Priscilla had applied so much mascara her lashes felt weighted down, and the plum lipstick and liner made her lips look as if she'd had them injected with collagen.

Wayne and Priscilla insisted the effect was dramatic and startling, but Grace thought she looked more like Morticia from the Addams Family.

Men were definitely taking notice, though, as she teetered the two blocks from the parking lot to the offices of Rosenkrantz and Maclellan. It was seven forty-five Wednesday morning, and Noah Burnside was supposed to be back at work.

Wayne had called his switchboard contact to find out exactly what time the lawyer would limp through the legal firm's waiting area. It was essential that Grace be sitting there, God help her, with her legs crossed and her breasts heaving.

CRUTCHES MADE NOAH CRANKY. Everything about having a broken foot made him cranky, and he'd decided he might as well be out of sorts at the office. Three days at home had convinced him madness was a very real possibility if he stayed there much longer.

They'd told him at the hospital to use the crutches for a full week. With help from a cabdriver who'd held doors open and retrieved his briefcase when he dropped it in the middle of the sidewalk, Noah finally made it, sweating and swearing under his breath, into the reception area at R and M.

"Morning, Mr. Burnside. *So* sorry to hear about your accident. How are you feeling?"

Cindy's solicitous greeting grated on his nerves. He knew damned well that the office telegraph had broadcast every detail of his mishap to every living person at the firm, and he despised being the subject of office gossip.

"Fine, thanks," he snapped ungratefully. "Any messages?"

"Agnes already picked them up. Um, Mr. Burnside, this lady has been waiting to speak to you? I did mention that you're not accepting new clients?"

Cindy gestured toward the seating area behind the fish tank that was old Maclellan's pride and joy, and a woman uncrossed long, shapely legs, rose gracefully to her feet and came over to stand beside him.

"If I could just have a few moments of your time, Mr. Burnside?" Her voice was husky and apprehensive. "I promise I won't take long. My name is Gracie Madison, and I—I badly need some advice."

She was gorgeous. Sexy. She was dressed to emphasize her assets. Testosterone that had been on sabbatical for the past few days returned with a vengeance, and Noah almost forgot about his foot.

"Okay, I think there's maybe a half hour before my first client arrives. Come this way." He tried to swing the crutches in a jaunty fashion as he led the way down the hall to his office and through the alcove where Agnes sat like a guard dog.

"Morning, Mr. Burnside, nice to have you back." Agnes's agate eyes photographed Ms. Madison and filed her away for future reference.

"Morning, Agnes."

The door to his office was a problem, but Ms. Madison reached smoothly past him and opened it. She also closed it firmly once they were inside.

The cleaners had done the office with the usual lemon disinfectant, but Noah could smell Ms. Madison's perfume over it, spicy and subtle. Her hair was short, somewhere between brown and blond, and the casual, windblown style didn't match the hooker clothes she was wearing, but who was he to question women's taste? Dress for sex was fine with him.

"Please sit down, Ms. Madison."

She did, on the armless but comfortable client's seat and, as he made his way behind the desk, he sneaked another peek at her legs. Damned if she wasn't wearing stockings instead of panty hose. He could see the tops and a nice slice of bare thigh under her skirt.

Spectacular.

He dumped the briefcase and the crutches on the floor and tried not to look as relieved as he felt when he finally landed in his own soft leather chair.

Sitting, he could pay more attention to the details of her appearance, the light dusting of freckles across her straight nose, the intelligent hazel eyes that looked out at him from behind impossibly long lashes lavishly coated with mascara. Under a pound of lipstick, she had a mouth made for kissing. She wasn't wearing a wedding ring, but that didn't prove anything.

Stop ogling and get some info, Burnside.

"Is it a matrimonial dispute, Ms. Madison?"

"Oh, no, I'm not married." She shook her head and her soft, short hair swirled. "And please call me Gracie. It's so much friendlier, don't you think? See, I have a business? And I think I'm being sued by this guy?"

She'd reverted to the same school of diction Cindy had attended, ending each statement as a question. It usually irritated him, but for someone like Ms. Madison, he figured he could probably overlook it.

She ducked her head and glanced up at him from under the messy eyelashes. "I think by two guys, actually? Clients, and I don't know what to do?" She gave him a helpless, vulnerable smile that made him want to sit up straighter and expand his chest. Maybe beat it a little.

"Explain exactly what your business entails and what these clients are unhappy about."

When she had, he was vastly relieved that it wasn't the world's oldest profession. The thought had crossed his mind.

He listened and made notes as she spoke in that soft, uncertain voice. She rambled a little, and he had to keep bringing her back to the point. She uncrossed her legs and crossed them again, giving him tantalizing glimpses of black lace and flashes of pale soft upper thigh that caused him some exquisite discomfort.

She fished in her handbag for scraps of paper with names and addresses. "It's quite warm in here, do you mind if I...?"

He shook his head and swallowed hard as she slid her green jacket off, forcing her breasts to thrust against a thin white blouse. He could almost see her nipples. She wriggled her shoulders and gestured with her long-fingered, narrow hands and smiled and frowned and pouted, and he wished he could take his own jacket off. Maybe his pants, too.

It wasn't easy to concentrate, but he asked questions and put together in his head a composite picture of her business and its legal requirements.

"So what you're looking for is an attorney

who'll represent your business,'' he finally summed up.

She nodded, pinning him with those huge hazel eyes. ''I know you're not taking any clients, and you mostly do matrimonial, but I'd be so grateful if you'd make an exception? I've heard such good things about you, and I sense that you're someone I could trust.'' And her tone indicated that the gratitude could take wild and wonderful forms.

She intrigued him. His specialty was matrimonial law, but there was no reason he couldn't take on something different for a change. And Grace Madison was different. He wanted to know more about her.

Lights were blinking on his telephone, and he knew that Agnes would be in any moment to remind him a client was waiting.

''Okay, Ms. Madison. I'll make an exception and agree to represent your company.''

For a surprised instant, he thought he glimpsed fiendish triumph in those soft eyes, but he must have been mistaken.

''I can't tell you how relieved I am, and how grateful. Thank you so much, Mr. Burnside.'' She got to her feet and held out a surprisingly strong hand for him to shake.

He held on a moment longer than was strictly

necessary, and then, with one final, brilliant smile, she said goodbye and left the office.

Her perfume lingered, and it took some time to banish the memory of those soft inner thighs, but he managed.

Agnes appeared an instant after he'd buzzed for her.

"I want you to find out everything you can about this business and this woman," he instructed, handing her a paper with Gracie's info on it.

His partners, knowing his fondness for pretty women, had all been puzzled when he'd hired Agnes, who was middle-aged and had never been sexy. Noah offered her top wages and good benefits. From a mutual friend, he knew about her background: she'd worked for ten years as a clerk in a Royal Canadian Mounted Police office. She'd learned everything there was to know about digging up a person's carefully buried secrets, and she had excellent contacts for ferreting out information not publicly available. She also had the instincts of the bloodhound she resembled, and hiring her was one of the smarter moves he'd ever made.

It took her exactly two hours and forty-seven minutes to get the goods on Grace Madison.

Agnes laid the perfectly typed report on his desk and gave him a satisfied smile. Without a single comment, she went out and closed the door softly behind her.

CHAPTER SEVEN

NOAH PROPPED his aching foot on the desk, tipped his chair back and skimmed the report. Then he went back and read it in detail. At last he shook his head, thought it over and burst out laughing.

The wily brat. The sneaky little sexpot. Those revealing clothes, and her slightly stunned manner, had all been a clever disguise.

So she was a Gamonski, was she? And she'd figured out what she believed was a foolproof way to keep him from taking any legal action against her idiot brothers, not that he'd planned on it anyhow.

Just how far would she go with this charade? What was she really like? He glanced at the report again, confirming the name of the guy she'd been married to.

Lloyd Madison. He was a lawyer, Agnes had indicated. So somebody at the firm must have heard of him. Vancouver wasn't that big.

Again, Noah put Agnes on the job, and it didn't

take long to find out that Madison was an adequate property tax lawyer who'd dumped Grace and married again before the ink on the divorce papers was dry. One of the legal secretaries at the firm was related to a cousin of the woman Madison had married, and knew the story. Madison's new wife had been Grace's partner.

Idiot, Noah thought, for no good reason, because how was he to know the details of their breakup? He knew nothing about the real Grace Madison, but he realized that he very much wanted to. How far would she go with the ditzy act she'd put on today?

On impulse, he looked up the number for Engaging Events and dialed, surprised when Grace herself answered.

"Noah Burnside here, Gracie." He grinned, wondering if she really liked being called Gracie. "I have several things I'd like to discuss with you. We really ought to get a letter of intent signed, and I wondered if we might do it over dinner? I'd like to hear more about your company, and that way we could take as much time as we wanted. I'm swamped here at the office."

There was a long pause, and he hoped it was because she was squirming with discomfort. "That sounds very enjoyable," she finally said.

What else could she say? Noah had her, and he knew she knew it.

"Where shall I meet you, Mr. Burnside?"

"Call me Noah." And then he gave her directions.

FEELING NERVOUS and very uncomfortable, Grace walked into the quiet little restaurant on Robson Street. She saw him immediately. His crutches were propped against the wall, but he didn't reach for them. Instead he used a chair back as support and struggled gallantly to his feet as the elegant maître d' led her to the table.

"Hello, Gracie."

She tried not to wince at the nickname, and she plastered on as ingenuous a smile as she could manage.

"Hello, Noah. What a super restaurant."

This time she was a little more prepared for the visceral effect Noah Burnside had on her senses, but the tingle of awareness she'd felt the previous day was very much apparent when he took her hand in his and smiled.

He had a quiet smile, a narrow but well-shaped mouth and, just as her mother had pointed out, a deep cleft in his strong chin. But it was his eyes more than his lean, dark looks that mesmerized Grace. Deep set and dramatic, they were somewhere between the chocolate her mother had indicated and coal. They had a depth and a sadness of expression that got past the defenses she'd erected. Because of those eyes, he just didn't look like an avaricious lawyer, damn his hide.

On guard, Grace. Don't let him fool you.

She kept on smiling and sat down in the comfortable chair the maître d' was holding for her, making sure the slippery silk skirt of her black chemise slid enticingly up her thighs. The dress was one she'd bought on impulse and never worn until now.

"So, Noah, how did your day go?" And how long was she going to be able to play the part of the bimbo?

"Very well, productive and busy, but no major calamities. And how about yours, Gracie?"

Was he overusing her name, or was she imagining it? She tried to think of a diminutive for Noah and couldn't.

"Oh, you know, brides, brides, brides, what can I say?" she said, with a wave of the hand and an attempt at a giggle.

God, playing dumb was difficult. How did some women make a career of it?

The waiter arrived and they both ordered fish. Noah selected wine, and in a few moments their goat cheese hors d'oeuvres arrived.

"Tell me about yourself, Gracie. You come from a big family?"

Slippery slope here. "Three of us kids, not really big. How about you, Noah?" She nibbled, admiring his dark gray suit and maroon shirt. He must have an excellent tailor. But then, he could well afford it, couldn't he?

"No siblings," he said easily. "I'm an only child. My parents divorced when I was in university, and my dad died a couple of years ago. Mom never remarried. What about your folks, Gracie? Divorced? Still together?" He reached across and poured her another glass of wine. She couldn't remember drinking the first one. She really had to get hold of herself. *Pay attention, Madison.*

"Oh, they're, um, in the process of separating." How on earth had they gotten into discussing parental marriages anyway? She reached into the basket for a piece of hot bread and recklessly slathered it with butter, concentrating hard on the task so she wouldn't have to look at him. She had the uncanny impression those dusky eyes would be able to see right through her, straight down to her dishonest soul.

She heard him chuckle and, startled, looked up.

"I know, Grace." Amusement made the corner of his eyes crinkle and his smile brought out creases in his lean cheeks. "I represent Lucille, remember? By the way, it *is* Grace, isn't it? As opposed to Gracie?''

For an instant, she considered throwing the buttery roll right at him. How *dare* he make a fool of her like this? But honesty forced her to admit that he'd simply turned the tables on her. After all, hadn't *she* been determined to put one over on him?

Her skin suddenly felt as if she'd been in the sun too long. "Did you know all along?" She was pleased that she managed to sound haughty, but it was a huge relief when he shook his head.

"Nope. I did some sleuthing after you left the office yesterday and found out you were Lucille's daughter."

Belatedly, it dawned on her that *he* was the one who ought to be furious. But he wasn't. There was an amused twinkle in his eyes and that darned sexy mouth of his was smiling even wider than before. He had wonderfully white, even teeth. Or maybe they just looked that way because his skin was tanned.

"So, Grace Madison, shall we start over?"

"From the very beginning?"

"Yup."

"Well, I was born at Grace Hospital, so my mom named me Grace. I weighed eight pounds eleven ounces, a real butterball, which has pro-

foundly affected my entire life.'' She held up the
roll, lathered with butter and took a hearty bite.

He wasn't smiling anymore. He'd tilted his
head back and was laughing aloud. If his smile
registered good, his laugh hit excellent. It rumbled
from deep in his chest.

''I didn't really mean *that* beginning, but go
on.''

She had nothing to lose. She could be outrageous and honest and silly. She'd probably never
see him again anyhow. She slid her toes out of
the stiletto-heeled sandals that were killing her in-
steps. She settled back in her chair, took a hearty
gulp of the excellent wine and let her tummy relax
for the first time since she'd met him. God, it felt
good.

''I tell you three things about me, and then you
have to tell me three things about you,'' she said.
It was a game Wayne had created when he first
came to work for her.

''We start with three things we love.'' She
closed her eyes and bit into the roll again. ''I love
bread.'' She chewed and swallowed. ''I love En-
glish mystery novels. I love waking up and knowing I have a day off.'' She opened her eyes and
grinned. ''Your turn.''

''Hmm. Okay. I love windy days. I love fishing. I love my job.''

"Your job? You truly love your job?" Her skepticism showed in her tone. "I would have guessed that matrimonial law was a pretty stressful way to make a living."

The waiter arrived with their dinners. When he left again, Noah said, "It is stressful. There's lots of animosity involved. But there's also a sense of accomplishment when I see couples fairly dividing their assets. It wasn't always that way. In the past women often got far less than their legal share of the matrimonial assets."

Grace knew that was true. She also knew this was a subject that would lead straight to Lucille, and she didn't want to go there. In the interests of client confidentiality, he couldn't talk about it, and she didn't want to. She forked up some of her fresh halibut.

"This is scrumptious."

He laughed again.

"What?" She swallowed and sipped at her wine.

"I haven't heard anybody actually use scrumptious for years."

"So I'm old-fashioned. Live with it. Now what made you choose matrimonial law as your particular specialty?"

"My mother."

It was Grace's turn to laugh. "She stood over

you with a whip and said, 'Noah Burnside, you're gonna devote your life to women's rights'? Hey, I really like your mother.''

He laughed again. "I like her, too, she's a great lady. She's an artist." His tone was proud, but it hardened a little and took on a steely tone. "She gave up years of her life for my father, a prince of a guy who was both controlling and domineering. Divorce was the best decision Mom ever made."

"Have you ever been married, Noah?" She'd have bet not, so she was surprised when he nodded assent.

"For all of six months, a long time ago. It wasn't my finest moment, and it taught me marriage isn't what I'm best at."

"I guess that makes two of us." Her tone was rueful.

"But it was your ex who sued for divorce."

"You really did your homework, didn't you?" But strangely, it didn't bother her that he knew her history. "I knew things weren't perfect between Lloyd and me, but I honestly thought it was just part of adjusting to marriage." She gave him a wry grin. "And all the time, Lloyd was actually adjusting to a passionate affair with Melanie, my best friend and partner. Anybody as naive as me oughta stay away from legal commitments, don't you agree?''

"The guy was obviously an idiot and a total jerk."

His words and the unguarded admiration in his eyes sent a warm glow through her. "He sure was," she agreed. "But that doesn't make me want to rush out and try again. My parents' track record doesn't exactly inspire me. I have a job that I enjoy, friends that I love, even guys that I date occasionally." Was her nose growing? "I'm pretty happy with my life as it is." She had to be. There weren't really any options, were there?

"Seeing anybody special?" The question was ultra cool.

"Nope. I stay pretty casual with relationships." How could she lie so easily? But the truth was too embarrassing. "What about you?"

"No. Like you, I date. I like women, but not any particular one."

Now why should that make her heart leap? Wasn't he as much as admitting he was a womanizer? For some reason, she didn't care. She didn't want to be, but she was powerfully attracted to this man. *Get a grip, Madison. He's a lawyer, for heaven's sake.*

The waiter arrived to remove their plates and

she was amazed to find she'd eaten everything. They both passed on dessert and ordered coffee.

"I've found I get bored easily in relationships. That's what happened in my marriage," Noah commented.

"Bored, huh?" Grace's high spirits flagged a little. Would it take three weeks, or four? "I can see where that would cause problems with commitment."

"It does." He shrugged. "I don't see myself getting married anytime soon."

"That's good, because I couldn't do your wedding anyway. I'm booked solid for the next three months at least," she joked.

He smiled and said, "You know, you didn't go into details about what exactly happened at those weddings you think you're getting sued over. Tell me about them."

So over coffee, she explained about bridesmaids getting caught in stirrups, horses biting fathers, grooms getting stabbed with swords, suits of armor nearly braining guests, and by the time she was done, he was laughing full out.

"Tell me horrific stories about your work now," she demanded.

So he reciprocated. He described clients who spent two years in litigation over the custody of a dog, and a man who could only talk to Noah with his smelly feet bare.

She wanted more. "You grew up in a small town. Tell me what you remember."

He smiled. "Walking through the graveyard at night with my first girlfriend when I was ten, terrified but loving the way she clung to me. Floating down the river on inner tubes on hot summer afternoons. Fishing from the railroad bridge."

And she got around to telling him what it was like having two outrageous younger brothers and parents who either locked their bedroom door every afternoon to make love, or divorced each other.

They talked nonstop until a glance around the room revealed that they were the only ones still there.

Grace put her shoes back on. Noah paid the bill, and then he retrieved his crutches and they made their way out to the parking lot where Grace had left her pickup.

"I'd like to invite you dancing, or for a walk, or even for a ride," he said wistfully. "But this damned foot really makes it hard to show a lady a good time. We could go to a jazz bar and sit for a while," he said hopefully, but she shook her head.

"It's late, and this lady already had a really

good time,'' she said softly, aware of how close he was to her. Impetuously she added, "Would you like a ride home?"

"Yes," he said, so quickly and in such an emphatic voice they both laughed. "I should have guessed you'd have a truck," he remarked. "You're a take-charge woman. I like that."

Pleasure made her feel warm. "I need it for the job, but I also just like trucks," she explained. They got in and Grace started the motor. "I don't know where you live."

He gave her instructions to an apartment building not far away, on the very edge of Stanley Park.

"Where do you live, Grace?"

"I rent an apartment in Kerrisdale," she replied. "It's actually the top floor of an old house, and it's within walking distance of my business."

"Smart planning."

"Luck," she corrected. "The landlord's a friend of my father's."

Miraculously, there was street parking in front of his building. Grace pulled in and turned the motor off.

"Would you like to come up and see my etchings?" His wicked grin was contagious. "I can't chase anyone with this cast on my foot."

She hesitated, but only for an instant. She very

much wanted to know more about him, see where and how he lived.

They went up to the fourteenth floor in the elevator, and he unlocked the door. He'd left a lamp burning, and the soft light illuminated a spacious living room with a sliding glass door that led to a large deck. A recliner and a brown sofa were arranged in front of an oversize television. One wall held bookshelves filled with books.

She went over and looked at the titles. There were classics and bestsellers and legal tomes, and even several volumes of poetry.

"What would you like to drink. Wine, coffee, soda, juice? Tequila, rum, vodka, scotch?"

"Any herbal tea?"

"Damn, no. Sorry. I'll put it on my shopping list."

"Nothing, then, thanks. I'm full from dinner." She was beginning to wonder just what she was doing here.

He went over to a sound system and flicked a switch. Rod Stewart's edgy voice filled the room, singing "If We Fall In Love Tonight."

Her legs suddenly felt weak, and she sank down on the sofa.

CHAPTER EIGHT

NOAH SAT IN THE RECLINER. He wanted to sit beside her, but he didn't want to scare her away. He silently blessed the fact that his cleaning service had been in today and tidied the unholy mess he'd made of the place. He couldn't have asked her up with used towels, dirty socks, empty bottles and discarded underwear festooning the room.

"What sort of things do you do for fun, Noah? When your foot isn't broken, that is? I've heard you work out at a gym," she added with a mischievous grin. "What other sports interest you?"

Contact sports. Intimate contact.

"I swim, and ski, and I've got a little skiff that I sail when the weather's right. I used to ride horses when I was a kid, but I haven't done that for years," he said. "How about you, Grace?"

"I jog," she said. "It never approaches a run, and when it starts to get tough I slow down and walk. I'm not interested in going for the burn. I play football with my dad and brothers sometimes. Mostly I rely on the business to keep me in shape. We're always loading and unloading props and tables and chairs.''

"You have any problems with employees?"

"Never." She shook her head and her soft, gleaming hair floated and settled. He wondered how it felt to touch. She was so beautiful. Her golden skin glowed, sun kissed and smooth. The silky black dress she wore slid and slipped around her breasts and hips, enticing and provocative.

"I've got the best employees in the world." She described them, and Noah raised his eyebrows and grinned at her. "Let me get this straight. Wayne is the expert on wedding gowns, and Priscilla rides a motorcycle?"

She nodded. "Wayne's father's a sportswear designer for Jantzen, and his mother's a talented seamstress who often helps Wayne make gowns for some of our customers when they can't find what they're looking for," she explained. "Priscilla's an artist. She and I spark each other's imagination when it comes to being original. She's also the best person you could ever have in an emergency—cool and levelheaded and incredibly strong. They're both loyal and honest. I'd trust them with my life."

He felt a twinge of envy as he thought of the people he worked with and realized there wasn't one of them, except for Agnes, that he felt he could truly trust.

He told her so, and then the conversation shifted to books and movies and they argued a little over which directors and writers they preferred.

And far too soon, she glanced at her watch and got to her feet. "Gotta go, work tomorrow. It's getting late."

He got up. He was getting better at maneuvering, not as clumsy as he'd been. She was standing an arm's length away, and he reached out and gently took her hands in his, drawing her toward him, taking a chance, unable to stop himself.

She didn't resist, and he was incredibly relieved.

He balanced on his left foot and slid his arms around her waist. Her body felt warm and firm.

"I have to kiss you, Grace." He was amazed at himself. He hadn't announced his intentions in that regard since high school, but for some reason it felt right.

Her arms came up and touched his shoulders, and he dipped his head and found her mouth. It was soft and full, sweet and shockingly arousing. She tasted like coffee smelled—indefinable, addictive, delicious. He kept it light at first, but the kiss rapidly took on a life of its own, and he stopped thinking and surrendered to intense sensation as her lips opened and her tongue met his.

A powerful need to make love to her overwhelmed him, and it was hard to control himself.

She drew away far too soon, her breathing as unsteady as his. She looked into his eyes for a long, silent moment, her hazel eyes unreadable, her expression thoughtful.

"You're a very accomplished kisser, Noah," she said, as if it had been a scientific experiment. But her voice trembled.

He took a shaky breath, forgot about his injured foot and lost his balance, cursed and half fell back on the sofa.

She giggled. "Don't get up," she said. "I can let myself out."

And before he could grab his crutches and hoist himself back on his feet, the door had closed quietly behind her. He swore and let himself flop down again, but instead of turning on the television and watching the news as he usually did, he sat deep in thought, replaying the entire evening in his mind.

Grace Madison was nothing like the women he usually dated. They were like—he groped for a simile.

They were like fast food, great for satisfying hunger, fun to enjoy, but lacking in sustenance.

He met them at the gym, on the ski slopes, at pubs, and until now he'd believed they were exactly what he wanted. They made no demands on him; if they did, he simply stopped seeing them.

There had been several who started making noises about commitment, and he'd had to be brutally honest. But they'd been the exception. Most of his ladies weren't really interested in conversation. They liked hot music, fast cars, a deep wallet and a good time. If he wanted an intellectual conversation, he took Agnes out to lunch.

By contrast, Grace was a gourmet dinner, fresh and filled with sustenance. She challenged him. She made him think. She reminded him that some hidden corner of his dreams had always whispered of a different sort of relationship, had promised in the face of all odds that the disparate parts *could* come together in one special woman.

And the sexual attraction was there, in spades. He imagined how she'd taste and feel and sound when he made love to her, and a hungry shudder went through him. *Soon.* He wanted it to happen soon. Now that she'd come into his life, he couldn't bear to waste time.

He'd call her tomorrow. He'd ask Jaimie how that show was, and if it was good, he'd get tickets. He'd take her to the jazz club he liked. He'd buy her the new mystery she'd mentioned, the one that was only out in hardcover.

Adrenaline shot through him as he realized that this was the best of all possible worlds for him. Grace didn't want commitment any more than he did. If either of them got bored, they were intelligent enough to part without recrimination.

"Damn," he whispered, punching an exuberant fist into a pillow beside him. "Damn, Burnside, you are one lucky man."

"TELEPHONE, GRACE." Wayne handed the receiver to her, his green eyes dancing with mischief. He hissed, "It's you-know-who, he needs his morning fix."

Grace gave him a withering look and turned her back on him, but she could hear him chortling.

"Morning, Noah. If you hang on a minute, I'll take this in my office." Grace hurried into the back. It had been eight days since her first dinner with Noah, and not a day had gone by that she hadn't heard from him. They'd gone to the theater, to the movies, and on Sunday, he'd packed a picnic lunch and a fancy bottle of wine and taken her to hear a jazz concert in the park. He'd bought her books and flowers and handmade chocolates from the most decadent shop in Van-

GET 2

HOW TO GET YOUR
2 FREE BOOKS AND FREE GIFT!

1. Peel off the MIRA sticker on the front cover. Place it in the space provided at right. This automatically entitles you to receive two free books and an exciting mystery gift.

2. Send back this card and you'll get 2 "The Best of the Best™" novels. These books have a combined cover price of $11.00 or more in the U.S. and $13.00 or more in Canada, but they are yours to keep absolutely FREE!

3. There's no catch. You're under no obligation to buy anything. We charge nothing — ZERO — for your first shipment. And you don't have to make any minimum number of purchases — not even one!

4. We call this line "The Best of the Best" because each month you'll receive the best books by some of today's hottest authors. These authors show up time and time again on all the major bestseller lists and their books sell out as soon as they hit the stores. You'll like the convenience of getting them delivered to your home at our special discount prices . . . and you'll love your *Heart to Heart* subscriber newsletter featuring author news, horoscopes, recipes, book reviews and much more!

5. We hope that after receiving your free books you'll want to remain a subscriber. But the choice is yours — to continue or cancel, anytime at all! So why not take us up on our invitation, with no risk of any kind. You'll be glad you did!

6. And remember...we'll send you a mystery gift ABSOLUTELY FREE just for giving "The Best of the Best" a try.

SPECIAL FREE GIFT!

We'll send you a fabulous surprise gift, absolutely FREE, simply for accepting our no-risk offer!

Visit us online at
www.mirabooks.com

BOOKS FREE!

The Best of the Best™ — Here's How it Works:

Accepting your 2 free books and gift places you under no obligation to buy anything. You may keep the books and gift and return the shipping statement marked "cancel." If you do not cancel, about a month later we will send you 4 additional novels and bill you just $4.24 each in the U.S., or $4.74 each in Canada, plus 25¢ shipping & handling per book and applicable taxes if any.* That's the complete price and — compared to cover prices of $5.50 or more each in the U.S. and $6.50 or more each in Canada — it's quite a bargain! You may cancel at any time, but if you choose to continue, every month we'll send you 4 more books, which you may either purchase at the discount price or return to us and cancel your subscription.

*Terms and prices subject to change without notice. Sales tax applicable in N.Y. Canadian residents will be charged applicable provincial taxes and GST.

couver. If she didn't know better, she'd think he was courting her.

She knew better. It would end as quickly as it started, the instant he got bored. It was a fast ride on a short road.

But wow, was she enjoying the trip. She closed the office door and snatched up the phone. "Hi, I'm back." She loved the sound of his voice in her ear.

"Hello, lovely lady. My ten-o'clock appointment is late, so I thought I'd give you a quick call. I wondered if you'd like to come over to my place tonight? I'll order in a pizza and pick up that Australian movie you were telling me about. Come about seven?"

Her heart skipped two beats and then hammered. She'd known the time was coming when they'd make love, and now she sensed that it was here. Their kisses had been escalating into caresses that left her aroused and longing for more, and there was no doubt he felt the same. His body graphically telegraphed his desire every time he touched her.

"Sounds great, what can I bring?" It came out breathless because she was.

There was a long, charged silence. "Your overnight bag would be nice." His voice was intimate and husky, and it touched her that he sounded a trifle uncertain.

"I'll see if I can locate it." She tried for lightness, but her voice wobbled.

She hung up the phone and floated from her office to the front of the shop.

Wayne and Priscilla were seemingly deep in conversation with an Oriental bride and her extended family. Neither of them so much as glanced at Grace, but she noticed they'd changed the classical CD she'd had on the player.

Celine Dion was now crooning, "It's getting serious."

THE SONG TITLE STUCK in Grace's mind all afternoon, and it was still there after she and Noah had eaten Hawaiian pizza, watched *Shine* and sipped herbal tea. They were side by side on the sofa, his arm cradling her shoulders.

"That was a powerful story," he commented about the movie. "I think it's easier to just be ordinary the way I am than to be a genius."

"I wouldn't say you're a genius—it would go straight to your head and make you insufferable—but I don't think of you as ordinary, either," Grace remarked. "You're way too smart and sexy and original for ordinary."

"Sexy, huh? Smart is nice, but sexy I really

appreciate." His arm tightened and he tipped her chin up with his knuckle and kissed her. His lips were familiar now, but familiarity didn't lessen the sensations.

He took his time kissing, and she liked that. She liked the way his broad chest pressed against her breasts, the way his hands slid down her back and around her rib cage, the sound he made deep in his throat as the kiss intensified and his palms cupped her.

A shudder ran through her as his tongue came into her mouth, caressed, retreated, repeated. Her heart hammered, and her body caught fire, yearning for more than kisses.

His breathing and the runaway pulse just where her lips touched at the base of his neck increased her desire. It was obvious he was as aroused as she.

"Will you come to my bed now, beautiful Grace?" The question was little more than a husky whisper.

"Lead the way."

"I'd love to scoop you up in my arms, but that'll have to come later." His chuckle was rueful.

"I don't mind walking." Her legs were none too steady, however, as she followed him down the hallway and into the large, softly lit bedroom.

It wasn't all anticipation that made her shaky, either. Making love with him would change their relationship, move it into new and unfamiliar territory. What if she wasn't all that he anticipated?

He sank down on the edge of the navy bedcover and dropped his crutches. "Come here, beauty, and lie beside me." He reached for her hand and drew her down, then moved them farther back on the huge bed. He settled a pillow beneath her head, traced her cheek with gentle, strong fingers.

"You have skin that glows," he told her. He lowered his head and kissed her, deeper now, more urgently, but still unhurried. "I couldn't pay attention to the movie," he confessed. "All I could think about was this."

"Me too. We'll have to watch it again."

"Later. Much later."

The last remnants of her nervousness retreated as desire grew. She relaxed, slipping her hands under the loose shirt he wore, absorbing the firm, smooth texture of the skin on his back, the muscles that rippled underneath her palms.

"Let's get some of these clothes off." He tugged her T-shirt up and over her head, kissed his way down from her forehead to her chest and slipped his own shirt off.

His fingers traced the pattern of the lace on her

white bra and then unclipped the front clasp. Her nipples became hard, hot peaks of sensation as he touched them.

"Beautiful lady." He dipped his head and suckled first one nipple and then the other, and now she didn't want slow. The urgency building in her wasn't patient. It demanded release, and she moaned and moved her hips.

"In a moment, love." His voice was thick. He found and unfastened the hidden zipper on her skirt, and he stripped it down and off, taking her panties with it. With difficulty, he slid his khakis and briefs past his cast and at last, skin met skin, hot and damp and needy.

She loved the thick, dark pelt on his chest and abdomen. She drew back and studied him, reveling in the dusky coloring, the beauty of his body. She rubbed herself against him like a kitten, pressing her nose to his skin, drawing in the distinct and arousing odor that was Noah. Her body burned as if she had a fever, and she looked into his eyes.

"Please hurry now. I want you to love me."

His fingers were exploring her folds, finding and fondling, and she writhed, loving the sensation but needing so much more.

Her hands slipped down and found his erection,

and she took pagan delight in his sharp, indrawn breath and the involuntary surge of his hips.

He protected himself and straddled her, and her legs came up and around him, drawing him tight. He pushed deep into her, hot, demanding, and then with a groan of abandonment, he moved and moved, and she forgot to breathe as she balanced on a cliff and then tumbled down and down, in ever-increasing waves of heat and pleasure, into a place of incredible, indescribable joy. She heard the sounds she made faintly, faraway, as if the person crying out in that abandoned fashion was distant, apart from her. She was aware of him holding her as she writhed.

She'd closed her eyes, and when she opened them he was waiting, dark eyes fierce and hungry, focused intently on her face. He held her gaze and drove himself into her, looking deep into her eyes. He'd kept his strength and power harnessed, but now he released it fully. She clung to him, and as his climax erupted, she felt tears trickle slowly down the sides of her face.

CHAPTER NINE

NOAH HELD HER as she slept. The arm cradling her head gradually grew numb and the muscles in his injured foot ached from being stationary for too long, but he didn't change position.

Her soft breath was warm and fragrant against his neck, and he could smell her spicy perfume, faintly underscoring the more pungent, musky scent of their lovemaking.

The depths of passion their loving had unleashed, both in her and in himself, sent a shiver through him. Why should this most basic of acts suddenly transcend what he'd known before, and become almost holy? And why with this particular woman? Was it some mystifying genetic thing, the connection he felt? Or was it simply because their chemistry coincided, so each instinctively knew what the other wanted? Whatever it was had shaken him to the roots of his being.

And now, having her sleep in his arms, wanting her to stay there, this was also new. Normally he preferred to sleep alone. He'd never been fond of waking up to find last night's sexual partner beside him in the morning.

Not that he was sleeping. His mind was running like a halfback with the ball heading for the goalposts, and now it took off on another tangent. Making love with Grace had brought up the question of whether it was ethical to go on representing Lucille. He had an appointment with her in the morning.

Grace had mentioned that her mother knew she was seeing him and was pleased about it. Noah thought about ethical conduct and decided he'd suggest transferring Lucille's file to another lawyer. There weren't any hard and fast rules that forbade him representing her. He'd just feel more comfortable not being involved.

LUCILLE FELT OTHERWISE, however, and she was vocal and adamant.

"I came to you because I have confidence in you," she said, recrossing long legs that reminded Noah forcibly of her daughter. "I absolutely refuse to change horses in midstream, and that's that." The stubborn set of her determined jaw—which also reminded Noah more than a little of Grace—softened, and she purred, "Besides, I feel so much more relaxed with you, knowing you and Gracie are dating.''

He certainly didn't feel relaxed about it, and he was pretty sure Grace didn't, either. He'd have to talk to her. They'd been too involved with other urgent matters to discuss it last night, or this morning.

The morning's activities went dancing through his mind like a delicious X-rated movie, and he hoped Lucille didn't have some hidden psychic streak that allowed her to read thoughts. He was having a hard time keeping his attention on the issues at hand.

''Okay, if you feel that strongly about it, we'll go on as we are,'' he told her, stifling a sigh. ''I'll see if I can hurry the disclosure statements along so we can proceed with the separation agreement.''

''The sooner the better,'' Lucille agreed. ''I saw a lovely little condo right on the water that I might consider buying when my money comes through.''

A condo on the water would cost a small fortune, Noah thought, although he didn't say it. How Lucille spent her settlement money wasn't his business. At least, not once his account was paid. At forty-eight, Lucille was an exceptionally sexy, attractive woman, and wherever she settled, Noah didn't think she'd be living alone very long.

Over the next two weeks, it became clear to Noah that he didn't want to be alone, either. He wanted Grace with him every moment they weren't working, and if that meant nights instead of days, so much the better.

It was the beginning of the third week, and he was talking to Grace on the phone one morning when Agnes buzzed, signaling that Mrs. Judy Jackson, his ten-o'clock appointment, was waiting.

"Gotta go, my darling. I'll let you know how I make out with the unveiling." He was scheduled to get the cast off his foot that afternoon, and he'd planned a celebration, a special dinner and a ride around Stanley Park in a horse-drawn carriage. He'd also bought Grace an antique silver bracelet. It was in his pocket, and he was as eager as a child to give it to her.

"How about meeting me here at six-thirty? I have a late appointment, and then we can go straight from here to dinner. And this is the last time you'll have to drive, unless my foot's rotted off under this thing."

Grace was agreeable. He lowered his voice to a whisper and told her exactly what sort of wicked things he had planned for later in the evening, and he hung up with an idiotic smile on his face that he couldn't subdue.

He buzzed Agnes and told her to send Mrs. Jackson in, wondering how he could feel this degree of anticipation about seeing Grace. Shouldn't he be getting bored anytime now? Normally he'd be looking for ways to slow things down, and instead he was counting the hours until she appeared and thinking of things they could do together next month. Next month, hell. He'd looked at travel brochures and daydreamed about a holiday in Antigua next January, and it was only the middle of May.

That gave him pause for thought. The fact that he wasn't bored yet didn't mean he wouldn't still wake up one morning knowing it was over, he reminded himself.

He'd deal with that when the time came. For now, he was happy. More than happy, he was filled with a sense of elation, a joy he hadn't felt since he was maybe eight years old. He whistled a love song under his breath and grinned at his client when she walked in.

"Morning, Judy." She was fifty-nine, finally divorcing the wealthy contractor husband who'd played around on her for more than half their married life, and Noah was trying to piece together the man's financial status. It helped that Judy was a bookkeeper, and had done the books for her husband's company until three months ago, when she'd arrived home early from a weekend visit with her grandchildren to find Sydney Jackson in bed with not one but two women young enough to be his daughters.

It took courage at Judy's age to divorce, and Noah had great sympathy for her. And as always, he was determined to get her a fair share of the mutual assets.

He held out a ledger from the business, pointing at an entry that confused him.

"I don't understand these amounts, Judy. Why are separate checks, identical amounts, going to the same businesses on the same day?"

She glanced at the book. "Oh, we always paid certain tradesmen with two separate checks," she said casually. "Half and half, some businesses request that method of payment. They keep different accounts."

"Two sets of books?" Noah was familiar with the practice. As long as income tax was paid, there was no law against it.

"There were only four businesses Sydney paid that way," she explained. "See, they're listed here." She flipped to another part of the ledger, pointing.

Noah looked, and his eyes widened. Third on the list of names was Gamonski Plumbing.

In the course of litigation, Noah had sent out demands to Gamonski Plumbing for discovery of documents. The business records that Hugo Gamonski had provided showed no record of a second accounting system. Noah had studied the documents in minute detail.

The ramifications of this rolled over Noah, and his elation disappeared like the air from a popped balloon.

Hugo Gamonski was obviously hiding what could amount to an enormous amount of money, money Lucille had no idea existed. Did Grace know, or her brothers? Noah thought it was unlikely.

Ordinarily, Noah would have been jubilant to have uncovered such information for a client, but instead his stomach churned with dread and he felt physically sick.

If Hugo Gamonski was hiding money and not paying tax, he could face criminal charges. At the very least, Grace would feel betrayed when she found out about this, and betrayal was an old wound for her. Lloyd Madison had made certain of that.

This information would cause a major crisis in Grace's family. It could send her father to jail, and somehow Noah didn't think Grace was going to appreciate the fact that it was Noah who'd found out about it.

He wished to God he hadn't.

The awful thing was, he had no choice in the matter. As Lucille's attorney, he was duty-bound to pursue it.

The moment Judy left, Noah called Agnes in and explained what he wanted her to find out. Notes in hand and the light of battle in her eyes, she marched off, leaving Noah slumped despondently in his chair, wondering exactly what degree of nuclear disaster he'd just set in motion.

AGNES WAS AS METICULOUS and thorough as always. By three that afternoon, she'd located the bank account to which Hugo Gamonski had been depositing money.

It would take several more days to ascertain whether or not there were other accounts. The one she'd located didn't contain an enormous sum, and she'd already learned that he'd paid income tax on it—she had a contact at Revenue Canada who was a genius at uncovering confidential information.

Noah stared down at the report Agnes had compiled, and his heart felt as though it had taken on a load of lead. There was no avoiding it. He now had to tell Lucille what he'd discovered, and he knew that was like setting a match to a powder keg.

With great reluctance, he picked up the phone and dialed her number.

CHAPTER TEN

AT SIX-THIRTY THAT AFTERNOON, Grace walked into the deserted reception area at Noah's firm and marched down the silent hall to his office.

She'd spent an hour and a half listening to her mother castigate her father. Then she'd driven to Gamonski Plumbing and watched her father come close to breaking down.

After that, she'd done her best to soothe her brothers' hurt and angry reactions at the knowledge that their business partner, and father, had hidden away money they should have known about.

She should have been exhausted, but the anger that had been building ever since her mother's unbelievable phone call was carrying her along on a riptide of energy.

Noah's door was open, and she swept in.

"Hi, darlin'." Noah was sitting behind his desk, and he got up and came toward her, limping a little but missing the cast. "Look at this, I'm free at last—"

He took a good look at her face, heaved a sigh and gave up on pretense. "I guess Lucille told you."

"Damned straight she told me." Grace put her hands on her hips and glared at him. "Do you have any idea how much pain you've caused my entire family, Noah Burnside? No matter what else my mother thought of my dad, she never *once* questioned his honesty. And neither did Barney or Theo—or me either, for that matter. Not until you came along."

"Look, all I did was find out what was going on," Noah said. He was leaning back on his desk, hands in his pockets, a defensive expression on his face. "Don't shoot the messenger, okay?"

"No, it's not okay. You've caused my entire family a whole lot of pain, and personally, I don't think it was necessary." Her voice rose. "Who elected you Dick Tracy, Noah? What gives you the right to poke around in my family's business and break their hearts?"

A part of Grace knew she was being unreasonable, but the other, more powerful part was filled with such anger and despair she couldn't stop herself.

"Your mother made me responsible for safeguarding her rights in a divorce proceedings, Grace." Noah's voice was soft, so soft she had to strain to hear. "That means that whatever information I find must be brought out into the open and dealt with."

"No matter how much it hurts, Noah? You keep saying you enjoy being with me, you pretend to care how I feel."

"I do care." But he didn't sound as if he did. He sounded grim and remote. "I happen to be a lawyer, Grace. There are standards that have to be met."

"And those standards have everything to do with money and nothing to do with people's feelings," she raged. "You don't know my dad—you've never even met him. He's the kindest, sweetest man..." She choked, on the verge of tears. She fought hard to stop them.

"I'm sure he is," Noah said in a tone that to her indicated he thought the opposite. "The simple fact is, he didn't tell the truth about his finances. If you own a business and don't produce documents on demand you can go to jail."

She thought he sounded righteous, and it infuriated her. "If he was a crook, don't you think he'd have found a smarter way to hide money?" Grace was shaking. She clasped her hands in front of her to hide it. "Dad put that money away because he wanted to take Mom on a holiday. See, you don't really know my mother, Noah. She has serious problems with money. She routinely spends more than my father earns. He even had her come and work in the office two years ago, just so she'd see that there was only so much income, but it didn't do any good. And that was when he opened that separate account, because he wanted to surprise her, take her on a cruise for their wedding anniversary, and he didn't want her to know the money was there. Because sure as hell she'd spend it long before he could buy the tickets.''

He nodded, but his tone was cool. ''Whatever the reason, the only thing that concerns me is that he didn't admit the account existed.''

''And of course you'd never call him up and just ask him why he had it,'' she stormed.

''You must know I can't do that.'' His jaw was set now, and he'd crossed his arms on his chest. ''And when you calm down, you'll realize that none of this is my fault, Grace. You're overreacting. I realize you're upset, but—''

''Don't you dare patronize me, Noah. I'm not one of your bimbos.'' She'd struck a nerve. His eyes narrowed and his mouth tightened. She hurried on before he could interrupt.

''And when I calm down, I'll realize exactly what I know right now. I shouldn't have allowed myself to get into a relationship with you in the

first place. You and I just don't think the same
way. You'd have seen that soon and dumped me,
so I'm saving you the trouble. I'm ending whatever there's been between us, here and now. I
don't want to ever see you again, Noah.''

"Grace, for God's sake..." He straightened
and took a step toward her, and she hurriedly
stepped back. The chemistry was powerful between them. Even in the midst of her anger, she
was aware of it, an electric undercurrent in the
room. She couldn't let him touch her. She'd lose
her focus. She took another step backward to the
open door, and then she turned and fled.

"Grace." His bellow echoed down the hallway. "God damn it all, don't do this. I love you,
Grace. Do you hear me? I love you...."

She was at the front door, and momentum kept
her moving. She hit the street at a run, and she
was in her truck in the parking lot before she allowed herself to think about what she'd heard him
say.

But of course he'd say he loved me, she rea-
soned as she started the motor with hands that
shook so badly she could barely get the key in
the ignition. She was probably the first woman
who'd ever walked out on the great Burnside, instead of waiting around for him to get bored and

do the dumping. His ego was smarting, so he'd pulled out all the stops. That's all it was.

So why did it feel as though her heart was breaking in half?

something else

CHAPTER ELEVEN

I LOVE YOU?

The unfamiliar words had come out of Noah's
mouth of their own volition, and they'd shocked
him speechless. Besides that, he knew for sure
he'd blown the rest of their conversation, and he
needed to tell Grace that he was sorry about it.

He called her at home, leaving messages asking
her to talk to him, at first politely. But as the evening wore on with no response from her, his temper got the better of him.

"Grace, this is damned well juvenile. The least
you can do is talk to me," he growled into her
machine. His voice rose. "We're supposed to be
adults here. If you're there, for God's sake, pick
up the phone," he heard himself bellowing.

No response. He slammed down the receiver
and felt like kicking something, but there was his
newly healed foot to consider. He'd get a cab and
go over to her house, he decided.

But by the time the cab arrived, Noah had

changed his mind. He needed to think about what he wanted to say to her, and Grace was so mad she probably wouldn't listen to whatever he came up with anyway. There was no point in pushing the issue tonight. He'd give her time to cool down. That was the mature thing to do.

He'd call her in the morning, take her to lunch tomorrow. By then she'd realize she'd made a mistake and they could discuss the quarrel rationally, put it behind them and move on.

Exactly where they'd move on to was what he needed to consider. What *did* he want, besides having her back in his bed? He finally crawled into it, but he slept badly. The bed was big and empty. How had he become this dependent on a woman? He got up and made himself brandy with a dash of hot milk, but the hollow feeling in his gut got worse as the night progressed.

He was at the office by seven the next morning, and at seven-fifteen his phone rang. Knowing it was Grace, he snatched it up and shouted hello.

"Is this Burnside, the lawyer?" The voice was deep and gruff and male.

Feeling duped, Noah grumpily confirmed that it was.

"I'm Hugo Gamonski."

Grace's father. For one tense moment, Noah

thought that Hugo was going to tell him to stay away from his daughter.

"This money you're so steamed about," Hugo said instead, his deep voice resonant with sadness and resignation. "Tell Lucille she can have it, every last cent. I'd tell her myself but she won't speak to me. I tried a dozen times and she just hangs up."

Noah felt sympathetic. Obviously Lucille had gifted her daughter with more than her legs.

Hugo was still speaking. "And the assessed value of half the business, she can have that, too. I'll come up with the cash. It'll just take me a while. I'll hafta get a mortgage."

"That's very generous of you, Mr. Gamonski."

A deep sigh came over the line. "Yeah, well, what good's money if there's nobody to enjoy it with you?"

Noah should have felt exuberant at having settled his client's case so favorably, but Hugo's words struck a raw nerve. What good was *life* if there was nobody to enjoy it with you?

A cold shiver went over him as he realized that he was now thinking long-term here. *Did* he want to spend the rest of his life with Grace? The idea of long-term commitment terrified him. It would take some getting used to.

In the meantime, he called Lucille and gave her

Hugo's message verbatim. Lucille burst into sobs, and with a garbled, tear-choked wail, hung up in his ear.

Noah then called Grace again, and this time, she answered.

"It's me." *Brilliant intro, Burnside.* "We need to talk."

"No, we don't. I've given this a lot of thought, Noah." Her voice was weary and so calm it frightened him.

"You were absolutely right yesterday. I shouldn't have blamed you for what's going on with my family."

His heart soared. She'd come to her senses, just the way he'd known she would.

"But I was right about you and me, Noah. There's no future for us, and I think it's best if we end it now."

No future? A sense of panic began to come over him. *What did she want, a proposal of marriage, for God's sake?* That idea shook him to his core. Marriage just wasn't in the cards. She knew that, they'd talked about it. But monogamy—that was something different. He hadn't looked at or given a single lecherous thought to any other woman since he'd met her. Why, he even thought there was a chance he was in...

The words that had come out of him so spon-

taneously the previous afternoon were on his lips
again, begging to be said, but he stifled them. She
hadn't paid any attention yesterday, and he had a
gut feeling she wouldn't now, either. And saying
them scared the hell out of him. Besides, he had
some pride left, hadn't he? He would not be re-
duced to begging. He swallowed hard and opened
his mouth to reply, but she didn't give him a
chance.

"We both know it wouldn't be long anyway
before you got bored with me," she rushed on,
her voice brittle. "You said yourself a few months
is your limit. I know it hasn't been that long, but
I don't feel like waiting around for it to happen.
So I'd appreciate if you'd not call or come
around." She sounded as if she'd rehearsed this,
or was reading it from a script.

Aghast, Noah burst out, "You're giving up
what we have together because of something that
you think might happen at some undetermined
point in the future?" Surely logic would force her
to see how ridiculous that was. His door was
open, and he could see Agnes putting her purse
in a drawer and settling things on her desk. He
knew she was also listening. Agnes liked Grace.
She'd told him Grace was the first lady friend
he'd had that used her head for more than a hat
rack.

"Look, I have to see you, Grace. This isn't something we can discuss properly on the phone. Let me check my Day-Timer here—damn it all, I've got court this morning but I can take a couple hours this afternoon, I'll pick you up and—"

"No." The response was firm and definite and final. "I don't want to see you, not today, not ever. And I don't want to discuss anything with you, either." She sounded a little like Lucille had, as if hysteria and tears might take over at any moment, and he was alarmed. A dose of desperation was also beginning to set in. "Grace, just listen for a minute—"

"Sorry, no. I've spent so much time listening I'm fresh out," she said, her voice rising. "My family is using up every ounce of my energy, and I've got a business to run. *Please,* Noah, please, just do as I ask." Her voice trembled and his heart melted. He didn't want to make her unhappy. That was the last thing he wanted to do.

"Noah, I'm on overload here. I can't take very much more."

"Okay." He had no choice when she put it that way. "Okay, Grace. If that's the way you want it, I won't be in touch." *For a while. Until this settles down.*

"Thank you. Goodbye, Noah." She hung up without waiting for a response.

Noah smashed the receiver down and cursed, a long and heartfelt stream of invective. Agnes got up from her desk, gave him a look and then quietly and firmly shut the door on him.

IT HAD BEEN TEN DAYS since her breakup with Noah, and Grace was sitting in her office staring at nothing when a soft tap sounded on the office door and Priscilla stuck her head in.

"Grace, can I talk to you for a minute?"

It was an indication of how out of sorts she'd been that Priscilla should even have to ask.

"Sure, c'mon in and sit down." Grace felt vaguely ashamed, but she couldn't seem to dredge up anything much in the way of strong emotion these days. She felt utterly drained and tired all day, and then when night came she couldn't sleep. Everyone said that getting over a love affair was just a matter of time, but so far, it wasn't working for her.

"I wondered if I could have a couple of extra days off next week? I'll be here for the swing wedding on Saturday, but I thought maybe Monday and Tuesday?" Priscilla's face turned a rosy shade. "Waldo and I are going down to Seattle. There's a big motorcycle rally, with a picnic and dance and everything. The kids are with Gina for a week, so it seemed like a good chance for us to…" Her voice trailed off and her color deepened. "Get to know each other better," she mumbled.

"Sure, we've got nothing big happening until the following weekend. Wayne and I can handle things here." Grace smiled, hoping it didn't look as ghastly as it felt. "You two seeing each other now?"

Priscilla nodded. "We get along really well, and his kids are so sweet." She shrugged. "His ex is nothing but trouble, but I figured what the heck, nobody has an ideal relationship—I might as well give this a chance."

"Good for you. I hope it works out."

Priscilla nodded, and then blurted, "I'm sorry about you and Noah, Grace. You guys made such a great-looking couple."

Grace had to smile. Trust artistic Priscilla to see the visual side of things. "I guess looks ain't everything," she joked feebly.

"It's such good news about your mom and dad, though, getting back together."

"Yeah, it is." Even better was the fact that Lucille had agreed to go for counseling to deal with her spending habits. Hugo, bless his heart, had stuck to his guns and insisted after Grace and her brothers lectured him.

Grace hadn't been able to summon much enthusiasm for her parents' reconciliation, however. Her mother had moved back into the house and Theo and Barney said their parents seemed to be getting along really well, but Grace didn't trust Lucille. Her mother made mercury look stable.

Priscilla went back to work, and Grace knew she should be out front, giving Wayne a hand, instead of hiding in her office and obsessing over who Noah was dating.

Before she could move, the office door opened and Grace's heart sank. The last person she wanted to see this morning was her mother. Lucille would undoubtedly babble on about Noah, and Grace didn't think she could stand it.

Lucille had badgered her incessantly about the reasons for her breakup with Noah, insisting that Grace should try again; after all, wasn't Lucille being an absolute model of compromise? Typically, her mother didn't see anything ironic about that declaration, and each time Grace heard Noah's name, it was like a nail hammered straight into her heart.

"Hi, Mom. Sit down. I'll plug in the kettle—I've got some instant coffee here somewhere." She tried to sound welcoming, but her voice was flat.

Lucille, wearing off-white raw silk trousers, took a tissue from her bag and wiped the chair seat before she gingerly sat. "You really ought to do something with this place, Gracie. It's your office, and surroundings are so important. I saw a lovely antique armoire on Granville that would go perfectly against that wall."

"I don't think so, Mom." Grace felt a sense of foreboding. What was her mother leading up to now?

"I have an eleven-o'clock appointment with Valerie, my counselor," Lucille explained. "But I want to talk to you first."

"Okay." Grace braced herself. Talks with Lucille could go anywhere, and if this was about Noah again, she was liable to explode.

Lucille leaned forward, pretty face beaming. "Your father and I have decided to renew our wedding vows."

"You have?" It was about the last thing she'd expected, and it took a moment to absorb. "Well, that's nice, Mom. That's great. I'm glad for you."

Lucille was practically bursting with excitement. "We're going to go on a cruise with that money your father put away—your father's idea, by the way, not mine. But before we go we want to have a special ceremony, a celebration of our life together, with our family and friends in attendance."

Grace was beginning to guess why her mother

was here, and she felt more wary than ever. "Exactly what sort of ceremony were you thinking of?"

"I want us to be married all over again, on the Orient Express," Lucille announced triumphantly, excitement practically sparking from her.

Was there a 911 number for spendaholics?

Grace knew enough about the Orient Express to know that plumbers and their wives had to be in the minority on board the luxurious, expensive train that ran from Singapore to Bangkok.

"Just how are we all getting to Singapore?" It wouldn't surprise Grace to hear that Lucille had booked tickets and billed them to Hugo's charge card.

"Not the *real* Orient Express, silly. The Starlight Dinner Train that runs from West Vancouver to someplace up Howe Sound. I've heard it's *so* romantic," Lucille exclaimed. "I want you to arrange the whole thing. My counselor's helping me work out a budget for the party this morning, and after your father's approved it, we can get into more details. But I wanted you to think about it in the meantime. Isn't this *exciting,* Grace?"

Actually, it was. The Starlight Dinner Train was an old steam train with eight passenger cars that had recently been refurbished to take guests on a five-hour evening trip that included dinner and dancing and spectacular scenery. Grace hadn't done a wedding on it yet, but she could see the possibilities. A tiny spark of interest replaced the lethargy that had gripped her for days.

"When do you want this to happen?"

"Oh, the middle of June. That gives you two weeks to get it arranged. That should be lots of time."

Grace didn't bother saying that most weddings were planned at least six months in advance. Such a concept would be foreign to Lucille. If something appealed to her, she wanted it immediately. She'd always opened her gifts the moment they appeared under the Christmas tree.

"Okay, Mom, I'll do this, but there are two conditions. The first is we stick absolutely to the budget Daddy approves, and no changing your mind as we go along, no deciding to divorce all over again, just when I get this whole thing organized." Grace gave her mother a stern look.

"I promise." Lucille clasped her hands on her stylish black T-shirt, in the vicinity of her heart.

"And the second is that you *never* mention Noah Burnside to me again, and you absolutely don't even think of calling him and mentioning me."

"Oh, darling." Lucille frowned and reached across and took Grace's hand. "I feel so responsible for that whole shmozzle. He's such a hunk, and a gentleman, and I know you liked him, and I still think you two are perfectly—''

"Mom." Grace drew her hand away and glared at Lucille. "What did I just say?"

"Sorry, sorry, sorry." Lucille held up both hands, palms out. "It won't happen again, I promise. I won't say another word. To either of you."

"Okay." Grace swallowed the lump in her throat. "Now let's see. I'll have to hurry up and reserve this train. We'll have to figure out how many guests. Do you think a twenties theme as far as clothing goes? Elegance and opulence with a strong note of untamed exuberance." If there was a period in time that suited Lucille, it had to be the Roaring Twenties.

Lucille's eyes widened. "Oh, perfect. Brilliant, Gracie. Oh, I can see my dress now—a blue flapper dress with the rows and rows of fringe. I look so good in blue, and I'll get Terry to do my hair in tight waves, and I'll buy a shawl, one of those pashmina things—''

"Mom, pashmina costs the earth. You're gonna have to stick to a budget." Grace had the feeling she should tattoo the words on her left arm so she could just hold them up and show them to Lucille over the weeks to come—she knew she'd be using them constantly.

"Right, not pashmina, maybe just angora—oh, good Lord, look at the time, I've got to run. One thing Valerie's a stickler about is being on time for appointments. Apparently it has something to do with self-discipline.'' Lucille raced off, and Grace let her breath out in a whoosh and closed her eyes.

For once, her mother had actually been helpful. In one fell swoop, she'd made certain Grace wouldn't have a second's free time for the next two weeks to obsess over anyone. And Lucille had promised not to mention that anyone ever again.

Grace tried to feel good about it, and failed utterly.

CHAPTER TWELVE

As MAY TURNED TO JUNE, Noah spent ever-increasing amounts of time at the gym. He was playing racquetball, and now that his foot was entirely healed, he'd started running around the park some afternoons. He was also giving serious thought to buying a racing bike.

Exercise took his mind off things, like what Grace was doing, what she was thinking, dreaming, saying, wearing, making, seeing, eating. Most of all, who she was dating. He could actually make it through a couple of hours now without seeing her in his mind's eye. If he worked out really hard.

"You're gonna turn into one of those muscle-bound apes whose eyes bulge out farther than their biceps," Jaimie had warned Noah. It was Friday, and Jaimie wanted Noah to come over to his house to meet his wife's best friend's sister, who was allegedly single, sexy and eager to have a good time on a short-term basis. She was in town on a banking seminar.

Noah declined. "I'm going to the gym. Nothing against your wife's—whatever. I'm just off women for the time being, sort of like taking a sabbatical."

"More like a fast. Still hung up on Grace, huh?" Jaimie knew about Grace dumping him. Hell, the entire office knew about Grace dumping him. Maybe every legal firm in Vancouver knew about it. Agnes had sworn she hadn't said a word, but someone must have.

"You know what they say when a horse throws you," Jaimie lectured. "You gotta get back on right away. Wait too long and you'll end up losing your nerve totally."

Noah didn't bother explaining that he'd tried several times to get back on, but Grace would neither see him nor talk to him.

"Thanks for that gem of wisdom, Jaimie. I'll give it serious consideration."

"Yeah, well, don't wait too long. And lay off with the weights. You're starting to make the rest of us look like ninety-pound weaklings."

Noah thought about what Jaimie had said as he loaded an extra five pounds on the bench-press machine. The gym was quiet for a Friday evening. Big date night, Noah thought, lying flat on the bench and preparing to lower the weights to his chest and lift them again. He used to date women on Friday nights himself. It seemed like a long time ago.

"Hey, Noah Burnside? We need to talk to you for a minute."

The male voice was all too familiar, and a sideways glance confirmed what Noah already knew.

"It's about Grace."

Theo and Barney Gamonski were looking down at him, one on either side of the weight bench. Noah strained to put the bar back as fast as he could, so he could get up, but the weights shifted. He struggled to regain control, and a sense of déjà vu sent a bolt of panic through him.

In tandem the brothers reached out and steadied the bar, smoothly setting it back in place on its holder.

Noah rolled to his feet and whirled to face the two muscular young men, adrenaline coursing through his veins.

He was in better physical shape than he'd ever been in his life, and if Grace's brothers were looking for a fight, they'd come looking for the wrong guy.

WAS THERE JUST ONE right guy for every woman? The question haunted Grace at every wedding she arranged these days, and it was foremost in her mind on this soft June evening.

She stood in the Starlight Train's gently rocking Stardust car, tears spilling from her eyes and trickling down the front of her coral twenties-style minidress.

The minister, a round little man with a deep, resonant voice, was leading her parents through a renewal of their vows.

"I now ask you, Lucille, and you, Hugo, to repeat the wedding vows that you shared thirty years ago. During those years, you have experienced the birth of three children together, and the loss of beloved parents. You have endured sickness and enjoyed health. Your relationship has not been easy, but it has endured, and with love, caring, understanding and tolerance it will flourish. Please repeat after me..."

The small group of invited guests were gathered around, and Grace, flanked by her brothers, stood right beside Hugo and Lucille.

Outside, the flowering cherry trees and rainbow-colored flowerbeds of Ambleside Park slipped slowly past the wide windows as the steam train chugged along.

Over the next hours, dinner would be served as the spectacularly scenic route unfolded. The train would make its stately way along Howe Sound, with breathtaking views of deep green ocean and purple mountains. They'd reach Porteau Cove near Squamish in the early evening.

Grace had arranged for a jazz band. She'd carefully chosen show tunes from the twenties, and at Porteau Cove the band and the guests would get off the train. There'd be dancing for several hours in the park, and then everyone would reboard. Wedding cake, various desserts and brandy would be served on the return journey.

"...do you, Lucille, once again take this man to be your lawful wedded husband?"

Just for an instant, Grace held her breath, and she felt a similar sudden tension in her brothers. Barney and Theo were each holding one of her hands, and their grips tightened in tandem. All three siblings knew their mother was unpredictable; there was always the possibility she'd change her mind, even at this last possible moment.

Lucille was radiant in a silver sheath, with an ostrich feather sprouting from her beaded headband. She gazed up at Hugo, her lovely eyes brimming with tears, and she nodded her head.

"I certainly do. I will walk with you, my husband, hand in hand through all the remaining days of our lives together, and my solemn vow is to love you, my dear Hugo, forever and a day."

Grace could hear quiet sobs from the female

guests, and even some of the men were discreetly dabbing at their eyes.

The minister pronounced Grace and Hugo husband and wife, and the guests cheered as the female lead singer launched into a twenties song called "I'll Be with You in Apple Blossom Time."

Champagne corks popped, the train made a short stop at a crossing, and Grace was kept busy chatting with guests who'd known her since she was a baby. She was also keeping a watchful eye on the serving staff, making certain that hors d'oeuvres trays circulated constantly and wineglasses were refilled. Dinner would begin in half an hour.

The band had segued into a rendition of "My Man" when Lucille slipped an arm around her waist.

"Gracie, darling, where are the boys? The photographer wants a family photo, and I can't seem to find them."

"They're probably in the observation car. I'll go get them."

Grace made her way back through the eight luxuriously appointed and aptly named coaches. She strolled through Indigo, Moonglow, Twilight, Rainbow, Apollo, Continental and finally Manhattan. There was no sign of Theo or Barney.

Puzzled, Grace turned and made her way back, looking more carefully this time. Where *were* her brothers? How could both of them disappear like this on a *train*, for heaven's sake? There were only a limited number of places they could be. Mildly annoyed, she asked invited guests and other passengers if they'd seen the young men.

"Two guys got off back there when the train stopped at that crossing," one man said. Grace thanked him, but she knew it couldn't have been her brothers. She checked washrooms and every conceivable corner, but there was no sign of the Gamonski boys.

Back in the Stardust car, the party was in full swing. The band was playing "Toot Toot Tootsie, Goodbye." Laughter, champagne and elegant food combined to create what looked like a perfect wedding, which should have given Grace a feeling of satisfaction and accomplishment.

It did, but along with it came an emptiness she'd grown familiar with in the past weeks, a sense of loneliness so intense it brought tears to her eyes and a physical ache in her chest. She slipped into one of the powder rooms and stared at herself in the mirror.

Her hair was good, her makeup perfect. She looked fine, unless someone studied her eyes. They were bright with unshed tears, and they reflected the deep sadness and sense of loss that had overwhelmed her ever since the breakup with Noah.

She leaned against the antique wooden vanity, rocking with the movement of the train, and admitted to herself that nothing felt really good or complete anymore. It was as if a portion of her heart was missing, and that portion had a name. She'd tried to block his face, his voice, his touch, out of her mind, but he was there the moment she relaxed her guard.

Noah.

"Noah." She dared to murmur his name aloud, allowing the pain of loss to wash over her fully. Her face crumpled, and a wrenching sob escaped.

Not here, not now. Pull yourself together. You can break down later. You've got the rest of this wedding to get through.

She took a deep breath and then another, becoming aware that the slow, steady rhythm of the train's engine had changed during the last few moments. A glance out the window confirmed that they were slowing down. The sound of brakes being applied told her they were stopping, but this wasn't Porteau Cove. It was far too soon.

She hurried back to the wedding party. The band was playing something she couldn't quite identify, and an air of heightened excitement greeted her. Everyone was grouped three deep along one side of the coach, peering out the opened windows.

"Gracie, oh Gracie, my goodness, what a brilliant idea." Lucille's eyes sparkled like the new diamond ring Hugo had placed on her finger. "My gosh, what fun having masked men hold up the train. It's so exciting. And you didn't whisper a word to me about it, you brilliant little sneak."

"What masked men? What are you talking about?" Grace pushed her way to the window and stared out, hardly able to believe her eyes.

The train had come to a halt in a clearing in deep woods, and three men on horseback were staging a holdup.

At least, Grace hoped they were only staging it.

They were dressed like western desperadoes, with Stetsons and long-sleeved shirts, blue jeans and leather chaps. They wore gun holsters low on their hips. Red-checked handkerchiefs were tied over their faces so only their eyes showed under the brim of their hats. They were riding spirited horses that reared as loud reports sounded from pistols Grace could only pray were fake.

"Oh, this is so *thrilling*," one of the female guests shrieked. "I'm going to have you do exactly this for my daughter's wedding, Grace."

She squealed with delight. "Oh, look, everybody, two of them are getting off their horses. Oh my word, they're boarding the train."

Visions of total disaster formed in Grace's head. What if those guns were real? What if the holdup was real? Some of the women were wearing expensive jewelry, and the men had wallets.

Sudden terror made her knees wobble, but it was her party and she was responsible. She shoved past guests until she was standing directly in front of the two masked men who'd shouldered open the door at the end of the carriage.

"Just *what* do you think you're doing?" Fists on her hips, Grace glared at them. One of them brandished a pistol in either hand.

"Everybody stay exactly where you are."

The women giggled and the men guffawed. They still thought the whole thing was a gag. One of the outlaws took two long strides toward Grace.

"Sorry, ma'am, but you're coming with me."

"Noah?" It was impossible, it couldn't be. But Grace knew that deep, assured voice as well as she knew her own, and when he pulled her into his arms, there wasn't a shred of doubt. She'd know those arms anywhere.

Before she had time to do more than squeak, he'd slid an arm down to her waist and another around the back of her legs. He picked her up and tossed her over his shoulder like some muscled hero in a B-grade movie.

Between the shock and the broad shoulder shoving into her rib cage, Grace could hardly breathe.

"The rest of you just stay calm and nobody'll get hurt," she heard the other desperado growl.

"*Barney?*" It was her brother. Even upside down, breathless, and horrified about the shortness of her dress and the generous view of beige lace panties that might well be flashing the guests, Grace knew it was Barney.

"What are you maniacs *doing?*" she shrieked. "Noah, put me down this *instant.*" She pounded her fists on a broad back that felt as if it was molded in steel, but then she let out a scream of fright as her captor shoved backward through the doors and jumped off the train steps to the ground.

They landed hard and he gave an audible grunt and an *oof.* For a moment he lost his footing and Grace had visions of flying through the air and landing on something harder than his shoulder.

But Noah caught himself and dumped her to the ground. Before she could even get her bearings, Barney grabbed her from behind in the same hammerlock he'd taught her years before, and Noah mounted the horse that—Grace squinted into the setting sun—yup, it was her other idiot brother, Theo, holding the horse's reins.

"You cretins are going to pay for this," Grace warned through gritted teeth. But the threat ended in another yelp as Barney picked her up and tossed her onto the horse, and into Noah's arm.

"Hang on, darlin'." Noah touched the horse with his heels and Grace reflexively grabbed the horse's mane as the horse dramatically wheeled and galloped away from the train. Behind them, guests cheered and hollered from open windows and the engineer gave two long, shrill toots of the steam whistle.

Grace heard the engine pick up steam and begin to move along the tracks, gathering speed as it went.

As the sound of the train faded into the distance, Noah slowed the horse to a sedate walk. He guided it along a wooded path and down an incline until they were on a narrow beach littered with driftwood and layered with sand.

On the indigo waters of the inlet, a freighter steamed majestically out to sea, and the sails on two boats caught the sunset breeze and puffed off into the distance.

"Whoa." Noah dismounted and reached his arms up to catch Grace as she slid down. Instead of releasing her, his grasp tightened and he pulled her close, crushing her to his chest.

"Don't say a single word until I've said what I have to say," he begged. "I'm crazy, insanely, madly in love with you. You're the only woman I've ever met who never bores me. I can't stand not being with you. I can't stand waking up in the morning without you in my bed. I've been so lonely and so bored without you I think I've gone a little mental."

His desperate words were a banquet for her hungry soul, but she wasn't going to let him get away with this fiasco scot-free.

"I think you've gone *more* than a little mental," she agreed. "Exactly whose idea was this kidnapping thing?"

He smelled delicious, like sweat and horse and Noah. His arms were more muscular than she remembered. In fact, his whole body felt more muscular than she remembered.

Heavens, his whole body felt luscious. She couldn't wait to explore it.

"Barney and Theo thought it up, and Hugo arranged it with the engineer."

"Dad?" Was her father more romantic than she'd ever imagined? "You planned this with my *father?*"

"Well, yeah, I did. I asked him if he'd mind if

I proposed to you. I hope you don't mind, Grace.''

''You asked my father for my hand in marriage? Before you'd even asked me?''

''It's traditional. I wanted to do things right this time. And you didn't give me much opportunity to ask you anything.'' He let her go and turned to dig in the saddlebags. He pulled out a black velvet ring case and dropped to one knee in the sand. Close behind him, the horse moved restlessly.

''Don't you think you should tie that animal up first? He's liable to step on your foot, and you know what having a broken foot feels like.'' For the first time in weeks, Grace was enjoying herself.

Noah was visibly losing patience. He got to his feet and clicked his tongue to the horse, leading it over to a chunk of driftwood and loosely tying the reins.

He turned back to Grace, but she'd moved away, over to the water's edge. She was sitting on a log. She'd kicked off her shoes and taken her panty hose off.

''Want to go wading?'' This had been a long time coming, and she wanted to savor every moment. She wasn't going to let him rush her. Besides, she didn't want to be predictable. He did get bored easily.

He walked over, took hold of both arms and lifted her up so he was looking straight into her eyes.

"I intend to keep you captive here until you agree to marry me, Grace," he said in a dangerously soft tone. "The forecast is for sunshine for the next week. I checked. I have food and blankets in those saddlebags, and there's a stream nearby for water, so this can take as long as you want it to take."

Heavens, this was sounding better and better. She'd never been held captive before. It was thrilling. There were possibilities in this whole kidnapping scene for some very unusual weddings.

"You haven't asked me anything yet."

"I'm trying to. Just stay put for a minute."

He let her go and knelt in front of her.

The sun was setting, and the inlet was ablaze with softly colored light. Gulls swirled and cried high overhead.

"Grace, I love you. I want to spend the rest of my life with you. Will you marry me?"

Maybe she'd postpone saying yes for at least the night. It was Sunday tomorrow. He was a smart lawyer, let him figure out some wickedly ingenious ways of persuading her—not that she needed persuading, but she wasn't about to tell him that.

She looked down into his beloved face. She saw the uncertainty in his eyes, the apprehension in his expression, the tension around his mouth, and her heart melted.

"Okay," she said. "Sure. I will. Yes, Noah."

Elation overcame her as he slipped an enormous emerald on her ring finger and she tipped her head back and held her arms up to the sky.

"Yes," she caroled. "Yes, yes, yes."

They'd get married on a beach just like this one, at sunset. There'd be bagpipes playing, at first far away, then coming nearer. She loved bagpipes. They'd have bonfires, and she'd wear—

His arms came around her before she could envision her dress, and when his lips claimed hers, she knew the details of the wedding didn't matter.

What mattered was love, the overwhelming, humbling, massive love she felt between this man and herself. What mattered was the promise she was making to him in her heart, here and now.

I, Grace Madison, do solemnly swear to love and cherish you, and never bore you, Noah Burnside, until the day I die, and beyond, into eternity.

He was kissing her again, and suddenly the name of the tune the jazz band had been playing just before her abduction popped into her head.

It was an old twenties tune called "Love Will Find a Way."

MALONE'S VOW

Sandra Marton

CHAPTER ONE

SHE WAS A BEAUTIFUL WOMAN, but not the kind a man should even consider marrying.

Not a man like Bill Thornton.

Liam Malone knew it the minute he saw her.

Bill wasn't her type. He was too good, too gentle, too trusting. He didn't stand a chance at being able to handle a woman like Jessica Warren. She was all quicksilver heat, while Bill was a glowing ember.

Hell, Liam thought as he stared out the window of Bill's study, past the rolling green lawn to Lake Washington glittering in the distance. He wasn't much given to thinking in metaphors, but that was what he'd thought of last night, at the rehearsal dinner. One look at his oldest friend's fiancée and he'd known Bill was making a big mistake.

Bill, of course, was clueless. He'd never been able to read women worth a damn. Liam always could. Jet-lagged as he'd been after the flight from Singapore to Seattle, one glance at his old friend's bride-to-be had told him everything he really didn't want to know.

"Wait until you meet Jessica," Bill had written in the letter that had followed Liam halfway around the world. "This is like a fairy tale, Liam, with me as the frog the beautiful princess turns into a prince. I still can't believe Jessica is going to be my wife."

Liam could. He'd spent enough years on the fringes of what most people called polite society to know that men and women married for lots of reasons, and hardly any had much connection to anything as banal as love.

More than one woman had called him a cynic, but Liam didn't agree. He was simply a realist. He understood that "love" was a catchall word people used instead of less poetic terms, especially in the rarefied strata of the very rich. Successful men married beautiful women as a balm to their egos. Beautiful women married successful men for the security of their wealth. He'd never sat in judgment on such arrangements. The tradeoff was fair enough. It could work, assuming both parties to the deal were still willing to settle for those things a year or two into the marriage.

The men usually were. Arm candy was arm candy, after all. But the women often became restless. They wanted both jewels on their fingers and pleasure in their beds, and they went looking for it. One glance at Jessica Warren and Liam had known that Bill wouldn't satisfy her for very long. She'd need more than his kindness and money to keep her happy.

It would take more than that to keep her at all.

But the poor bastard didn't know it. He was marrying for love, and in his case, "love" really did mean a bucketful of syrupy clichés. One man, one woman. Forever after. Until death do us part. Bill was ready to swallow all of it, hook, line and sinker.

And that was the problem.

Give it a couple of years and Bill would still be crazy about his wife but she'd be bored to tears and looking for greener pastures. For all Liam knew, she was bored already. The flash in her eyes last night, when she'd caught him watching her, had said it all. She'd managed a nice girlish blush and a quick downward sweep of her lashes, but that hadn't changed anything. She'd been interested. His best friend's bride-to-be, interested in another man, the night before her wedding.

Interested in him.

Liam's mouth thinned.

It wasn't the first time a woman with a rich man in her life had given him that kind of look. Not all that long ago, he'd been the guy with the looks that turned women on and the empty pockets that turned them off. He'd lived by a combination of luck and his wits, but even so, he'd refused those invitations. He wasn't into playing games with women who belonged to other men. At best, he'd found that kind of come-on amusing.

Not this time. A single glance from Bill's fiancée, and he'd felt himself respond.

"Damn," Liam muttered. He swung away from the window, tucked his hands into his pockets and paced the length of Bill's study.

Of course, he'd responded. What man wouldn't? The message in those eyes had been clear, a promise of satin sheets and silken skin, of heated whispers and sizzling caresses. In one swift instant, his brain had stripped away the expensive suit, undone the classically styled hair...

Well, why not? He wasn't a saint. He was a healthy, heterosexual, thirty-four-year-old male. Yes, she was Bill's fiancée but a man's hormones had a way of ignoring the niceties. He knew that just as surely as he knew that a woman who was signing on for a happy ending with one man shouldn't look at another the way Jessica Warren had looked at him.

The trouble was, he had no idea what to do about it. He couldn't collar Bill and say, "You can't go through with the wedding this morning. The marriage won't work.''

Bill would laugh in his face. As far as he was concerned, Jessica was the only woman in the world. As soon as she'd gone to the powder room, he'd leaned in close and confided that he'd never been this happy in his life. Jessica was all the things he'd ever wanted. She was beautiful and good-natured; she was bright and charming. And when Liam had cautiously hinted that she was getting a good deal, too, that marrying a guy with an old family name and money wasn't exactly a bad thing for a woman, Bill had happily agreed.

''Everything Jessica has, Liam—her education, her career—she got on her own.'' His smile had turned soft and loving. ''It's going to be a joy to spoil her—if she lets me.''

She'd let him, Liam knew. She was, already. The rock on her finger, the expensive watch on her wrist...oh, yes, Jessica Warren would let her husband spoil her. The sad part, or maybe the good part, depending on your point of view, was that Bill's gifts would make both of them happy, he to give them and she to receive them. The question was, would the jewels, the furs, the cars, be enough to keep the lady faithful?

Liam doubted it. He knew how this particular fairy tale would end, and he was helpless to do anything about it without telling Bill the way Jessica had looked at him...and the way he'd looked at her.

A muscle ticked in Liam's jaw. He picked up a decanter of brandy and poured some into a crystal snifter.

There had to be some way to protect his oldest friend. They'd met at Princeton, where they'd made a strange pair. Bill had probably been enrolled the day he was born. Old-line money and a family that had come over on the *Mayflower* tended to do that for a man. Liam, on the other hand, was at Princeton courtesy of a glib tongue and money from the U.S. Army. His great-great-who-knew-how-many-times-great-grandfather had come to America either to escape the Irish potato famine or the long arm of the law, depending on who was telling the tale. Money and status weren't exactly part of the Malone family history.

Liam smiled.

Still, he and Bill had clicked. They'd fallen easily into an older brother, younger brother relationship, especially after Bill lost his parents in a plane crash in his sophomore year. Bill had financial consultants but it was Liam, the man of the world, who'd counseled him about Life. Bill, for his part, had saved Liam's tail more than once.

Liam had been plagued with something an endless succession of advisors had called ''an attitude problem.'' Put simply, it meant he'd have been kicked out of college half a dozen times, if it hadn't been for Bill and his connections.

It was time to return the favor.

''It's good to see I can still read your mind at a hundred paces, Liam, my man.''

Liam swung toward the door. Bill, resplendent in his morning coat and striped trousers, grinned at him.

''Can you?'' Liam said, and managed a smile.

''Sure.'' Bill walked to where Liam stood, reached past him for the decanter and poured himself some brandy. '''What's Malone doing now?' I asked myself a minute ago.'' Smiling, Bill lifted his glass to Liam's. '''He's stalking around my study,' myself replied, 'fortifying himself with brandy while he works up to telling me I'm on the verge of making the biggest mistake of my life.''' Bill laughed at the look on Liam's face. ''I'm right, aren't I?''

''Absolutely, as long as you've asked.''

''I knew it. What else would a confirmed bachelor like you think on my wedding day?'' Bill downed half his drink and grimaced. ''I needed that. My stomach's been going up and down like an elevator all morning.''

"Bill." Liam put down his snifter. "Look, I know you think you're in love with this girl..."

"Woman," Bill said, and grinned. "Jessica has very definite opinions on the male-female thing."

"Yes," Liam said coolly, "I'm sure she does."

"Wouldn't go out with me at all, even though we'd been working together almost a year. Said it wasn't right for a woman to date her boss."

"But you managed to change her mind."

Bill didn't seem to hear the sarcasm in Liam's tone. "I did," he said, and gave a lopsided grin. "Bet you didn't think I could talk a woman who looks like that into dating a guy like me, huh?"

Liam's brows lifted. "This isn't your first brandy today, is it?"

"It's my first in this room," Bill said, and chuckled. "Hey, you'd be edgy, too, if you were about to take a wife."

"You don't know what you're doing," Liam said bluntly, and felt better for finally having spoken the truth.

Bill sighed, sank into his favorite leather armchair and sipped his brandy. "I wondered how long it would take you to get around to that."

"Well, dammit, what choice do I have? You're about to make the biggest mistake of your life—"

"See? I even got the wording right."

"Bill, I'm serious."

"So am I, Liam. I love Jessica and she loves me."

"You know nothing about her."

"I know everything about her. I told you, she's had to make her own way in life. Her father never managed to hold on to a dime. He died when Jess was eighteen and she lost her mother only a year later. She's never been married, she has a degree in business studies—"

"You know nothing about her," Liam insisted. "You've only been dating her for, what, four months?"

"Only because she wouldn't go out with me sooner."

"Are you sleeping with her?" Liam said brusquely.

Bill blushed. "Direct, as always, Malone. Why do you want to know?"

A good question, Liam thought, and came up with what wasn't quite an answer. "It's normal for a man and woman who love each other to share a bed."

"So?"

"So, if you haven't slept with her, maybe you should consider why."

"Liam, I know you've been with a lot of women but Jessica is—"

"Different. Yes, I figured you'd say that. Look,

you have to know that there are women who use sex to snare a man.''

''Well, Jessica hasn't. Not that it's any of your business, but she hasn't slept with me yet. I haven't asked her to. She's not that kind.''

Liam snorted.

''She isn't, dammit!''

''There are all kinds of ways to use sex, Bill. Withholding it is only one of them.''

''Oh, for...'' Bill shot to his feet. ''Listen to me, Liam. Jessica is about to become my wife. Keep that in mind when you talk about her.''

''Dammit, Thornton, haven't you grown up at all? You're as naive as you were when you needed me to save your skinny tail from the weird babe with the purple hair. You were certain she was the love of your life, too, remember?''

''Oh, give me a break! I was eighteen, not thirty.''

''And not much smarter, from what I can see.''

Bill's mouth thinned. ''Back off, okay? I love Jessica, and she loves me.''

''What if it's your money she loves? Your name? The step up you'll give her by marrying her?''

''It isn't.'' Bill walked to Liam's side, smiled and clapped a hand lightly on his back. ''She loves me for myself, hard as that may be for you to believe, considering that it's you, with your black Irish good looks, the ladies always drool over.''

''Dammit, hear me out.''

''No.'' Bill threw an arm around Liam's shoulders. ''No, for once, Malone, *you* hear *me* out. This is love. The real thing, and don't judge it by your need to bed every good-looking female in sight, or by figuring a man with a bank account is always a hostage to his money.''

Liam looked at his old friend. He thought of telling him he'd changed that attitude when he'd finally decided there were better ways to indulge a love of risk than on the fall of the cards, but then he'd have to explain more than that, and this wasn't the time to do it. Not on Bill's wedding day, and it looked as if this really was going to be his wedding day.

Hell. Maybe Bill was right. Maybe the marriage would work. The bottom line was that there was nothing more he could do, except hope he was around to help pick up the pieces if, and when, the time came.

''Liam?''

Liam looked up.

''You could, at least, try and look happy for me.''

"Sure." Liam sighed. "I hope it works out. You know that."

"It will," Bill said solemnly. "Jess is the best thing that ever happened to me. Once you get to know her, you'll think so, too. Come on, get that sour look off your face and admit the truth. You're just jealous 'cause I've found the perfect woman."

Bill smiled. Liam tried to, and wondered if he'd succeeded. "I hope you're right."

"I know I am. Now, drink up, wish me luck and then get out there and do your duty. I fielded half a dozen phone calls after the rehearsal dinner last night, every last one from a lady aching to know more about my best man."

Liam grinned. "Only half a dozen?"

"All right, a dozen." Bill grinned, too, and touched his glass to Liam's. The men finished their brandy, put down the snifters and walked to the door together. "You know how come you're such a cynic, my man? It's because the ladies let you get away with murder."

"The Malone charm," Liam said lazily. "Love 'em and leave 'em, that's me."

"Yeah, well, sooner or later, you'll meet a woman like my Jessica and you'll change your tune."

"Sure," Liam answered, because an intelligent

man always knew when it was time to admit defeat. "Maybe in the next century."

Bill laughed. "Go on out and charm the ladies."

Liam strolled through the house to the music room, where the ceremony would take place. Pink and white roses filled the air with their perfume, and strains of Vivaldi drifted from the library. A pair of bridesmaids, ethereally lovely in gowns of palest pink, flashed him welcoming smiles.

Welcoming smiles to what he knew was going to end in disaster.

Liam turned on his heel and made his way through the house and out a side door to a garden with narrow, hedge-lined paths winding through it. He'd done what he could to convince Bill he was making a mistake. He was his friend's best man, not his conscience.

From this moment on, everything was up to fate.

UPSTAIRS, in one of the guest suites of her fiancé's home—the home that would soon be hers—Jessica paced restlessly from one wall to the other.

She'd longed for a perfect wedding day, and she had one. Blue skies, bright sun, not a single cloud to obscure the silhouette of Mount Rainier on the horizon...rare things in Seattle, but then, this was a special day. She was marrying the man she loved.

"Fate has really smiled on you, Jess," her maid of honor had said just a little while ago.

It was true. Jessie had never put much stock in fate, but how else could she explain all the wonderful things that had happened in the past few months? She and William had gotten to know each other. Their mutual respect had become friendship, and friendship had become love.

Jessica looked at her reflection in the mirror and smiled. How could the day be anything less than perfect? Not just the weather but everything. The music she and William had selected. The menu they'd planned. The vows they'd written together.

I, Jessica, do solemnly vow that I will love you, William, for the rest of my life, that I will always be at your side...

Her stomach did a slow, dangerous roll.

She was nervous, that was all. And that was normal. Everybody said so, from the seamstress who'd put a couple of quick darts into her ivory satin gown to the stylist who'd plaited tiny pink tea roses into her hair. Even Carrie, her maid of honor, had said the same thing when she saw Jessie's hands trembling.

"Butterflies," Carrie had assured her. "All brides have them."

Where *was* Carrie, anyway? How long could it take to look for a bridal bouquet? Jessica glanced at the platinum-and-diamond watch William had given to her last night at the rehearsal dinner. "Something new," he'd said softly. The "something old" was the emerald-and-diamond engagement ring on her finger, which had belonged to his mother and grandmother.

The watch had caught her completely by surprise.

"Oh, it's too much," she'd blurted when she opened the long blue box and saw the wink of diamonds. William had laughed, kissed her gently and said that nothing was too much where she was concerned.

"I love you, Jess," he'd said softly.

Jessica swallowed dryly. She loved him, too. Her fiancé was a kind, generous, wonderful man and she was the luckiest woman in the world, and yes, the day really was going to be perfect...if she could just stop trembling.

"Butterflies," Jessie whispered to her image in the mirror. "All brides have them."

Was that true? She didn't know much about brides, perhaps because she'd never thought she'd be one, not after watching her mother endure a marriage to a man who'd made a mockery of the word. Jessie's father had been a handsome rogue. He couldn't stay in one place for very long or, as it turned out, be faithful to one woman, but her mother had adored him anyway.

Jessie grew up knowing she'd never be that kind of fool. Why would a woman have to be blinded by passion to fall in love? Love could be something that happened slowly and gently. That was the best way, the way that would last.

She smiled.

That was the way she'd fallen in love with William.

She'd worked for him for almost a year before he'd asked her out and even then, she'd turned him down. She knew that dating your boss was never a good idea, but he'd been gently persistent and, at last, after a late night at the office, she'd agreed to dinner. Saying no under those circumstances would have been silly. Soon they'd begun spending all their time together. When he'd proposed, saying yes had been the most natural thing in the world.

Now she was less than an hour away from becoming Mrs. William Thornton the Third. It was hard to believe it was happening.

One man, one exchange of vows, for the rest of her life. Maybe it wasn't fashionable to believe

in forever-after anymore, but Jessie did. It worried
her a little that she'd never yet wanted more than
William's tender good-night kisses, but she was
sure that would change. Given time, her skin
would tingle when he touched her. Just looking
at him would make her breathless. She'd feel the
way she'd felt last night, when she'd first laid
eyes on Liam Malone.

Jessie took a step back, felt the bed hit behind
her knees and sank down on the edge of it.

"Oh, God," she whispered, and shut her eyes
as if she could block out the memory. What was
she doing, thinking about another man on her
wedding day? She hadn't even been looking forward to meeting Liam. William had talked about
him endlessly, until she'd been weary of hearing
the name and the stories that went with it. How
Liam traveled the world. How he made fortunes
and lost them on the turn of a card. How he went
through women. She'd been appalled by some of
the stories, fascinated by others and aware, almost
immediately, that her sweet, sensible William was
wistfully envious of Liam's free and easy life.

She'd come up with a picture to go with the
tall tales. Liam would be sexy as sin, gorgeous as
the devil and twice as persuasive. In other words,
he'd be the kind of man she most disliked.

As it turned out, she'd gotten it almost all right.

The rehearsal dinner had been in full swing; William had been holding her hand and telling her how happy they were going to be. Suddenly he'd dropped her hand, leaped from his chair and said, "Liam, my man, you made it!" She'd looked up and there, in the doorway, she'd seen Liam Malone for the very first time, exactly as she expected: tall, broad shouldered, with a handsome face, a shock of silky black hair and emerald-green eyes.

What she hadn't expected was the jolt of electricity that slammed through her when those green eyes met hers. Her heart had gone into overdrive and a pervasive heat had slipped under her skin. She'd felt all the reactions she'd sworn she'd never feel for any man, and she'd felt them for her fiancé's best friend.

She'd wanted to bolt from her chair and run. Instead, she'd torn her eyes from Liam's, stared blindly down at the table, and hoped, prayed, that the floor would open up and swallow her.

"Jessica, sweetheart," she'd heard William say, and she'd forced herself to look up and smile. William had his arm slung around Liam's shoulders and he was smiling, too, but Liam hadn't smiled at all. He'd just watched her through narrowed eyes set in a face that might have been chiseled from granite.

Somehow she'd stood up, said all the right things, extended her hand and tried not to jump at the tiny spark that leaped from Liam's fingers to hers.

"Static electricity," she'd said with a forced laugh.

"Indeed," Liam had replied, and the slightest smile had curved his mouth, a smile that said he knew exactly what she was feeling. "It's a pleasure to meet you at last, Jessica."

And that had been the end of it.

Jessie let out a breath she hadn't realized she'd been holding.

What was the matter with her? That *had* been the end of it. The moment had come and gone. Liam pulled up a chair, William settled in beside her again, and she'd listened while the two friends talked about old times. Her gaze had met Liam's once again but she'd looked quickly away and, before she knew it, the evening ended. Come stay with us, William had said, and she'd found herself fearing the answer, but Liam had thanked him politely, said he already had found a place and went off to wherever it was.

"A hostel, for all I know," William had said cheerfully, "or a penthouse. It depends on whether his luck's been good or bad."

Good, Jessie thought now, remembering the expensive cut of Liam Malone's gray suit. Or maybe bad, considering the longer-than-it-should-have-been, black-as-midnight hair that curled over his collar. She thought, too, of what William had told her, that Liam liked to gamble. Poker was his specialty, William said, but Jessie knew that women would be Liam Malone's specialty, women who were willing to trade one night in his bed for a lifetime of hot memories.

She stood up quickly and smoothed down her skirt. Where was Carrie? Better still, where was William? She needed to see him, put her hand in his, feel the warmth of his smile.

"Got 'em!"

Jessie swung around. Her maid of honor stood in the doorway, holding a bouquet of tiny pink roses, trailing baby orchids and lacy-white stephanotis in her hand.

"Would you believe the kid who delivered the flowers left your bouquet on a table in the—"

"Have you seen William?" Jessie hadn't meant to sound so shaky, but the look on Carrie's face told her she hadn't succeeded.

"What's the matter, Jess?"

"Nothing. I just want to see him, that's all."

"You can't see him. It's bad luck for the bride and the groom to see each other before the ceremony."

It was worse luck to think about another man before the ceremony, but Jessie knew better than to say that.

"That's just a silly superstition."

"Maybe, but do you really want to tempt fate?"

"No." Jessie gave a choked laugh. "That's the last thing I want to do."

"Jess." Carrie's voice softened. "Honey, I keep telling you, all brides are jittery."

"I know. And I'm not jittery. I just—I need some fresh air." Jessie gathered up her skirt so the hem wouldn't drag. "I'm going for a walk in the garden."

"What?" Carrie stared at her as if she'd lost her mind. "You can't! It's only half an hour until the ceremony."

"That's plenty of time."

"What if someone sees you?"

"Nobody will. I'll go down the back stairs."

"But—but you'll get grass stains on the hem of your gown."

"I won't. See?" Jessie hoisted the gown higher.

Carrie sighed. "Well, who am I to argue with the bride? You want to go for a walk? Fine. We'll go for a walk."

"No!" Jessie swallowed hard. "No," she said,

more calmly, "really, I need a few minutes by myself."

"It's cold outside," Carrie said worriedly. "At least take a jacket."

"It's okay," Jessie said, "I know what I'm doing."

But she didn't. And the enormity of the lie scared the life out of her.

THE GARDEN WAS QUIET. All the hullabaloo was taking place inside the house. Liam was glad he'd decided to go for a walk where he could escape the necessity for social niceties.

He felt a lot better, too. For all he knew, Bill was right. Maybe he'd misread everything. The newlyweds would settle into a pleasantly dull marriage. A couple of years down the road he'd look at Jessica and know that he'd been wrong about her.

But if he was, then what was that invitation he'd seen in her eyes last night? What would she have done if he'd taken her up on it, if he'd walked straight across the room, pulled her out of her chair and kissed her?

Slugged him, probably, because whatever else the lady was, she wasn't a fool. Bill would have slugged him, too, but at least he'd have learned if that soft, pink mouth tasted as sweet as it—

There was a whisper of sound just behind him. Liam drew a breath. Even before he turned around, he knew she'd be there.

"Miss Warren," he said with deliberate courtesy.

Her chin lifted, her cheeks pinkened. Could she possibly know what he'd been thinking?

"Mr. Malone," she said, just as courteously. "I didn't expect to find you here."

His smile didn't reach his eyes. "Is it customary for brides to wander around, alone, moments before they wed?"

"I might ask you the same question about groomsmen. What are you doing in the garden?"

Liam looked at the woman who was about to marry his best friend, into the smoky blue eyes that had haunted him through a long and sleepless night.

"Looking for you," he said, and before she could respond, he reached for her.

CHAPTER TWO

PEOPLE ALWAYS TALKED about time standing still or going too fast, but in Jessie's experience, time was more like a treadmill. It moved at a steady, predictable pace.

Now she knew she'd been wrong. Liam reached for her and time hung suspended by a silken thread. She had all the opportunity she needed to anticipate what was about to happen. He was going to take her in his arms, gather her close and kiss her. And she'd let him do it. The dreams that had kept her awake half the night because, yes, she'd dreamed of him, yes, she'd imagined this happening...those dreams would come true.

She sighed, lifted her head, closed her eyes, waited to feel the hardness of Liam Malone's body, the race of his heart...

Waited to betray William.

She took a quick step back, her hands upraised. "No," she said, but it didn't stop him. Liam caught her hands, drew them down. "Liam," she said sharply, "think of William!"

He lifted his head and stared at her through eyes that were dark and hot. Slowly, like clouds receding after a storm, the wildness in his eyes faded. A shudder racked his body, and his hands fell to his sides.

"My God!" He spoke in a choked whisper. "We must be crazy."

Jessie opened her mouth, then closed it. The truth was ugly, but she couldn't deny it. She'd been a part of what had almost happened.

"Nothing happened." Panic lent her words harsh urgency. "Nothing," she repeated, as if saying it again would make it so.

"No." Liam nodded. He turned his back to her and she saw the rise and fall of his shoulders, heard the sound of breath being dragged deep into his lungs. "Nothing happened. And anyway, it didn't mean a..." He swung toward her, anger etched into his face. "The hell it didn't! I'm Bill's best man. You're his bride. And we almost went at each other like a pair of—of sex-starved teen-agers. And you say, nothing happened?"

"Mr. Malone..."

"Oh, that's great. That's terrific. Another minute, we'd have been down on the grass and you're calling me 'Mr. Malone'?"

Jessie stiffened. "There's no need to be crude."

"Crude is you not remembering that you're marrying my best friend this morning."

A breeze rustled through dried autumn leaves still trapped in the hedge. Jessie shivered and wrapped her arms around herself.

"I remembered it, and so did you. That's why nothing happened."

"I came within a breath of betraying my friend. You came within inches of violating the promises you've made him. Seems to me that something happened."

The wind lifted a strand of Jessie's hair. Her hand trembled as she smoothed it back. He was right. They'd almost kissed. Pretending they hadn't wouldn't change the fact, but there had to be an explanation. She'd never hurt William. Never.

"All right." Her voice quavered. "But—but it's been a stressful week."

"Now, why didn't I think of that?" Liam said coldly. "You're stressed. I'm jet-lagged. And that makes it all…" He paused, then blew out a ragged breath. She was right. Nothing they could do would erase that one moment but, the truth was, they hadn't done anything. The best solution was to shove the memory into a dark corner and forget it was there.

"Okay. We made a mistake. Let's leave it at that."

"That's what I've been saying." Something in his eyes—contempt, perhaps, or a suggestion of it—stirred Jessie's anger. "And if you want to be specific, Mr. Malone, we didn't make a mistake. You did. I'm not the one who—who…"

"Do us both a favor, okay? Let's not waste time lying." His mouth twisted. "You and I both know what's going on here. You looked at me last night exactly the way you did a couple of minutes ago."

"I don't know what you're talking about." Jessie gathered up the skirt of her bridal gown. "And I have better things to do than stand here and talk nonsense."

"Yeah," Liam said coldly. "You have to step up to a judge, take Bill's hand and promise to love, honor and cherish till death—"

"I know the vows I'm going to take, Mr. Malone."

Liam's eyes narrowed until there was just the barest flash of green. "I thought you were all wrong for him. Now I know it."

"Is that what this—this little episode was all about? The Liam Malone quality control test?"

Jessie said, trying to keep her tone as cold and even as his.

"Bill deserves better than you. A man deserves a woman who loves him without reservation."

"And that's just the way I love William," she said heatedly. "He knows that."

"Right." Liam smiled tightly and rocked back on his heels. "I'm sure he'd agree that the last few minutes prove it."

"You can't tell him! You'd break his heart!"

"I know that. No, I won't tell him. Neither will you. You're right. Nothing happened." He paused, and a seductive softness crept into his voice. "But it could have."

Jessie knew what he was thinking. How it would have been, if they'd kissed. The mingling of breath. The taste. The feel of his arms around her, the heat of their bodies pressed together.

"This is a pointless conversation," she said, and some small part of her mind gave a brisk nod of approval that she could sound so calm when she was shaking inside. "William is waiting. The wedding—"

Liam caught her wrist as she began to turn away. "Why didn't you slap me?"

"Mr. Malone. Liam. I thought we just agreed—"

"It's a simple question. You knew what I was

about to do. How come you didn't haul off and slug me?"

"Is that how the women you come on to generally react?" She smiled sweetly before her lips hardened into a thin, accusing line. "I don't understand how William can think of you as his best friend. You're not like him at all."

"No," Liam said softly, "I'm not."

He took a step toward her; she retreated, but the bench was behind her and she was trapped. Her heart pounded. She'd been right about Liam Malone. He was sexy as sin and gorgeous as the devil. Why hadn't she realized he'd be as dangerous as the devil, too?

"Keep away from me!"

He smiled, a quick glint of white teeth against his tanned face. "Maybe that's what appeals to you, Jessie." Lazily he ran a finger over her cheek. "Maybe you know there's no way you could wrap me around your little finger, or buy me off with a smile and a promise."

"You're right. I should have slapped you. You're a horrible man."

"I must be," he whispered, his fingers curling around the back of her neck, "because I'm going to finish what I started a few minutes ago. What you want, despite all your self-righteous protests."

He watched her face as he drew her to him and told himself he was only doing this because she was twisting things, making it sound as if he were the only one who'd wanted the kiss. One whisper of dissent, just one, and he'd back off. But when she looked up at him, he saw that her eyes had gone from blue to the color of the sky just before sunrise in the mountains, and not all her protests or his excuses could keep those eyes from telling him everything he needed to know.

"Jessie," he said softly, and she sighed, tilted her head back and met his descending mouth with hers.

It was a gentle kiss, only the brush of his lips over hers. It was the kiss a man gives a woman when he knows he can never claim the taste of her again. And because the kiss was gentle, because Jessie knew that there would only be this once between them, because she could no more have stopped the rotation of the earth than rid herself of the need for it, she let it happen. She let him draw her closer, and when he did, she laid her palms flat against his chest, rose on her toes and parted her lips to his, let him slip his tongue into her mouth.

A wave of white-hot flame consumed her. She moaned, curled her fingers into the lapels of Liam's morning coat and let everything she'd spent the night dreaming about happen. His kiss was all the poets said a kiss could be. It was more. It was turning her inside out, dissolving her flesh, melting her bones. It was...

She lifted her arms, wound them around Liam's neck and stopped thinking.

The wind scurried through the garden again. Jessie trembled, but not from the cold. Liam drew her, hard, against him. His hands swept down her back, cupped her bottom, lifted her against him, into him. Sounds drifted on the air. Music from the chamber orchestra. The distant buzz of conversation.

And, from somewhere nearby, Carrie's voice.

"Jessica? Jess, where are you?"

Jessie tore her mouth from Liam's. Panic raced through her blood. "Liam!"

His arms tightened around her as she tried to pull away. "Come back here," he said thickly.

"Liam, for the love of God, someone's coming!"

He blinked, shook his head, whispered a word that might have been a blessing or an oath and stepped back, as if putting distance between them could change what had happened.

"I didn't..." He stopped, cleared his throat. "Jessie, I never meant—I never meant this to happen."

"Then—then it didn't," she said frantically. "Do you hear me? This never happened." Her lips felt dry. She touched them with the tip of her tongue, tasted Liam and felt as if she wanted to die. "William must never find out. Do you understand?"

"Dammit," Liam said harshly, "don't you think I know that? But we can't just forget. We—"

"Jess?"

Jessie spun around. Carrie stood a few feet away, staring at them. "Everyone is waiting," she said slowly. "The judge. The guests. William."

"Of course." Jessie gave in to the temptation to touch her hand to her hair. She could feel some strands that had come undone, but the wind could have done that. Only the wind. She'd simply been out here, having a pleasant chat with William's best man. Nobody had to know the truth, not ever. Nobody but Liam. And she. Oh God, she would know, she'd always know. "Certainly," she said, and smiled. "I'm ready."

Carrie cleared her throat. "I think—why don't you just let me fix your makeup, Jess? Your lipstick. And your hair. The, uh, the wind must have…" Her voice trailed away as she hurried forward and clasped Jessie's arm. "Come on up to the house, okay?" She smiled brightly. "A bride should look perfect on her wedding day. Isn't that right, Mr. Malone?''

Liam nodded. It was the best he could manage.

''Why don't you go tell William we'll just be another five minutes? He can wait that long for the woman who's going to be his for the rest of his life, don't you think?''

The message might have been subtle, but the way Jessie's maid of honor looked at him wasn't. Could what they'd done be so obvious? Liam cleared his throat and decided to see if he could get out something more than a croak.

''Yes,'' he said, ''I'm sure he can.''

''Good.'' Carrie wrapped an arm around Jessie's waist. ''Now, come on, honey. This is your big day. You don't want to spoil it.''

''No,'' Jessie said. ''No, I don't.''

Her eyes met Liam's, and the terrible secret they shared burned hot between them.

''Jess?'' Carrie said, and Jessie smiled brightly and let her maid of honor hurry her toward the house.

Liam waited until they were out of sight. Then he let out a breath that was almost a moan and ran his hands through his hair. How could he let her go? He'd only had one taste of Jessie, only held her in his arms for a moment.

''Stop it,'' he said in a harsh whisper.

He walked deeper into the garden, found a bench, sank down on it and put his face in his hands. How could he have done this? She was to be Bill's bride. Bill, who was the best friend he'd ever had. If only there were a way to wipe away what had happened.

But there wasn't. And the longer he thought about it, the more he knew that nothing could have stopped him from kissing her, or make him regret the kiss. Now he knew how soft Jessie felt. How sweet her lips were. How it was to take her sigh into his mouth as she opened to him.

How right he'd been in his assessment of her.

Damn Jessica Warren to hell, and himself along with her! How could he let her marry Bill? And yet, he had to. He couldn't tell Bill what had happened, not if saving him meant destroying him. Time slipped past as he tried to find a solution but, at last, he knew he had to admit there was none. He had to play his role in this farce. There was no other choice.

At last, Liam sat up straight. He had no idea how long he'd been sitting there but it was time to put a smile on his face and do what was expected of him.

Liam stood, smoothed down his shirt, took a couple of deep breaths.

"Liam?"

Bill was hurrying toward him, his face tense, and for one awful moment, Liam thought he'd found out what had happened. But Carrie was trotting alongside him, looking just as bad.

"What is it?"

"It's Jessica," William said. "She's—she's gone."

"What?" Liam eased an arm around Bill's shoulders, led him to a bench and sat him down. "What do you mean, she's gone?"

Carrie knelt on the grass and took Bill's hands in hers. She spoke to Liam, but her eyes never left Bill's pale face.

"She wrote a note," Carrie said, "and left it on the bed with her engagement ring and watch."

Liam shook his head. Maybe he wasn't crazy. Maybe it was the rest of the world that had gone insane. "Bill?" He squatted down beside the bench. "Talk to me. How can she be gone? Gone where?"

Bill took a piece of paper from his pocket and handed it to Liam. "You can see how upset she must have been," he said shakily. "Just look at how she scrawled the words."

Upset? Oh, yes, Liam thought as he took the note, yes, indeed, the lady would have been upset. Beside herself, was more like it, afraid—no, ter-

rified—that he'd break his promise and tell Bill
what had happened.

Dearest William: I'm sorry. So terribly sorry.
You're a wonderful man. A fine man. That's
why I can't marry you. You deserve more
than I can ever give you. Forgive me, please.

He read the note again and again, until anguish
blurred both his anger and the words Jessie had
written. He had done this. He'd given in to a moment's desire and this was the result.

Slowly Liam rose to his feet.

"Carrie? You took Jessie back to the house.
What happened after that?"

"I started to fix her hair, but she said she
wanted to do it herself. She asked me to go down-
stairs and make sure everything was ready. When
I got back, she was gone." Carrie gave Liam a
look filled with loathing and accusation. "She
was fine before she went out to the garden. Just
bridal jitters, that was all. She was fine!"

Liam nodded. There was a bitter taste in his
mouth. He'd come back to Seattle to join in a
happy celebration. Instead, he'd kissed a woman
who wasn't his to kiss, and now his best friend
was behaving as if his life had ended. Like it or
not, he knew what he had to do.

"Bill?" He squatted down again, put a hand on Bill's knee. "Bill, you have to go after her."

"Go where?" Bill looked up, his face tear-stained. "She gave up her apartment when I asked her to move into the guest suite here."

"Well, what about family? Friends?"

"Jessica has no family. And her friends are all here, at the...in the house."

"Call the police," Carrie said. "Hire a private detective."

"No. No, I can't do that. Jess isn't a fugitive. She's my fiancée and if she's run away, it has to be my fault. I must have done something to make her—"

"You didn't," Liam said, so sharply that Bill stared at him. "I mean, there's no reason to think that. You'd know if you'd done something to drive her away."

"The only thing I know is that I have to get her back." Bill clamped his lips together, bowed his head. Seconds passed before he looked up again. "Liam? You have to find her for me."

Liam shot to his feet. "No. Not me."

Bill stood up slowly, looking as if he'd aged five years in the past five minutes. "She'd run if she saw me. She has no reason to run from you."

"Bill," Liam said, "Bill, please—"

"And you know something about running

away. You used to talk about it, remember? About how you'd run away all those times when you were a kid?''

''Yeah, but that was—''

''Let's be honest, okay? I'm—what's that phrase of yours? I'm a desk jockey. If I were going to run away, I'd probably tuck a couple of credit cards in my pocket and ring for the chauffeur to bring the car around.'' Bill gripped Liam's arm. ''I'm afraid for her. I can't imagine where she'll go. Carrie says she didn't even change her clothes or take anything with her. What will she do for money?''

''She took her car,'' Carrie offered excitedly. ''A white Civic. It's not in the driveway anymore.''

''Well, then, she'll drive until she runs out of gas.''

''Who knows where she'll be by then?'' Bill's hand dug into Liam's flesh. ''I'm begging you, man. You're like a brother to me, you know that. You've got to do it.''

There'd been times in Liam's life when he hadn't much liked himself. He'd thought that those times were all behind him. But as he looked into the pleading eyes of his oldest friend, he knew he'd never hated himself as much as he did at this moment.

"All right," he said slowly, "I'll find her for you."

Bill expelled a breath. "Thank you."

"Don't thank me until this is over."

"I know you, Liam." Bill put out his hand. "You'll find my Jessica, and you'll do the right thing."

Liam looked at his oldest friend's outstretched hand, clasped it and forced a smile to his lips. "I'll do the right thing," he said softly. "I promise you that."

CHAPTER THREE

LIAM SAT BEHIND THE WHEEL of his rented Corvette as Bill leaned through the open window.

"Call me as soon as you find her, okay?"

"Look, I can't guarantee—"

"Tell her I love her, that whatever's wrong, we can work things out." He gripped Liam's shoulder. "I don't know how to thank you, man."

"Don't," Liam said quickly. "Not until I've brought Jessie back."

"Jessica." Bill's voice broke. "Her name is—"

"Sure." Liam shifted into gear. "I'll be in touch."

Bill said something else but Liam didn't wait to hear it. He stepped on the gas and the Vette's tires squealed as he shot down the long driveway. Another couple of minutes listening to Bill talk about Jessie and how he couldn't think of a reason in the world she'd have done this, and he'd have blurted out the truth.

"I know the reason," he'd have said. "It's because I violated our friendship and my principles over a woman I don't even know."

"Hell," he said softly, and clamped his hands more tightly on the steering wheel. If there was one thing he'd learned, it was that there was no percentage in reliving the past. You made a mistake, you set it right and you moved on. That was exactly what he was going to do. Find Jessie, make her see reason, return her to Bill and move on.

He drove fast, slipping in and out of traffic, heading for his hotel so he could trade his morning coat and striped trousers for something that wouldn't make him stand out in a crowd. The only thing as noticeable as a woman driving around in a bridal gown would be a man pursuing her rigged out in a silly suit. Besides, who knew what story Jessie might tell if people asked for explanations? The last thing he needed was interference from some helpful soul who might take him for the groom she was fleeing.

Liam dressed quickly, trading his formal wear for faded jeans, an ancient Princeton Tigers sweatshirt, sneakers and a leather bomber jacket he'd had so long that it felt like an old friend. Then he got into the Vette, doubled back toward Lake Washington and got on the road Jessie would have taken. An excited guest had told him she'd headed toward the city, but where would she go? No apartment, no credit cards, no cash...well, not exactly. Carrie had remembered that Jessie kept a fifty-dollar bill and her driver's license in the glove compartment of her car.

"Mad money, she called it," Carrie had explained, while Bill clutched her hand like a lifeline. "I always told her that was just making it easy for a thief, but—"

"It's okay," Liam had replied. "She won't get far on fifty bucks."

Now he tried putting himself in Jessie's place. What would she use the money for? Like him, she'd want to get out of that bridal regalia. And she'd want a place to go to ground, but in a city like Seattle, how could anybody afford clothes and a hotel room on fifty bucks? That was the question, although the bigger one was what he could possibly do or say when he found her to make her see that kiss for what it really was.

Liam glanced in his mirror, gave the Vette a little more gas and switched lanes.

It was simple, really. What had happened between them was lust. That good old male-female, down-and-dirty, I-want-to-get-you-between-the-sheets thing called lust. They'd been sexually attracted to each other, she'd been all nerves, and he'd taken advantage. End of story.

He wasn't a gentleman like Bill. And he couldn't let a moment's stupidity and weakness on his part ruin what Bill wanted. A wife, a couple of kids, a dog and a cat.

Some people were made for fairy tales.

Liam looked at the speedometer and eased his foot off the gas. He was driving too fast, and he could just imagine trying to explain this to a cop.

"Well, you see, Officer, I came on to my best friend's bride maybe ten minutes before the ceremony, and she ran away."

Oh, yeah. That would go over big.

Dammit, where had she gone? Forget the change of clothes. She was upset, probably close to hysterics by now. Her first priority would be a hotel room, but without money...

A horn blared as Liam shot across two lanes of traffic and made for the exit ramp. He looked in the mirror, saw the guy he'd cut off tell him what he thought with a universal gesture, and fought back the urge to respond. The guy was right. There was no need to be angry at him. Jessie, dammit, she was the one who'd made him lose control, made a mountain out of a molehill, ruined what should have been the best day of Bill's life, and for what?

"For a kiss," Liam said, with a snort of disbelief. Just a kiss. Just a moment torn out of time, when he'd held her in his arms and never wanted to let her go....

There she was!

He stood on the brakes, made a hard turn into a lot dominated by a huge Kmart, and brought the car to a jolting stop. A slender figure in ivory satin, little pink roses braided into her honey-gold hair, was marching—there was no other word for it—straight toward the store entrance, her satin train sweeping behind her.

Liam eased the car forward a safe distance, pulled into a space, shut off the engine and watched. Someplace between her car and the door, she'd picked up a gaggle of followers. Kids, a few housewives, a guy in coveralls, all of them shuffling after her, grinning at each other, peering around as if they suspected they might be on *Candid Camera*. Well, he couldn't blame them. A bride in full regalia, going into a store that sold everything from aspirin to zippers, was definitely not an everyday sight, even in a city as sophisticated as Seattle.

Jessie had to know she was drawing a crowd, but her chin was up and her spine was as straight as it had been when she'd faced him down in the garden.

He got out of the car, pocketed his keys and started after her. He knew he'd have to approach her with caution. She might bolt or even scream. Given the insanity of the world, he'd probably end up trying to convince the crowd and then the cops that he wasn't a mugger or worse. So he followed her into the store at a discreet distance and asked himself what a bride on the run could possibly want in a Kmart?

Everything, it turned out.

Jessie grabbed a shopping cart and sailed down the aisles. Her cheeks glowed with color, so he knew she wasn't as oblivious to the gawkers as she tried to appear. She moved from counter to rack, snatching things only when there was a sale sign on view and dumping them into her cart. Jeans. A T-shirt. A desperately ugly lime-green nylon jacket whose claim to fame had to be the big sign that said not just Sale but Fifty Percent Off. She added a pair of sneakers to the stack, a tote bag, a toothbrush and things he'd always thought of as female survival gear.

Finally she headed for the register.

Liam hung back, observing her from behind a display that advertised a Blue Light Special on dinnerware. The clerk rang the items up, Jessie handed over a bill and got back only a couple of coins. Goodbye cheap motel room. He started forward as she scooped her packages from the cart, but she reversed direction so fast he almost stumbled as he scooted back behind the dinnerware.

When it was safe, he followed.

She led him straight to the rest rooms and disappeared into the ladies' lounge. He leaned against a counter a couple of aisles over, folded his arms, crossed his ankles, looked down at his feet like any other guy, bored as he waited for the missus. Obviously, she was going to change her clothes, but then what? Maybe Carrie was wrong, and she had more than fifty bucks.

The minutes dragged by. Jessie's followers wandered off. Liam shifted his weight, unfolded his arms, tucked his hands into the pockets of his jeans and planned his next move....

And then the door to the ladies' room opened, and all coherent thought flew away.

Bill Thornton's bride was gone. Proper, elegant Jessica had been replaced by Jessie, a woman ready to try anything, the quicksilver woman Liam had sensed was inside her from the beginning.

She'd stripped the roses from her hair and brushed it out so that it hung in honey-colored waves down her back. She was wearing the clothing he'd watched her buy, even the ugly lime-green jacket. But it didn't seem ugly now. As

Liam looked at her, at that face scrubbed clean of makeup and artifice, he knew, with gut-wrenching certainty, that everything he'd been telling himself was a lie.

He wanted Jessie still, wanted her in a way that frightened him. When she lifted her head and saw him, she suddenly stiffened. But what he read in her eyes in that single, unguarded moment told him that she wanted him in exactly the same way.

She turned and ran.

Liam went after her, let her keep her lead through the store, through the parking lot, picking up his pace only when she neared her car. Then he caught her by the elbow and swung her toward him.

She swatted at him with both hands. "Let me go," she panted. "Damn you, Liam—"

"Jessie." He clasped her wrists, gripped them tightly, held her hands captive against his chest. "Jessie, listen to me."

"What for? Haven't you done enough?"

He hadn't. He'd only kissed her once, held her once, but that wasn't why he was here. He'd come after her for Bill. She belonged to Bill.

"Forget what happened," he said gruffly. "It's history."

"History?" She laughed. "We were climbing all over each other five minutes before I was sup-

posed to say 'I do,' and you say that's history?"
Angrily she jerked against his hands. "Maybe you
can forget what we did, but I can't."

"Of course you can. Okay, we did something
neither of us is proud of, but—"

"I'd never be able to look at William again
without thinking of how I betrayed him."

"Dammit, we all make mistakes."

"Yes," she said coldly, "but not all of us are
so callous that we can pretend they didn't happen."

Liam let go of her. "Bill wants you back."

"Well, I'm not going back."

"You have to! Otherwise—"

"Otherwise, what?" She smiled thinly.
"You'll have to admit to your part in this mess?"

"This has nothing to do with me," Liam said
quickly.

"Oh, give me a break." Jessie's eyes narrowed. "You're no better than I am. You decided
to find me and fast-talk me into going back to
William so you wouldn't have to live the rest of
your life dodging the sight of yourself in mir-
rors." Her mouth twisted. "Spare me the lies,
Liam. This has everything to do with you."

He stepped forward, his eyes hard and cold.
"Okay. I'm not proud of what I did, but I'm not

the one who decided to handle it by running away and leaving Bill at the altar.''

Jessie's face fell. "Was he—was he very upset?"

"Was he..." Liam laughed. "Hell, no. The woman he loves leaves him a note and takes off just before she's supposed to become his wife. Why would he be upset?"

"I didn't want to hurt him," she whispered. "I'd have done anything—"

"Anything but go through with the wedding."

"How can you say that to me, damn you?" Her face lifted, and there was the glitter of tears in her eyes. "He's your friend. Do you really want him to marry a woman who—who was in another man's arms right before the ceremony?"

Not another man's, Liam thought. *My arms. Mine....*

"There's no point in ruining Bill's life because of a moment's stupidity," he said gruffly.

Jessie stared at him. Then she swung away and unlocked the door to her car. "And what about my life?" Her voice broke. "Did you ever think of that?"

"Dammit!" Liam grabbed her and turned her toward him. "You love him. You said so. What am I supposed to say, huh? 'Bill, look, maybe it's better all around if the wedding's off?' "

"Say whatever you like. Just—just don't break his heart by telling him the truth."

"Look, let's start again, okay? Bill asked me to find you, and to ask you to come back to him."

"Why didn't he come himself? Oh, don't bother answering. William knows you're a master at convincing women to do things they don't want to do."

"Fine. That's how you want to play it?" A muscle knotted in his jaw. "I'll take the responsibility. All of it, if that makes you feel better. What happened was my fault."

"It was! I certainly wouldn't have…" Jessie hesitated. "No. It wasn't. I wanted you to kiss me, Liam. I thought about what it would be like, all last night."

"Don't say that," Liam said quickly, trying not to think about the rush of pleasure he felt hearing her confession.

"Why shouldn't I? I can't tell William the truth, but I'm tired of lying to myself." Her voice wobbled again but her gaze was steady. "You're right. We made a mistake. Period. End of story— except that mistake made me face something I think I've known for weeks. I'm not right for William or maybe—maybe he's not right for me. Either way, I'm not going to marry him. Tell him I wish him all the best. Tell him…" Tears filled her eyes. "Oh, God," she whispered, "I'm so ashamed."

Liam didn't think. He reached out and Jessie went into his embrace as if she'd been born for no other reason.

He held her close, his face buried in her hair, his body warmed by hers. She wept softly, her face in the hollow of his throat, and he whispered to her, words he'd never even thought to use with another woman, words of comfort, of solace, and gradually her tears lessened.

"Liam," she said, and he felt as if a hand were reaching into his chest and closing around his heart.

She pulled back in his arms and looked up at him. Her eyes were tear dampened and swollen. He kept one arm around her, dug in his jeans' pocket, took out a folded white handkerchief, dabbed at her eyes, then held it to her nose.

"Blow," he said gently. She smiled a little and did as he'd asked, and he laid his hand against her cheek, threaded his fingers into her hair and tilted her face to his.

"I can't marry William."

Liam wanted to tell her that she could, but the words caught in his throat. A woman wasn't supposed to weep like this on her wedding day. He'd already made one wrong judgment, thinking she was after Bill's name and money, and he'd be damned if he wanted to make another.

"He's a wonderful man. And I love him, but not the way I should. I didn't realize that, Liam. I swear I didn't."

He nodded. He knew that, too.

Jessie gave a shuddering sigh. "Tell him I'll be fine. He mustn't worry about me. And tell him I'll get in touch with him, once I—once I get my head together."

"Come back with me. Tell him yourself."

She shook her head and moved out of his arms. "I can't. Not yet. If I did he might realize…he might see…" She opened the door of her car and got behind the wheel. "Goodbye, Liam."

"No," he said, "Jessie, wait—"

She moved quickly, heard his hands slap against the car as she put it in gear, and then she was moving and he was running across the lot. Seconds later, a shiny black Corvette was on her tail and she choked back a spurt of hysterical laughter. What else would Liam Malone drive, except for a car that was sexy and fast?

She drove recklessly, tossing aside her usual caution, but his car followed hers like a shadow. A horn blared. Jessie looked to her left, saw a white-faced driver shake a fist at her. Chagrined, she realized she was endangering everybody on the road, and she slowed her car. There was no reason to drive so fast. What was she running from? Liam? That was ridiculous. He couldn't make her do anything she didn't want to do.

Yes, he can, a sly little voice whispered inside her head. *All he has to do is kiss you, and you're lost.*

No, she wasn't. She'd never been the kind of woman whose head could be turned by a handsome man.

Well, then, the voice said, even more slyly, *maybe you're running from yourself.*

That was even crazier. Just because she'd turned to jelly in Liam's arms, just because he was all the dangerous things Bill wasn't, things she'd spent her life trying to avoid....

She had a plan. Maybe it wasn't great. Still, without money or credit, she had only one place to go where she could marshal her thoughts, and one way to get there.

Liam was right behind her as she took the exit ramp, but it didn't matter. She'd left her groom, her wedding and her carefully planned life. Now she'd leave the man who'd made her realize that she didn't want any of those things. If she had, she'd never have been unfaithful to William and yes, that was what she'd been, unfaithful, kissing a stranger, wanting him, still wanting him....

Jessie swiped at her eyes with the back of her hand, drove into the airport and pulled into the first parking spot she saw. Liam did the same thing. He was behind her as she locked her door and started briskly toward the AmericAir terminal.

"Jessie!" His footsteps pounded after her. "Jessie!"

He caught up to her, clasped her arm. She wrenched it free.

"Leave me alone, Liam."

"Do you think I'm just going to let you run away? We have to talk."

The terminal doors slid open. She stepped inside, walked to a departure board, checked it. If she remembered correctly, there'd been a morning flight to Miami as well as the one she and William had planned to take. Yes, there it was, Flight 937, leaving from gate twelve. With luck, she could swap her ticket and get on this plane. But there wasn't much time. She picked up her pace, almost stumbled when Liam did a quick two-step to get in front of her.

"You can't solve anything by running away from it."

She moved around him, dumped her tote bag on the conveyor belt at the security checkpoint and went through the gate with Liam right behind her. When she heard the buzzer go off, she heaved a sigh of relief.

Goodbye, Liam, she thought, and blinked back the tears that welled in her eyes again.

"Sir?" said a polite voice. "Would you empty your pockets, please?"

Liam bit back a groan, dumped his change into a receptacle and watched as Jessie merged with the crowd. By the time he started after her, she'd disappeared. He moved quickly from one gate to the next. She could be anywhere by now. If only he had some idea...

There she was, at the information desk at gate twelve. Liam looked at the sign behind the desk. Flight 937 to Miami, it said. Departing at 10:45. He looked at his watch. It was 10:15. Not that it mattered. Jessie wasn't going anywhere, not without a ticket. But she was. Everything clicked into place. No cash, no credit card needed, not if she'd made all her arrangements via the Internet. With luck, she could even switch to an earlier departure.

"Where are you guys going on your honeymoon?" he'd asked last night, as he'd tried to make conversation and get his mind off Bill's fiancée.

"Florida," Bill had replied with a quick smile at Jessie. "Hibiscus Key. Well—" he'd blushed

"—actually, it's a place called Couples' Cove."
He'd looped his arm lightly around Jessie's shoulders. "Jessica made the arrangements. She makes
all my travel plans on the computer, don't you,
dear?"

And Jessie had torn her eyes from Liam,
cleared her throat and said yes, yes, she did, and
they'd continued with some meaningless chitchat.

Liam swung away and ran through the terminal
to the AmericAir ticket counter while he dug his
cell phone from his pocket. There were two people ahead of him. "Emergency," he said, and
stepped quickly to the head of the line as he
punched in Bill's number.

"Hello?"

It was Carrie's voice. "Put Bill on," Liam said
curtly.

"He's resting. I hate to wake him, Mr. Malone.
He's had such a bad—"

"Give him a message. Tell him…" He looked
up. The ticket clerk was staring at him, eyebrows
raised. "Hang on," he said, and hit the mute button. "One seat, Flight 937 to Miami." He dug in
his pocket, took out his driver's license and his
credit card, handed them over. "Charge the ticket,
and there's my photo ID."

"Coach or first class?"

"First class. Look, pal, the flight's going to be boarding in—"

"It's already boarding, sir. If fact, I don't know if I can—"

"Just do it," Liam said tersely, and put the phone to his ear. "Carrie? Tell Bill… Tell him I…" Liam watched as the clerk began typing his ticket. Jessie was on that plane. She was leaving Seattle, putting three thousand miles between them. "Tell him that I've found Jessie. She's at the airport, and she's fine, and—" And what? "Tell him I'll be in touch," he said, and hit the disconnect button as the clerk handed him his ticket.

The attendant was just closing the door that led to the boarding ramp as Liam sprinted through the gate. "Wait," he yelled. "That's my flight."

The attendant opened the door and reached for the phone. "Talk about cutting it close—"

He thundered down the ramp to the plane. The flight attendant greeted him with a smile.

"Just about missed it," she said brightly.

He nodded, struggled to catch his breath. "Yeah," he said—and then he saw Jessie, sitting by the window, alone in the last row of the first-class cabin. She looked up and saw him, and for the first time in his life, Liam knew what people meant when they said they were terrified, because that was how he felt now, scared right through to the marrow of his bones.

His eyes never left hers as he walked down the aisle. "I almost missed the flight," he said softly when he reached her. "I probably could have bluffed my way into picking up Bill's ticket and using it, but I didn't want to."

Jessie touched the tip of her tongue to her bottom lip. "Why not?"

"Because I'm not standing in for Bill, or speaking for him. Not anymore. Do you understand that?"

Her mouth trembled as Liam sat down and took her hand. "Yes," she whispered. "Oh, yes, I understand."

Liam took Jessie's face in his hands. This time, when their lips met, it was in a kiss so tender that it almost turned him inside out.

CHAPTER FOUR

THE SEAT BELT SIGN BLINKED OFF when the plane reached cruising altitude.

Liam looked at Jessie. The softness of her smile, the undisguised joy with which she'd greeted him, were gone. Instead, she stared straight ahead, features rigid, face pale, her hand turning to ice in his.

"Jessie," he said, and she looked at him, her eyes wide with a fear he could only guess at.

He wanted to gather her into his embrace. He'd always liked having a woman in his arms, in bed or on a dance floor, but women in need of soothing made him feel clumsy. That wasn't how he felt now. He wanted to hold her, not to kiss her but to comfort her, warm her, rock her against him as if she'd just awakened from a bad dream and only he could chase away the demons.

"It's a long flight," he said to ease the tension.

She gave him a strained smile. "I know. Almost five and a half hours."

Liam cleared his throat. "How about some wine? Or some coffee? I can ask the flight attendant to—"

"No, I'm fine."

She wasn't. The shadows under her eyes looked like bruises and he fought back the desire to press his mouth to that tender skin, to draw her close.

"Well," he said briskly, "I think I'm going to read for a while." He let go of her hand and fumbled in the pocket of the seat in front of him. "Sometimes these airline magazines are pretty interesting."

Airline magazines were interesting? He was running away with his best friend's fiancée, he ached with the need to make love to her, and now he was going to bury his nose in a magazine?

Damn right, he was. Otherwise, he was going to take her in his arms and say things he didn't believe in, things he'd never imagined ever saying to any woman, much less one who belonged to Bill.

"Let me know if you need anything," he said, as brightly as a waiter hoping for a big tip. Then he whipped open the magazine and pretended that the print wasn't one enormous gray blur.

JESSIE STARED OUT HER WINDOW.

Liam was reading. Reading, she thought, and

clamped her lips together so hard her jaw hurt. He'd turned her life inside out, made her run away from her wedding, followed her through half of Seattle and onto a plane headed for the other side of the continent, and now he was sitting next to her, engrossed in a stupid magazine.

It was hard to know who she despised more, herself for letting him ruin her life or him for doing it.

"Excuse me," she said coldly, and shot to her feet. Liam looked up, his brows lifted as if he'd never seen her before. "I have to go to the bathroom," she said, even more coldly, and he rose so she could march past him. It seemed like a good move, but it turned out that her timing was rotten. She was halfway up the aisle when a man in the first row stood up and went into the lavatory.

Jessie blew out a breath, folded her arms and leaned back against the bulkhead. Perfect. He was the only other passenger in first class, and he'd made it to the bathroom ahead of her. Well, why not? The entire morning had been perfect, starting with the moment she'd been stupid enough to think she didn't want to go through with the wedding, stupid enough to think the rush of lust Liam Malone had stirred in her blood was anywhere near as important as the love she felt for William.

As for what she'd felt when she saw Liam board the plane—what she'd thought she'd felt—that had been nothing but surprise.

She glanced at her watch, frowned and looked balefully at the Occupied sign on the lavatory door. What was taking so long? Airplane bathrooms were little more than high-tech closets, first class or not. She wanted to splash some cold water in her eyes, think about the best way to tell Liam that she'd changed her mind, thank you very much, but she wasn't going to Hibiscus Key with him.

Did he really think she'd let him take William's place in their honeymoon bed?

The door to the lavatory opened. The man who'd been inside stepped out. He smiled. Jessie glared and moved into the narrow space. The guy's cologne engulfed her. William wore cologne, too. She'd thought she'd liked the smell— it seemed masculine and fresh—until Liam had taken her in his arms. He didn't seem to wear any cologne at all. He smelled of things she couldn't quite put her finger on. Soap, maybe, and fresh air and leather. And of himself. Pure male, intriguing, sexy...

"Oh, stop it," she said through her teeth.

Scowling, she locked the door, then met her reflection in the mirror. It wasn't a happy moment. The lime-green jacket had been cheap, but it was ugly as sin. The rest of her wasn't much better. Brushing the gel from her hair had left it an unruly mess. Her face was as shiny as a polished apple. Her nose was pink, her eyelids swollen. How Liam could still want her was...

Not that it mattered.

Her scowl deepened as she turned on the water, scooped it onto her face, then dried off with a towel. Who cared what she looked like, or whether or not Liam wanted her? She'd been crazy to run, crazy to think she wanted him, crazy to—

There was a tap at the lavatory door. What was with people, anyway? Occupied meant exactly that.

The tap came again.

"Just a minute," she said irritably. She balled up the towel, dumped it, took a deep breath and undid the bolt.

Liam stepped inside the narrow little room. Jessie stumbled back as he shut and locked the door.

"Are you crazy? Liam, dammit, what are you doing? You can't—"

"Just shut up," he snapped, "just shut the hell—" His arms went around her and his mouth came down, hard, on hers.

He *was* crazy. And so was she, because the

instant she felt his lips on hers, she moaned, threw her arms around his neck and kissed him back. He groaned, spread his hands over her hips, pulled her against him and slid his tongue into her mouth. Jessie whimpered, arched against him and he whispered her name, slid his hands inside her jacket, under her T-shirt, and cupped her breasts. She fell back against the sink as he ran his thumbs over her nipples.

"Liam. Oh, Liam."

For one wild, wonderful moment, they were lost in passion. Then Liam tore his mouth from Jessie's, put his hands on her waist and leaned his forehead against hers.

No way was he going to take her like this. Not the first time. He wasn't even sure how he'd gotten into the lavatory. He certainly hadn't planned it. One minute he'd been sitting there, telling himself he really was interested in reading a review of a new Miami restaurant and the next, he'd looked up, asked himself why he was acting as if he was on an unimportant flight when he knew, dammit, knew that this was the most important flight of his life. He'd shot to his feet and headed for the locked door and the woman behind it without really knowing why he was going after her or what he'd do when he got there. But when she opened the door, he knew he was there to hold her and taste her and remind them both that what had started in that garden was too powerful to deny.

She was looking at him now, a smile trembling on her mouth, and he sensed, without having to ask, that her anger had come from the same place as his fake disinterest. He sensed, too, that whatever was happening between them had never happened before, not to any man or woman on the planet.

"Jessie."

Her smile broadened. It lit her face, even her eyes, and he felt his lips curve in response.

"Liam?"

"I know what you're thinking."

She laughed. She blushed, too, and he realized he'd never seen a woman blush before, not quite like that, as if she really meant it.

"I know what you're thinking, too," she said.

Hell, she was really something. He wanted to kiss her again but he knew it would be a mistake. It was difficult enough to just stand here without taking her in his arms and finishing what they'd started.

"I didn't mean that." He grinned and stepped back the inch the cramped space permitted. "I mean, yeah, that's what I'm thinking, but—" he took a deep breath "—you're thinking you did the wrong thing."

Her smile faded. "Yes."

"That you shouldn't have run away."

"Maybe," she said in a little whisper.

"You're thinking you know Bill and you don't know a damn thing about me, and that you've never done anything so crazy in your life."

He saw her try to smile again, but she couldn't quite pull it off. "Yes and yes," she said, her eyes lifting to his.

"Well, neither have I." He reached out, tucked her hair behind her ears, smoothed down the collar of her lime-green jacket. Then he looped his hands loosely behind her neck and leaned his forehead against hers again. "I've never run away with a woman."

"Never?"

Liam shook his head. "I've done a lot of things on impulse, but nothing like this."

"I thought—I mean..." She licked her lips. "William always talks about how—how successful you are with women. And I just figured—"

"That I swoop in, snatch one, and carry her off when the mood's on me?" This time, she really did smile and he kissed her gently, capturing her only with the kiss. "This is a first for me," he said softly. "I wanted you to know that."

She nodded. "Thank you for telling me."

Her tone was solemn. Liam took the edges of her jacket and drew her close. "You're welcome," he said, just as solemnly. "You should know another thing, too." He looked into her eyes. "We're not going to Hibiscus Key."

"We're not?"

He shook his head. "I know a place off the Florida coast. Flamingo Island. It's beautiful. White sand beaches, bright emerald water, soft blue sky, privacy so complete you'll think we've gone back to the Garden of Eden and that we're Adam and Eve."

"Ah," Jessie said with a smile she hoped didn't show what she was feeling. "A personal recommendation from Adam himself."

Liam had been there, all right. He thought of explaining how and why, decided this wasn't the time, and shook his head. "Only on business, sweetheart. Never with a woman."

"I didn't ask."

"You didn't have to." He framed her face in his hands, lifted it to him. "Everything about the next few days is going to be a first, Jess. For you, for me...for us."

The next few days. Well, he'd told her what he expected and she had to admire him for his honesty. William had offered forever, but that had been love. This was lust. She knew it, Liam knew it, and it was silly to pretend it was anything else.

"Jessie? Will you go there with me?"

She lifted her head and in that terrible, wonderful moment when their eyes met, she knew that she'd go anywhere with him, if he asked, that she would stay with him, if he asked.

"That sounds..." She smiled. "It sounds wonderful."

Liam kissed her. Then he unlocked the lavatory door and stepped into the cabin.

"The coast's clear," he whispered.

It was true. Nobody was watching them. The flight attendant wasn't in sight, and the man in the front row was sound asleep. Still, Jessie didn't take an easy breath until she was seated beside Liam again, safe in the protective curve of his arm. He drew a blanket over them, tucked it in and brought her head to his shoulder. It felt as if they were in a cocoon, with the rest of the world locked away.

"Close your eyes," he said. "See if you can get some rest."

She nodded and burrowed closer. She was exhausted, but she was too wired to sleep. So much had happened. She'd done things she'd never have believed herself capable of doing. Her life seemed to be spinning out of control and she still couldn't decide if that was terrifying or exhilarating. All she knew was that she'd never felt more alive than she did now. And she felt safe with Liam's arm around her, but how could that be? Nothing about him was safe. He was everything she'd avoided, everything she'd been afraid to want.

Maybe there were times it was best not to think too much about what you were doing.

Maybe this was one of those times.

NIGHT HAD FALLEN by the time they landed in Miami.

Liam told her he'd made some calls while she slept. Everything was ready for them, he said, holding her hand as he led her through the terminal.

She caught people looking at them. Why wouldn't they? Liam was so handsome. *Gorgeous* was the word. And she was probably glowing with excitement. It was hard to remember how frightened she'd been a few hours ago. She gave a soft laugh, and Liam looked at her and smiled.

"What?"

"Nothing. I just—I can't believe this is me. I mean, I never..." Jessie hesitated. "It's awful, isn't it? That this feels so right when William—"

"Don't think about Bill," Liam said quickly. "Not tonight."

He was right, Jessie told herself as she waited near the cash register in a brightly lit terminal gift shop. "I need some stuff," Liam had told her, and she'd nodded, knowing he meant things like a toothbrush, knowing he'd probably also meant condoms, but trying her best not to think about it. Not that she didn't want him to buy condoms. She was glad he saw that as his responsibility. The problem was, she could feel her nerves starting to take over again, feel the anticipation giving way to wariness.

Any second now, she half expected her conscience would demand to know if she had any idea at all of what she was doing.

She did. And she was going to do it anyway.

Liam caught her eye and smiled as he headed for the register. She smiled back, tried not to think about the condoms, looked down at the counter and the cheap souvenirs arrayed on it. She picked up a plastic alligator boasting a mouthful of teeth and an articulated tail, toyed with it, put it down, picked up a small plastic globe that held a bright green palm tree standing on white sand, set against a tropical cardboard sea. She tilted the globe and the sand turned the placid scene into a hurricane.

"Would you like that?" Liam said, and she looked up to find him standing close beside her.

"No." She gave a little laugh, put the globe down. "I mean, it's just silly, but..." Her voice trailed off. "Well," she said briskly, "did you get everything you needed?" Color flew into her cheeks. "I mean—"

"Everything I need, for now," he said easily. "There are shops at the place we're going to. We can take care of the rest tomorrow."

"Fine," she said, even more briskly. "I won't be able to pay you back until after I return to—until I can get to my bank again."

"Jess."

"Hmm?"

"What's the matter?"

"Nothing. Why would you think—"

Liam picked up the little plastic globe. "You were looking at this thing as if it were a crystal ball."

"Was I?" She tried to smile, didn't quite make it and shrugged her shoulders instead. "It's just weird, that's all. I mean, one minute, the scene inside is so peaceful. Then you just give it a little tilt and it's as if this storm comes along and sweeps everything away." To her horror, her voice suddenly quavered. "It's frightening. That the world can tilt and your whole life can change in the blink of an eye.''

"Let the world tilt," Liam said softly. He put his arm around her, drew her against his side. "I promise, I'll keep you safe."

THE PLANE THAT AWAITED THEM was small, and they were the only passengers. It lifted into a black sky hung with a huge ivory moon. Ivory, like the color of her wedding gown, Jessie thought, and shivered.

Liam shrugged off his leather jacket and draped it around her shoulders. He put his lips to her ear so she'd hear him over the roar of the engine. "Cold?"

"A little." She hesitated, then put her mouth to his ear. "How far is it to—what did you call this place?"

Her breath tickled his skin, her fragrance rose to his nostrils. Liam closed his eyes, told himself to take a couple of deep breaths when what he really wanted was to take a fistful of her hair and bury his face in it. But that would only make her more skittish than she already was. Jessie was vibrating like a tuning fork and only an idiot wouldn't have realized that she was having second and third and fourth thoughts. The last thing he wanted to do was rush her, or let her see how much trouble he was having hanging on to his self-control. He never lost control. Never. And that was all he'd done today, all he'd done since last night.

He sat up straight and cleared his throat.

"Flamingo Island," he said calmly. "I'll let you know when it comes into view."

When he did, Jessie looked out the window. All she could see was a glow in an otherwise inky sea. The plane circled, began its descent, touched down lightly. Liam thanked the pilot, climbed out, helped her down and led her to a canopied Jeep waiting in the short grass alongside the runway. The driver greeted him by name as they climbed into the back seat, and they set off.

"You won't be able to see much in the dark," Liam said, putting his arm around her shoulders. "I'll take you for a tour tomorrow. Okay?"

"Fine," she said, and she'd have laughed if she hadn't been afraid the laugh would turn into a sob. What was she doing here, in the middle of nowhere, with a man she didn't know? With her entire life, her oh-so-safe life, a million miles away?

The driver said something about the weather. Liam answered. Jessie just sat there, taking deep breaths and planning how and when to tell Liam she'd changed her mind again because she surely had. She wasn't going to stay on Flamingo Island and she certainly wasn't going to sleep with him.

Not that he'd said anything about sleeping.

Carefully, as if he might not notice, she eased free of his encircling arm.

They were traveling a road that skirted the water. She could hear the boom of the surf, smell the salt tang, but Liam had been right when he'd said she wouldn't be able to see much. Jessie bit her lip. Actually, all she wanted to see was the desk clerk, so she could find out how to arrange for a flight back to the mainland.

Finally the Jeep slowed. Several small buildings, and then a much larger one, blazing with lights, were just ahead.

Thank God, she thought—but the driver didn't stop. Jessie craned her neck and looked over her shoulder. "Wasn't that..." She licked her dry lips. "Wasn't that the hotel?"

"That was the main building, yes. But we have a private villa."

A private villa. She was still processing that when the Jeep bounced to a stop. Liam leaned forward, exchanged soft words with the driver. The man handed over a key; Liam handed over a tip and helped her from the Jeep. From the effusiveness of the driver's thanks, she knew it was a large tip. She'd been right, then, when she'd figured that his luck had been good lately. That was the way it went for men like Liam Malone. Good luck, followed by bad luck. One woman, followed by another.

She spun toward the Jeep. "Wait," she started to say, but she was too late. The vehicle was roaring away.

"Jessie?"

Liam held out his hand. She hesitated, took it, and he led her up a narrow path of crushed white shells toward a villa that rose like a block of white sugar in the moonlight. She hung back as he opened the door and switched on the light.

Jessie caught her breath.

The villa was one enormous bedroom. White tile floors. Soaring white walls. Wood ceiling fans, blades turning lazily. A wall of glass looking out on a white beach. And a bed. An enormous four-poster bed mounted on a low platform like something out of a stage set, and draped in yards and yards of gauzy white lace.

Liam had brought her to a lover's paradise. Long, hot days in the sun. Longer, hotter nights in that bed. She felt as if a cold hand had wrapped around her heart. They weren't lovers, she and Liam Malone. They were a man and a woman brought to this place by lust, and once they'd sated their hunger, they'd go their separate ways. She'd understood that.

Except, she couldn't go through with it.

She took a quick step back. "I can't," she said. "I can't do this."

Liam shut the door, leaned back against it and folded his arms. "And just when, exactly, did you reach that decision?"

His tone was polite, his expression pleasant. But there was something just under his words, something flickering in his eyes, that made her shiver.

"Does it matter? I only know that—that—"

"That you can't do this." A muscle knotted in his jaw. "Is that how you ended up saying yes to Bill when he asked you to marry him?"

Her head came up. "What?"

"You heard me. Is that how it happened? Did you lie to yourself about your feelings, tell yourself you loved him when you knew that you didn't?"

Jessie stood straighter. She dropped the tote bag and put her hands on her hips. "I never lied to William."

A tight smile etched Liam's mouth. "I didn't accuse you of lying to him. I asked if you'd lied to yourself."

"That's ridiculous. Lie to myself? About my feelings?"

She tossed her head and the spill of her hair over her shoulders was like the swirl of a flamenco dancer's skirt. Liam unfolded his arms and dug his hands into his pockets. It didn't matter that she was beautiful, that he wanted her more than he'd ever wanted a woman in his life or that he could seduce her in a moment because, even if she wasn't ready to admit it, her need for him was as wild as his for her. What mattered was that she come to him on her own, that she put aside the lies and give herself to him fully. That was how he wanted her; it was the only way he wanted her. It was the way she wanted him, too, and he needed to hear her say it.

"Why would I lie? William's a wonderful man."

"You don't love him."

"He has so many wonderful qualities that I could never list them all."

"And you still don't love him."

"He's kind and good and decent, and he'd never, not in a thousand lifetimes, do what you've done."

"No, he wouldn't." Liam narrowed his eyes and stepped away from the door. "That's the difference between us, I guess. I see what I want and I take it.''

Jessie's skin prickled. ''Charming. I bet that goes over big with the ladies.''

''Maybe I should clarify that.'' He reached behind him, turned the lock, then came toward her as lithely as a big cat, his green eyes locked to hers. ''I only take what's offered to me. I'm honest in what I want, Jessie. I don't lie to a woman.''

''That's even better,'' she said, and hoped he couldn't see the pulse leaping in the hollow of her throat. ''Really a smooth come-on, Liam. You telling a woman you know what she really wants, even when she says you're wrong.''

He reached out, cupped her shoulders with his hands. ''Don't do this. If you don't want to be with me, say so. But, dammit, don't play games. Not now.''

''I don't want to be with you. Okay? Is that what you wanted to hear?''

''I want to hear the truth.'' His eyes were dark and angry. She felt the press of his fingers, knew the tension that was building inside him because it was inside her, too. ''Say it. Say that you want me.''

''You've no idea what I want, Liam. You—''

He kissed her. Not hard. She'd have fought

him, if he had. He kissed her gently, his mouth moving lightly over hers.

"Say it," he whispered. "Let the world tilt, sweetheart. Let it happen."

Jessie's heart thudded. How could he know her so well when he hardly knew her at all? He brought her hands to his chest. She could feel his heart racing under her fingers. A honeyed weakness was spreading through her bones. It would be so easy to do...

"Let go," she said sharply. "Damn you, let go of me!"

He did, so suddenly that she stumbled back. "To hell with it," he growled.

"Oh, that's nice." Her voice trembled. She grabbed her bag and stepped around him, heading for the door. "You can't get what you want so you say to hell with it?"

"*You're* the one who's not getting what you want, because I'm not about to deliver."

"What are you talking about?"

Liam grabbed her again and backed her against the wall. "You're a coward, Jessie. You're so afraid of behaving like a real woman that you want me to do it all. What did you have in mind, huh? Am I supposed to turn into a villain? Maybe you'd like me to play at being some kind of Don Juan, a guy who can talk a woman into bed even

if she keeps saying she doesn't want to be there."
He let go of her. "Well, I won't do it. You cast
the wrong guy in the part."

Her hand whirred through the air and cracked
across his cheek. His head snapped back; he
cursed and grabbed her wrist before she could hit
him again...and then she was in his arms, her
mouth pressed hungrily to his, her fingers knotting
in his sweatshirt as his fingers tangled in her hair.

"Jessie." He caught hold of her face and
brushed her mouth with his. "Sweetheart, I'm
sorry. I didn't mean—"

"It was my fault. I was afraid, Liam. Not of
you," she added quickly. "Never of you. I was
afraid of the way you make me feel."

The look on his face made her breath catch. He
swept his hand down her back, lifting her into
him, watching her eyes darken as he pressed
against her.

"Tell me how I make you feel," he said
thickly.

"As if..." Her jacket fell to the floor and his
hands, his hard, exciting hands, slid under her
T-shirt and over her skin. When he cupped her
breasts, her voice broke. "As if—Liam. Make
love to me. Please, please, pl—"

Liam kissed her, swept her into his arms and
carried her to the bed.

CHAPTER FIVE

WHAT HAD STARTED in the garden would end here. They'd known each other for little more than twenty-four hours. Still, as Liam drew Jessie to him, he felt as if he'd waited all his life to make love to her. He wanted to tell her that, but she reached her arms up to him and sighed his name, and words became meaningless.

All that mattered was touch. And taste. And scent.

He kissed her gently, moving his lips over hers, waiting for her mouth to soften and cling to his. When it did, he slipped his tongue between her lips, groaning with pleasure at the honeyed sweetness he found waiting for him. Her arms tightened around him, her body arched against his, and he rolled her beneath him, caught her bottom lip between his teeth and eased the small hurt with a kiss. Jessie moaned softly, and the need to take her pounded through his blood.

Slow down, he told himself, slow down. He'd

been a gambler most of his life and understood
that when you bet on the toss of the dice, you put
your money on today. Only a fool would bet on
tomorrow, or think that far ahead. Right now the
wheel of fortune had spun and the little red ball
with his number on it had dropped into the slot.
That was all he'd count on but, if he was very
lucky, he could make the moment last.

He tunneled his hands into her hair and swept
it back from her face. He kissed her temples, her
eyelids, her throat as she arched against him
again. Lord, she was beautiful, especially now, as
the wildness he'd sensed in her from the beginning burst free. Little sounds were breaking from
her throat; the musk of arousal rose from her skin.
Such silky skin. Such hot, golden skin.

"Liam," she whispered, and kissed him, her
mouth taking his mouth, her breath mingling with
his breath. She slid her hands under his shirt, laid
them against his chest. His body clenched like a
fist. Slow down, he told himself again, slow
down....

And then he stopped thinking.

He grasped the hem of her T-shirt and tried to
pull it up, but the thin cotton tore apart in his
hands, exposing her to him. She wore a sheer bra,
the color of her skin. No lace, no silk, bows or

ribbons, nothing but the lush roundness of her breasts and the tawny satin of her nipples.

The room swam out of focus. He bent to her, smoothed the tip of his finger over her breasts, kissed them, licked them. Jessie cried out, moaned his name as he kissed her and swallowed her cries.

He reached for the front clasp of her bra. Her hands, cold as ice, locked on his wrists.

"Wait," she said shakily. "Liam, please wait."

His body told him to ignore her plea. His mind, or maybe his heart, said something different. *I'm afraid of what you make me feel,* she'd said, and he'd reacted by ripping her clothes off.

He groaned, rolled over and threw his arm across his eyes. "Jessie," he said when he could trust himself to talk. "Sweetheart…"

He reached out to her but she moved quickly, clutched the blanket around her and stood up, facing away from him. "I'm sorry," she said stiffly. "I know you're disappointed."

Liam got to his feet. Gently he peeled the blanket from her hands and dropped it to the floor. "Jessie," he said again, and drew her back against him. Her body was rigid against his; he knew she wanted him to let go. Instead, he put his arms around her waist. "I'm the one who's sorry, Jessie. Can you forgive me?"

"There's nothing to—"

"There is." He turned her in his arms, stroked her back, pressed kisses into her hair. "I came at you with all the finesse of a sex-starved water buffalo."

She made a little sound, half sob, half laugh, against his shoulder. "How do you know how a sex-starved water buffalo would behave?"

Liam smiled. "It's something about males, I guess. Show us a beautiful female, we lose our cool." His voice roughened. "Especially if she touches some special place inside us."

Jessie lifted her head, leaned back in his arms. "Have I?" she whispered. "Touched something special inside you? Because—because that's how I feel about you, as if you've reached into me and—and..." She sighed and buried her face against him again. "And that's crazy. We don't even know each other."

"We will, though. I promise." Gently he scooped her into his arms. She looped her arms around his neck and sighed.

"You must think I'm an idiot."

"What I think," Liam replied as he made his way across the room, "is that we've damn near broken the how-long-can-a-human-being-stay-awake record.'' Jessie laughed. It was a real laugh this time, a wonderful sound, and Liam grinned at her. ''You like that, huh?''

''You made it up. There is no such record.''

''Well, if there isn't, there should be.'' He kissed her, then jabbed the light switch with his elbow. Velvet darkness swallowed the room. ''Okay,'' he said briskly, ''here's the plan.''

''The plan?'' Jessie swallowed. Liam was heading back toward the bed, washed in ivory moonlight. ''Liam?'' She hesitated. ''I think you should know…I mean, if you think it's the light— if you think turning it off will—''

''I know that, sweetheart.''

He laid her on the bed and stood over her. She caught her breath as he pulled off his sweatshirt. He was beautiful. The hard, masculine face. The broad shoulders. The wide chest and narrow waist.

''What I thought,'' he said huskily, ''was that we'd get some sleep.''

''I won't be able to sleep,'' she said quickly. ''I'm too—too—''

''Let's try, anyway.'' She heard the thud of his sneakers as he kicked them off. His hands went to his waist and he opened his belt, undid his zipper. The denim rustled as he stepped out of his jeans and stood before her, clad only in a pair of dark boxer shorts slung low on his hips. "The thing is, I can't sleep with the light on." A smile curved his lips. "Or with most of my clothes on, either." The mattress dipped gently as he sat down beside her. Jessie could hear her blood beating in her ears.

"Liam," she whispered.

"Shh." He took her hands, brought them to his chest, and she caught her breath at the feel of hot skin, tight muscle, silky hair. "That's not so awful, is it?"

No. Oh, no, it wasn't. It was wonderful touching him. He was so alive, so real, so excitingly male.

His fingers were at the front clasp of her bra. This time she didn't stop him. A languid heat was moving through her body. She could almost feel herself turning to liquid. When the clasp gave way, he drew the bra off and tossed it aside.

"I want to feel your skin against mine," he said. "That's all, I promise. Is that all right, Jessie?"

She didn't answer. She couldn't, but Liam seemed to understand her silence. He put his arms around her and when her naked flesh touched his, she caught her breath. He lowered his head to hers and kissed her. Desire, sharp and hot, began to boil in her blood.

''Let's just get you out of some of this stuff.''

She sighed her acquiescence, sat up so he could undress her. When she had nothing on but her panties, he eased her back against the pillows and kissed her mouth, her throat, her shoulders. She closed her eyes and waited, her skin tingling, for the feel of his lips on her breasts.

This was what she'd dreamed of last night. This slow, scalding seduction. Liam in her arms. A burning ache, low in her belly. When he finally stretched out beside her, she turned toward him, trembling, every breath searing her lungs.

''Liam,'' she whispered. ''Liam—''

He put two fingers lightly over her lips, drew the blanket over them. Then he gathered her into the strength of his embrace.

She almost came apart at the first touch of his body against hers, the first awareness of his erection pressed against her belly. She waited for him to move against her, to strip away the last flimsy barriers that separated them, yearned for it to happen.

''Go to sleep, darling,'' he whispered.

He stroked her back, kissed her temple. After a while, his breathing slowed. So did hers, but she knew it was meaningless. He was pretending and so was she. Neither of them would get any sleep, not pressed together like this, with their hearts beating in unison, her breasts against his chest. Nevertheless, his heartbeat steadied. Hers did, too.

He really had fallen asleep, she thought in surprise.

Moments later, so did she.

LIAM CAME AWAKE SLOWLY.

It was just before dawn. A pale pewter light was seeping into the room, and Jessie was still in his arms. She was asleep, cradled against him, and he fought back the desire to dip his head and awaken her with a kiss.

Only when she was ready. Not until then.

He put out his hand and smoothed a silken tangle of honey-gold hair back from her cheek.

The amazing thing was, he'd made it through the night. A smile angled across his mouth. What he'd pretty much figured was that lying with a half-naked Jessie in his arms would kill him. The first touch of her skin against his had almost been his undoing. He'd told himself to lie still, slow his breathing, convince her he was asleep. It must have worked because, eventually, she'd sighed and relaxed against him.

Holding her, keeping her safe through the night, wasn't much of a price to pay for having her come to him without fear or hesitation.

The funny thing was that he'd never much liked

to spend the night with a woman. Not that he was a guy who was into wham, bam, thank you, ma'am. He always held a woman after sex, shared her bed for an hour or two before getting up and heading home. If a woman asked him to stay the night, and most did, he said he was a restless sleeper. It wasn't a lie. He almost always awakened sprawled across the bed, the blankets off and the pillows on the floor.

Liam drew Jessie closer.

This time, though, he'd awakened just the way he'd gone to sleep, lying in the center of the big bed, Jessie in his embrace, her head on his shoulder. Sometime during the night, she'd put her hand on his chest. It lay just over his heart. He'd moved a little, too. He'd thrown his leg over hers in what any shrink would surely have defined as a subconscious gesture meant to keep her with him.

Strange behavior for a man who preferred to sleep alone.

Maybe the simple truth was that sleeping alone wasn't as important as waking up alone. Maybe he just didn't want to greet the day with a stranger beside him, even if she wasn't actually a stranger. He'd never been into one-night stands. The thing was, no matter how hot the affair, a man and a woman were forever separate entities, and making love to a woman was less intimate than sleeping alongside her. It might sound crazy, but it had always seemed logical—until now. He'd just slept beside Jessie, they hadn't even made love, and he'd known her for all of—Liam lifted his arm, squinted at his watch. For all of thirty-something hours.

Thirty-something hours, and in all that time he'd phoned Bill exactly once and left a message that told him nothing. But then, how did you go about telling a man who was crazy with worry that he had nothing to worry about, because you'd not just found his bride, you'd run off with her?

Liam eased his arm from beneath Jessie's shoulders and sat up. He took one last look at her, then pulled on his jeans and made his way to a small alcove near the patio where a rattan cabinet hid a minifridge, a stocked wine rack and an electric coffeemaker, ready to go.

He turned the coffeemaker on. That was one of the first things he'd changed when he bought Flamingo Island Resort.

"We don't provide any food or drink in the villas," the manager had told him with an officious little smile. "Most of our guests are honeymooners. They don't want to be bothered with such things."

Liam knew the officious smile probably was

the result of the rumor that said he'd won the place in a game of poker. So he'd smiled pleasantly and pointed out that that was precisely the reason the resort would provide champagne, wine, coffee and tea, plus a basket of fresh-baked breads to be left on each porch in the morning.

"And by the way," he'd added with a smile that was more than a match for the manager's, "just so we understand each other, Mr. Edding, I didn't win this place playing cards."

Edding had paled. "No, sir. I never said—"

"Be sure you don't."

They'd gotten along just fine after that.

Liam took a bright red mug from the cabinet and filled it with hot coffee.

Two years had gone by since that day. Flamingo Island, always successful, had become a world-class resort. Liam had added two more properties to the string, and hadn't played so much as a hand of poker in all that time. It had taken a while, but he'd finally figured out that a man couldn't go through life gambling on everything.

Until he'd stood in the departure terminal at Sea-Tac Airport and decided to bet his honor against his need for a woman he knew he couldn't have.

The hot tropical sun was rising over the ocean,

turning the water to shimmering gold as he stepped out onto the patio. He sipped at his coffee, leaned his elbows on the sea wall and tried to figure out what to do next. A man of principle would call Bill and tell him everything. Good Lord, how could he do that? What was "everything," anyway? What would he say? "Bill, I don't know how to tell you this, but Jessie and I are together. We're in our own private world, and she won't be coming back to Seattle for a while."

"Liam?"

He turned around. Jessie was standing in the doorway. She'd pulled on his sweatshirt but not her jeans. Her hair was a confusion of honey-gold waves. Her eyes were bright as the ocean, her skin as flushed as the morning sky, and he knew, in that moment, that he was never going to let her leave him.

"I thought I smelled coffee," she said with a hesitant smile. "Liam? About last night—"

He was beside her before she'd finished the sentence. He swung her into his arms, kissed her, and she put her arms around his neck.

"I wasn't ready last night," she whispered. "But I am now."

Liam carried her inside, lay down with her in his arms. He rolled her onto her belly, drew her hair away from her neck and pressed his lips to her skin. The scent of her rose to his nostrils, a delicious blend of flowers, salt air, and woman. Gently he eased up the sweatshirt, eased down her panties. He heard her catch her breath as he kissed the long curve of her spine, the dimple at its base before turning her over.

"You're beautiful," he said huskily, his eyes locked to hers.

She smiled. "You are, too."

He laughed softly. "Men aren't beautiful, sweetheart. Handsome. Magnificent. Muscular and altogether fantastic, yes, but not—"

Jessie grabbed his hair and dragged his mouth to hers. "I'll give you all the compliments you want, later. But first..." She sat up, tugged the sweatshirt over her head and tossed it aside. "Look at me, Liam," she said, "and tell me you like what you see."

Like? There were no words to describe what he felt, looking at her. Her body was as beautiful as her face, her skin all flushed, her breasts high and rounded, the tips already beaded with excitement.

"I love what I see," he said softly.

"Touch me, then." She reached up, stroked her finger gently over his mouth. "Kiss me. Make love to me."

He was on fire for her. Liam stripped off his jeans and shorts, and went into Jessie's arms.

He'd dreamed of this, but the reality was better than any dream. The sweetness of her breasts, of her belly, the startled little sound she made when he opened her to him, found the secret flower that was the essence of her femininity and kissed it.

Her cry of shocked pleasure combined with her taste and rocketed through his blood. When she began to tremble, to convulse under the sweet torment of his mouth, he moved quickly up her body and, on one long, possessive stroke, sheathed himself in her satin heat.

"Jessie," he whispered, and when her lashes fluttered open, he bent to her, cupped her face and kissed her deeply. "Look at me, sweetheart, and say my name."

"Liam. My Liam." A long, keening cry burst from her throat.

"Jessie," he said, and then he let go of everything, the years of loneliness and of doubt, and exploded deep within the welcoming warmth of the woman he loved.

CHAPTER SIX

JESSIE SAT on the sun-drenched patio, wearing a white, fluffy robe provided by the hotel and drinking coffee while she waited for Liam to return from what he'd smugly referred to as a "secret mission."

She smiled over the rim of her cup. It didn't take much effort to figure out what that "secret mission" was. She'd made a face when she'd started to dress, teased him about only men not shuddering at the thought of putting on yesterday's clothes, and he'd gotten a glint in his eyes. Suddenly he'd wanted to know her favorite colors, whether she liked short summer skirts or long ones, if she preferred bikinis or what he'd referred to as "you know, those clingy, one-piece jobs."

She put down her cup, stretched her arms high overhead, then lay back on the chaise longue.

He'd gone to buy her something to wear, she was sure of it. Still, she'd act surprised when he turned up with a swimsuit and a T-shirt and shorts and, yes, she'd stop being silly about it and accept them as gifts because it was pointless to stand on ceremony with the man who was your lover.

Her lover. She rolled over on her stomach and closed her eyes. It was such a lovely word. The only bit of darkness came when she let herself think about the emptiness she'd face when their days here ended.

And the pain she'd caused William.

"No," she said aloud.

She wasn't going to think about that, not yet. It was too soon to think about what lay ahead. She was happy, happier than she'd ever imagined possible, and she wasn't going to spoil her joy for anything.

She sat up, stretched again and took her coffee cup into the villa and rinsed it in the sink. The serving cart, bearing the remnants of the gargantuan breakfast Liam had ordered earlier, sat waiting in the corner. She thought of the waiter's smile when he'd delivered it, all that food for only two people, and how she'd felt herself blushing, knowing what he must have been thinking, that only a man and woman who'd spent hours making love could possibly be hungry enough to tackle waffles and eggs and a hundred other things.

And she thought of how Liam had taken her in his arms after the door closed, how they'd laughed while she fed him strips of bacon and he'd licked her fingers clean until laughter turned to sighs and sighs to passion.

She thought about how much she loved him.

There wasn't any point in trying to pretend she didn't, not to herself. It was impossible to fall in love with a man you hardly knew, especially when that man wasn't the kind she'd ever imagined wanting, but there it was. She loved Liam the way she'd wanted to love William, and what good would it do her?

"None," she said softly as she sank down on the edge of the bed.

Liam loved making love with her. He loved holding her, and he even seemed to love being with her. But he didn't love her. He'd never love just one woman. That was just the way they were, the Liam Malones of this world. Her mother had told her once, probably in a moment of desperation, that she'd made a terrible mistake thinking she didn't have to hear her man say those simple words, and thinking she could be happy with one who preferred wandering the world to making a real home.

Not that she'd have to be concerned about any of that with Liam. Even if a miracle occurred, which it wouldn't, but even if it did, and Liam looked at her and said those magical words, "Jessie, I love you..."

Even if that happened, he could never be hers because the shadow of William, and what they'd done, would always be there, chilling their happiness.

Tears rolled down her cheeks, and wasn't that ridiculous? Here she sat, weeping because there wouldn't be a forever-after when that was exactly what she'd walked away from, choosing, instead, a few short, sweet days in Liam's arms.

Jessie sat up straight, scrubbed her knuckles over her eyes. Liam would be back soon and she didn't want him to see that she'd been crying, didn't want to waste whatever little time they had left on tears or recriminations or—

A knock sounded at the front door. He must have locked himself out. She dabbed at her eyes again, ran her hands through her hair and went to open the door. But it wasn't Liam on the steps, it was a bellman with a load of gaily wrapped boxes in his arms. There were more boxes in the Jeep he'd parked alongside the villa.

"Packages for you, Miss Warren."

"There must be some mistake. I didn't order—"

"No, ma'am. Mr. Malone did."

"But..." She stepped back as the bellman

started past her. It took two trips before he'd transferred everything from the Jeep. Jessie looked from the boxes to the bellman's smiling face. "I don't—I'm afraid I don't have anything to—"

The man's smile broadened. "Mr. Malone took care of that." He put his hand to his forehead, flipped her a brisk salute. "Enjoy the day, ma'am."

Jessie nodded. "You, too," she said, or thought she said, as the door swung shut. For a few minutes she just stared at the packages. Then, carefully, she unwrapped one, then another and another. Silk skirts, cotton tops, cashmere shawls and lace underwear spilled onto the bed.

"Liam," she said, laughing with delight, "oh, you crazy, wonderful man."

She took off her robe, let it slip to the floor, pulled on a cropped white top and a long, gauzy skirt and looked at herself in the mirror. Her eyes were bright with pleasure, her mouth was pink from Liam's kisses, her hair was a mass of curls and waves. She hardly recognized herself. What had become of Jessica Warren? Who was this woman in the mirror, wearing such beautiful things, her hair loose, her feet bare, all propriety and dignity forgotten?

Jessie's smile faded. And how could a heart soar, then break, all in the same moment?

"Liam," she whispered, "how can I let you go?"

Falling in love wasn't supposed to be like this. But, oh God, it was.

FALLING IN LOVE wasn't supposed to be like this.

Liam walked slowly along the shoreline, his hands tucked into the pockets of his jeans. He'd left Jessie on the patio, lying sleepily in the sun after they'd consumed a room service breakfast so huge even he'd laughed, and he'd been the one who ordered it. It was just that she'd smiled and said "you" each time he'd asked her what she wanted for breakfast and he'd felt honor-bound to take her up on the offer. When he finally reached for the phone, he hardly knew his own name so he'd ordered waffles and eggs, pancakes and bacon, biscuits and toast, strawberries, mangoes and coffee.

They'd eaten on the patio, and it was a good thing the villas were heavily screened by bougainvillea, because when Liam groaned and said he couldn't eat another mouthful, Jessie made a stern face and said he had to finish what he'd ordered. Laughing, she'd fed him a strip of crisp bacon. But when he reached the final bit and sucked her fingers into his mouth, her laughter had died, and they'd made love on the chaise longue, with the hot sun beating down.

Great. He was thinking what it was like to make love with Jessie and turning himself on.

"Malone," he said lightly, under his breath, "you're some piece of work."

Indeed, he was. He was a man in love, and the world had suddenly turned into a wonderful place, and never mind the gray smudge on the horizon, or the brisk breeze. It was a beautiful day, and it would be even more beautiful in—he looked at his watch—in just about five minutes, when the things he'd ordered were delivered to the villa.

After he and Jessie had finished breakfast and made love, they'd showered together. Liam gritted his teeth and told himself not to think about the way Jessie's skin felt wet, or how her hair streamed down over her breasts, or how he'd soaped her body, all of it, all of her....

He cleared his throat.

They'd put on the robes the hotel provided. Jessie had scooped up her clothing and wrinkled her nose.

"What?" Liam had asked, and she'd laughed and said that only a man would look so perplexed when a woman shuddered at the thought of taking a shower and then putting on the same stuff she'd

worn the previous day. He'd clapped his hand to
his heart, as if she'd wounded him deeply, ac-
cused her of being the female equivalent of a
chauvinist pig, admitted she was probably right
before dropping a kiss on her smiling lips. Then
he'd put on his jeans and sweatshirt. "Stay just
the way you are," he'd warned, "while I under-
take a dark and dangerous secret mission."

And, he thought with smug assurance, he had.

He'd walked to the main building. First, he'd
seen to his own things. He kept simple clothing—
jeans, T-shirts, chinos and a blazer—in the
owner's suite. He'd packed some of it and arranged for delivery to the villa. Then he'd gone
to the gift shop and, well, maybe he'd gone just
a little bit overboard.

"I need some things for a lady," he'd told the
clerk. "She's…" He'd held his hand up, just
about at mid-chest. "She's, uh, maybe so tall.
And…" He'd started making curves in the air
while the clerk watched politely and he felt his
face turning red. "And she's, I don't know, a size
six or maybe an eight. Her hips are…well, her
waist is…"

The clerk had finally shown him some pity.
"Lisa," she'd called, and a girl had come out of
what he figured was the stockroom, a pretty girl

about Jessie's height and weight. "Is the lady similar to Lisa, Mr. Malone?"

"Yes," Liam had answered, because he knew better than to think anybody wanted to hear him babble that Jessie wasn't similar to any other woman in the world.

The clerk had dismissed Lisa with an imperious wave of the hand. "What kinds of 'things' did you have in mind, sir?"

Shorts, he'd told her, and T-shirts. Oh, and a swimsuit. And how about a couple of those long filmy skirts? Those little cotton tops? Those silk things, with the lace?

"Camisoles," the clerk had said with a quick smile.

"Camisoles, right. And sandals. And that dress, the one with the little flowers." He'd paused at a counter, picked up a little vial, opened it, sniffed it, smelled lilacs. "This, too," he'd said, "and that. And this—"

In the end, he'd ordered too much to carry, so he'd arranged for it to be delivered.

"Your lady is a lucky woman," the clerk had said, and Liam had replied that he was the lucky one....

It wasn't true.

His smile fled. He bent down, plucked a small white stone from the sand and threw it far out into the surf. He wasn't lucky, because this couldn't last. Jessie had made love with him, but she still belonged to another man. Not just any other man, either. She belonged to William.

Liam stared blindly over the water. Hell, no. Falling in love was not supposed to be like this.

He sighed and began walking again. Not that he was any kind of expert. Until now he'd figured love was a concept dreamed up by salesmen trying to sell soap. One man, one woman, bells ringing, fireworks going off—how could any of that be real?

But it was. You saw a woman, a special woman, and all that stuff happened. And if you were lucky, it was that way for her, too, so that both of you knew it could be like this for the rest of your lives. He knew, anyway, and even if Jessie hadn't said so, she knew it, too. It was there, in her eyes, in the way she kissed him, in everything she said and did.

She loved him, he loved her, and what could possibly come of it? Nothing but grief, all around.

"Dammit," Liam said. What else was there to say without putting back his head and howling his anguish to the gods who had to be looking down and laughing until their sides split? Fate sure had a hell of a sense of humor. Liam Malone, who'd figured love was about parts of the body that hadn't a damn thing to do with the heart, who'd thought that even talking about settling down marked a man as a sucker extraordinaire—that very same Liam Malone was in love.

"Find my Jessica," Bill had said, "and do the right thing."

Liam mouthed an oath, kicked at the sand and watched the shiny particles rise into the air. Maybe the day wasn't as beautiful as he'd thought. Little whitecaps danced on the restless sea and that dark smudge in the distance was growing. The woman at the gift shop had mentioned that a storm might be blowing in.

"It won't last," she'd promised. "Trouble in paradise never does."

She had it wrong. What never lasted was paradise. How come he hadn't remembered that? Life had a way of holding out happiness, waiting until you reached for it and then snatching it back. He should have told that to the clerk—although it was probably just as well he hadn't. She'd only have looked at him as if he was nuts. Not a good thing, he thought with a little smile, for the staff to label the owner. Not that it seemed so great that he owned Flamingo Island or that he'd turned his life around.

It would only mean something if he could share it with Jessie.

He'd kept it a secret from Bill because he'd wanted to tell him in person, how he'd awakened one morning with a fortune in his wallet and a French movie star in his bed. He'd been on a hot streak that month, winning hand after hand at high-stakes poker tables, dazzling the oil barons and investment bankers he'd outplayed, and he'd opened his eyes that particular day, looked at the famous face on the pillow beside his, then at the opulent gold-leaf ceiling in his posh hotel suite, and said, "Malone, just what the hell are you doing?"

So he'd kissed the movie star goodbye, dumped his money into the startup stock of an Internet company he'd heard about over a hand of poker. Two weeks later, he cashed out, rich. Rich beyond his wildest dreams. But it became boring, reading the financial news and watching his money make more money. He took a chunk of it, looked around for opportunities, bought this place for no better reason than that he found it peaceful and beautiful. The next thing he knew, he'd turned himself into a man he'd thought he'd never want to be. To his amazement, he liked the transformation—but he'd never planned on falling in love. Love hadn't worked for his parents, who'd probably died screaming at each other as their car hit the overpass abutment, or for the rich and famous he'd known over the last decade.

Except it had happened. With Jessie, the only woman he'd ever love. He'd tell her that, slowly. Work up to it, because as much as he loved her, it scared him.

The villa door swung open. Jessie smiled at him. She had on one of the outfits he'd bought, a little white top with a long, filmy skirt, and she'd left her hair loose, the way he liked it.

"Jessie," he blurted. "Sweetheart, I'm crazy in love with you."

She didn't say anything. Then, just when he thought he'd made the worst mistake a man could ever make, she threw herself into his arms.

"Liam," she said. "Oh, Liam, I was so afraid it was only me."

He swept her up, kicked the door shut and, for a little while, nothing mattered but showing each other exactly what being in love meant.

THEY LAY IN EACH OTHER'S ARMS in the center of the bed, safe and secure in the aftermath of their lovemaking.

Liam inhaled the fragrance of Jessie's hair. "You smell delicious. Is that the perfume I gave you?"

"Mmm-hmm. It's lovely."

"And what you were wearing. I loved you in that. You know, the long skirt and that top, the one that looks like somebody shrank it."

She laughed softly and snuggled closer. "You must have emptied out that gift shop."

Liam took her hand from his chest and brought it to his lips. "Did I buy the right size? If there's anything you don't like—"

"Everything was perfect, but I can't let you spend so much money on me."

"I'd give you the world, if you'd let me."

Jessie lifted her head from his shoulder and kissed his mouth. "Thank you," she said softly. "But even if the cards have been good to you lately—"

"Aha." Liam grinned. "So, Bill told, and the deep, dark secret's out, huh? That I used to be a gambler?"

"Uh-huh. Give you a deck of cards and you're...used to be?"

"That's right, sweetheart." He rolled over, gently eased her onto her back. "I've reformed."

"A reformed rogue." Jessie touched the tip of her finger to his mouth. "William will be pleased to...I mean, that's nice to hear." She smiled, though the smile was wobbly. "But I can't see you working nine to five."

"People change." A muscle knotted in his jaw.

"You think you know exactly who you are and what you want out of life. Then, I don't know, you walk down a street or read a book..." He cleared his throat. "Or you agree to be the best man at an old friend's wedding, and—"

"Don't." Jessie put her hand over Liam's mouth. "Please," she whispered, "not yet."

"We have to talk about it. You know that."

"Yes. But—"

"I love you with all my heart, Jess." His voice was deep, his words a whisper. "I want you to know I've never said those words to another woman, and I never will."

"Liam. Oh, God, Liam—" Her voice broke. "What are we going to do? I thought—I thought this was just a—a.... I don't know what I thought. When I first saw you—"

"I know. It was the same for me."

"It terrified me but I told myself it was only— that it was only—"

"Sex," Liam said softly. "Yeah, so did I. A couple of hours in bed." He pulled Jessie into his arms and held her close. "Then I got on that plane and saw the way you looked at me. Or maybe it was when I undressed you and you went into my arms so trustingly. I only know that I love you, that I'll always love—"

Jessie pressed her mouth to his. He could taste her tears in her kiss.

"I'll always love you, too," she whispered. "But—but you know that this is all we can ever have."

"No! Don't say that." He sat up. "I want to marry you, Jessie. I want to do all those things I never believed in. Buy a house. Have kids. Live happily ever after. Sweetheart, don't you understand? Without you—"

"My life will be empty, too." The words shuddered from her lips. "I tried to tell myself we could make a life together, Liam. But we can't. William will always be between us." She began to weep. "You know what we have to do."

He did know. Each beat of his heart reminded him of his promise to Bill. "I'll do the right thing," he'd said. But the right thing had changed. The world had changed. Right was wrong, and promises were pain.

"I'm not giving you up," Liam said fiercely.

"You love William as much as I do, and he adores you." She took an unsteady breath. "You're his hero."

"God." He let go of her, sat up and raked his fingers through his hair. "Some hero I turned out to be."

"He told me once that you and I are the two

most important people in his life." Jessie knelt beside Liam and took his hand. "It would be bad enough if one of us let him down, but if—if we betray him—"

Liam couldn't listen to any more. She was right but he wouldn't admit it, not to her, not to himself. Instead, he sprang to his feet.

"There's got to be a way!" He grabbed his jeans and stepped into them. "My mind's going in circles. I have to take a walk." He stopped and took Jessie's hands. "I'll come up with something. I'm not going to lose you, Jess. Not after I spent my life looking for you."

Jessie laughed, but by the time she rose from the bed and put her arms around him, her laughter had turned to tears.

"I know," she sobbed. "I'll never forget you, or this time we spent together. I'll always adore you, Liam, always."

He kissed her as if the world were going to end at any moment. And, in a way, it did, because when he returned to the villa less than an hour later, Jessie was gone.

CHAPTER SEVEN

RAIN BEAT DOWN on the island, and a driving wind rattled the fronds of the palm trees that towered over the villa.

Inside, a grim-faced Liam faced three hapless hotel employees.

"It's a simple question," he said coldly. "Surely one of you can answer it."

The desk clerk who'd arranged for Jessie's flight to Miami, the driver who'd taken her to the airstrip, even the chambermaid who'd gone to the villa hours ago to make the bed and had ended up, instead, directing Jessie to the office, looked at him, then at each other. No one spoke. Finally the desk clerk shifted his feet.

"I've explained, sir. The young lady phoned the desk. She said she wanted to leave the island. She asked—"

"I know what she asked," Liam snapped. "What I'm having difficulty with is that you didn't think to inform me."

"I'm sorry, sir. There didn't seem to be any…"
The clerk licked his lips. "We—we didn't know
that you'd object." He looked to his companions
for support. Both of them were nodding their
heads vigorously. "We were only doing what
your guest asked us to do, sir."

"I see." Liam folded his arms and glared at
the man. "Do you always do what guests ask you
to do?"

The clerk swallowed dryly. "We—we try to
accommodate all requests, Mr. Malone."

"Suppose a guest wanted to jump off the roof?
Would you let her do that?"

"No, sir. Certainly not. But—"

You're acting like an idiot, Liam said to himself, while the clerk stumbled for words. Just what
was it he expected these people to have done?
Tell Jessie she couldn't fly out without permis-
sion? Wait for him to give his okay? Guests of
the hotel were supposed to be treated with courtesy, and they'd done that. As for Jessie—she'd
done what had to be done, what he hadn't had the
courage to do despite his promise to Bill, and now
he was venting his anger on these poor people
rather than dealing with the truth.

He and Jessie could never have a life together.
One of them, at least, understood the meaning of
the word *honor.*

"—did the best we could, sir, by accommodating the lady's wishes, and—"

"That's okay," Liam said, interrupting the clerk's stumbling explanation. "You're right. I'm wrong." He dredged up a smile. "In fact, I was way out of line."

Color began seeping back into the man's face. "If we'd known you wanted us to speak with you first, Mr. Malone—"

"Forget it. It's a free country. The lady wanted to leave and that's that." Liam clasped the man's shoulder, then shook hands with all three employees. "There'll be something extra in your paychecks this week," he said briskly, and herded them to the door. "How's that sound?"

"Thank you," they said, "thank you very much, Mr.—"

Liam shut the door, let the smile slip from his mouth and sank down on the edge of the bed. After a moment, he buried his face in his hands. Jessie was gone and he couldn't go after her even if he wanted to. The smudge on the horizon had turned into a charcoal bank of clouds, spewing rain and wind. Until the weather cleared, there was no way off the island.

Besides, what was the sense in going after her? Their affair had been doomed from the beginning.

Jessie had said it all in the last few minutes they'd been together.

"You're his hero, Liam."

Liam groaned and fell back against the pillows. Oh, yeah. He was Bill's hero, all right.

If only he'd met Jessie a year ago. Six months ago. Hell, a day before Bill put that ring on her finger would have been enough. What a difference that little bit of time would have made. He and Jessie would have met, there'd have been that same wild, lightning-hot attraction....

No. He wasn't going to do that, play a game of "if only" that would do nothing but make the pain worse. Liam sat up and scrubbed his hands over his face. He'd lost Jessie, lost her forever....

To hell with that. Bill was his oldest friend, yes, but Jessie—Jessie was everything.

He sprang from the bed, grabbed his leather jacket, reached for the phone. No way was he going to lose her. He loved her. He adored her. He...

He had no right to her.

The jacket fell from his hand. There was no way around the truth. He'd betrayed Bill, made a promise he hadn't kept. Now he had to go back, face Bill as Jessie was going to do, admit his guilt and ask his forgiveness before fading out of the picture. Anything else—like loving Jessie—he'd relegate to the past.

Liam lifted his head. He could hear the faint sound of an airplane engine in the distance. He went to the door, opened it, looked up into a clear, rain-washed night sky. The small plane that ferried guests to and from the island, that had taken Jessie from him, forever, was coming in for a landing. He could tell the pilot to gas it up, turn it around.

Not yet.

Tomorrow was soon enough to fly west. Once he did, it would all be over. Could it really be only a couple of days since he'd first seen Jessie, days that had changed his life, forever?

Liam sank down on the bed again, lay back and put his arm over his eyes. *Jessie,* he thought, *Jessie, my love.*

Early the next morning, he was on a flight headed for Seattle.

IN MOST PARTS OF THE COUNTRY spring meant flowers, sunshine and birdsong. In Seattle, tucked between the rainforests of the Olympic Peninsula and the towering Cascade Mountains, spring meant rain.

Jessie had never minded that. She'd heard some people say the gray skies were depressing, but she loved the misty feel of the air, and those moments when the clouds parted and Mount Rainier was visible on the horizon always made her spirits lift.

Nothing could make that happen, not this spring.

Except for a stop at her bank, where she'd picked up a new ATM card and used it to take some money from her account, and then an hour spent buying a few things to wear, she'd been huddled in her hotel room ever since she'd arrived in the city. She'd intended to face William immediately but once she stepped into the hotel, she'd realized she had to get herself in hand first. She felt as if her life had stopped when the plane carrying her away from Liam lifted into the air. She'd watched their villa recede and then the hotel until, finally, the island had been only a small dot in the vast ocean.

"Liam," she'd whispered, and she'd wept for what could never be, the lifetime of love they might have shared. If only they'd met some other time, some other place.

Jessie sighed.

Perhaps not.

What she'd shared with Liam couldn't possibly last. She'd always known that. Such fire, such heat, would only burn out over time. For all she knew, it had already turned to cold ashes, otherwise why wouldn't Liam have come after her?

No. No, she didn't want him to do that. She wanted to set things right. If William was willing to take her back, she'd—she'd...

She'd never let it happen.

Yes, she'd beg his forgiveness, tell him he was a wonderful man and that he deserved to find a woman who'd make him happy, but she wasn't that woman. She loved Liam. She always would, for the rest of her life, even though she'd never see him again.

A sob caught in her throat.

"God," Jessie whispered, "help me, please."

She reached for the phone, punched in the number for the big house on the lake before she had too much time to think about what she was doing. Her heart was thumping; her hand was so wet her fingers slipped on the plastic handpiece. Who would answer? The maid? The cook? Or William, himself. What would she say to him? What—

"Thornton residence."

Jessie blinked. "Carrie?"

"Jessica?"

"Yes. It's...did I dial the wrong number? I'm sorry. I've been so—so upset that—"

"*You've* been upset?" Carrie gave a cold

laugh. "I hardly think so. William's the one who's upset."

Jessie closed her eyes. "I know."

"You don't know. How could you, when you and that man have been—have been..."

"William—William knows about—about Liam?"

"Certainly he knows. That man called from the airport. We know you and he flew to Florida. Together."

Each word was a brand and an accusation. "Carrie." Jessie took a breath, expelled it and rose to her feet. "Put William on the phone, please."

"I don't know that he'll want to talk with you."

"Maybe not. But ask him, will you?"

"He's busy. If he has time later, maybe he'll call you back."

The line went dead. Slowly, Jessie hung up the phone. William couldn't call, not without her phone number, and Carrie hadn't requested it.

Something had changed while she'd been gone, some delicate shift of power and loyalty. Jessie thought about it for a minute. Not that it mattered. William might, in fact, despise her, refuse to see her. He certainly had the right.

Still, she had to face him.

Jessie put on her jacket, picked up her car keys and locked the door to her room behind her.

LIAM PULLED TO THE CURB just before Bill's driveway and sat staring straight ahead as the car idled.

"Come on, Malone," he muttered, "get it together."

He had to before he faced Bill. It had all seemed so clear back on Flamingo Island. Confront Bill, explain that what had happened was nobody's fault but his, that he'd never intended to betray their friendship, wish him well and walk away. He'd worked it all out during a couple of endless hours spent pacing the first-class lounge at the Miami airport, refined it during almost six hours of flying time.

So how come he still didn't know what he'd say when Bill opened the door?

Liam smiled grimly. All things considered, he might not have to worry about it. He'd ring the bell, Bill would open the door and their conversation would begin and end with Bill delivering a hard right to Liam's jaw.

That was what he'd do, if a man stole Jessie from him. Not that one punch would do it. He'd want to kill the bastard. Jessie was his. She'd always be his. Nobody could ever take her from...

Liam crossed his hands on the steering wheel and pressed his forehead to his wrists.

She wasn't his. That was the point of this whole infuriating exercise. He'd come back to acknowledge the truth, that he had no claim on Jessie, even though he'd never stop loving her, that he was the worst friend a man had ever had, a lying, cheating, double-dealing, no-good bastard.

"Just admit you're a rat," he muttered, "and then get the hell out."

He straightened in his seat, put the car in gear, shot up the driveway—and looked up just in time to see a small white car come hurtling up behind him.

"Son of a—"

He jammed his foot on the brake pedal, felt the jolt and heard the glass breaking as the white car's headlights shattered. He threw open the door and jumped out.

"Damned idiot," he snarled, as he strode toward the other car. "Where'd you learn to drive?" This jerk needed driving lessons. That was fine. Better than fine, considering his mood. If Bill slugged him, he couldn't slug back, but if this idiot so much as made a sound—

"Get out of there," Liam said. He yanked open the door, reached in...and saw Jessie. Her face was pale, her eyes were red rimmed. From tears, he knew, because he'd cried, too, in his heart, and he knew, too, that the person he'd really been lying to was himself.

No matter what happened, he would never let her leave him again.

"Jessie," he said, and she was in his arms before her name had left his lips.

"Liam," she sobbed. "Oh, Liam, my love."

"Why did you leave me?"

"Why didn't you come after me?"

"I didn't want to leave you, but—"

"I wanted to go after you, but—"

They spoke together, words, voices, crossing in a hurried blur. Then they fell silent. Liam's arms tightened around her, Jessie raised her face and they kissed.

"I love you," Liam said fiercely against her mouth. "And I'm not letting you go."

"Don't." She sighed. "Oh, don't. Not ever. I need you, Liam, I need you and love you and—"

The door to the house swung open. Liam and Jessie turned and saw Bill and Carrie standing in the entrance. Jessie started to pull away, but Liam kept an arm around her waist, anchoring her to him.

"Well," Carrie said, "isn't this a pretty sight?"

Liam ignored her. "Bill," he said steadily.

Bill Thornton's expression was unreadable. "Liam."

"William," Jessie said, "William, I'm so sorry."

"It's my fault," Liam said. "Not hers." He dropped his arm from Jessie's waist and took her hand. Her fingers were icy, and he squeezed them reassuringly. "Jessie had nothing to do with what happened."

Bill's mouth thinned. "How noble."

"Bill, look. Neither of us planned this. I mean, we didn't expect..."

"And that's supposed to make it okay?" He took a step forward. "My best friend. And my fiancée. What a fine pair you make."

"William." Jessie's voice broke. "We never meant to hurt you. You have to believe that."

"The only thing I have to believe is that I never knew either one of you. I'd have trusted you with my life, Liam. And Jessica...I thought you were the most wonderful woman in the world, but now—"

"Watch what you say to her," Liam said, his voice hardening. "I'm the one who made a mess of things, understand? You want to take a shot at me, go ahead."

Bill stared at the two of them, then shrugged his shoulders. "What would be the point? It wouldn't change anything." A tired smile lifted one corner of his mouth. "Besides, the last time I tried that, Malone, I ended up almost needing to have my jaw wired shut, remember?"

Some of the tension eased from Liam's stance. "Yeah, but that was ten years ago, and you were dumb enough to think you could tackle me five yards from the goalpost."

"It was just a game of pickup football," Bill said. His eyes went to Jessie, then back to Liam. "You weren't defending something as basic as your right to fall in love with Jessica." He cleared his throat. "That's what this is all about, isn't it? You're in love with her."

Liam's jaw knotted. "Yes."

"And you, Jessica? Do you love him, too?"

"Yes," Jessie whispered. "I love him with all my heart." Tears rose in her eyes. "But you'll always be special to me, William. I want you to know that."

"Special," Bill said, and gave a bitter laugh. "And I'm supposed to take comfort in that?"

"I promised you I'd do the right thing," Liam said, his eyes steady on Bill's. "It's true, I made some detours along the way, but in the end, I know that what I'm doing now *is* the right thing." He paused, twined his fingers through Jessie's. "I love Jessie. And she loves me. She can't marry you because it would be a travesty. Everyone would end up cheated—you, me, and her—and not one of us would be able to live down the shame for the rest of our lives.''

After a long moment, Bill sighed. ''I guess that's one of life's toughest lessons, that the right thing isn't always easy to figure out.''

''No,'' Liam agreed, ''it isn't.''

''Anyway, I'm not blameless. Part of this mess is my fault, too.''

''That's not true,'' Carrie said, with indignation. ''You didn't do anything!''

''But I did.'' Bill took Carrie's hand and held it tightly. ''I didn't give Jessica any options. One night she agreed to have dinner with me and the next thing she knew, I was making her part of my life. Isn't that right, Jessica?''

''If you mean that you were wonderful...'' Jessie smiled shakily. ''You sent me flowers every day. You phoned all the time.''

''Sure. I figured if you were right for me, all I had to do was convince you that I was right for you. I guess I thought, well, if we were a great team in the office, we'd be terrific as husband and wife.'' He cleared his throat. ''Obviously, I was wrong.''

''Bill.'' Liam cleared his throat, too. ''I don't expect you to forgive us—''

"Good." Bill stood straight and tall, and looked directly into Liam's eyes. "Because I haven't. You want the truth, Malone? I don't know if I'll ever forgive you. Accepting what's happened is one thing. Forgiving it is another."

Liam nodded. "I understand. Let's—let's give it some time, okay?"

"Yeah," Bill said, "let's do that."

He stepped back, still clasping Carrie's hand, and the door swung shut. Liam stood motionless for a long moment. Then he swallowed hard, turned to Jessie and took her in his arms. She was weeping, and he drew her close and kissed away her tears.

"Don't cry," he said softly. "It's going to be okay."

"Poor William. He's so hurt." She sniffled, and Liam dug out his handkerchief and handed it to her. "He was right, you know." She smiled through her tears. "We were a great team in the office. We should have left it at that."

Liam smiled, too, as he took her in his arms again. "You liked being assistant to the CEO, huh?"

"Yes." Despite her tears, she tilted her chin in defiance. "Don't tell me you're one of those male chauvinists, Malone, who doesn't like the idea of his woman having a job."

"To begin with," Liam said gently, "you're not going to be my woman, you're going to be my wife."

Jessie sighed. "I like the sound of that."

"And you're right, I don't like the idea of you working for some guy."

"Now, wait a minute, Liam—"

Liam kissed her. "Working *with* some guy," he said, smiling into her eyes, "an equal partnership kind of thing, well, that's different."

"What are you talking about? Do you mean you're thinking of starting some sort of business?" She snuggled against him. "Oh, that would be lovely. But you don't have to do it for me. I know you like to bounce from place to place, and if that's what you want, it's what we'll do."

Liam wrapped his hand around the back of her neck and tilted her face to his. "I have a lot to tell you, sweetheart. About me, about my life..." He could feel his heart lift. "Let's just say I've got some irons in the fire that can use your skills and, no, we're not going to bounce from place to place, unless that's what you really want."

"I just want you," Jessie whispered. "Only you, my love."

"Always," Liam said softly. "For all the rest of our lives."

EPILOGUE

THEY WERE MARRIED less than a month later, in the solarium of the handsome house they'd bought on one of the beautiful San Juan Islands in Puget Sound.

Jessie had wanted to be wed in the garden, because a garden was where they'd met, but Liam convinced her to take pity on their guests and have the ceremony inside the solarium. The northwest was still in the grip of a chilly spring, but that day the sun shone. The first of the spring crocuses had pushed their heads through the snow and Jessie had decorated both the house and the solarium in the same soft lilac color.

She wore white silk; Liam wore a black tux. A guitarist played softly in the background. There was champagne and caviar, oysters and Dungeness crab, and on top of the five-tiered wedding cake, in place of the figures of a bride and groom, there stood a small globe that Liam had given Jessie at breakfast.

It was made of crystal and, inside it, a tiny porcelain bride who looked suspiciously like her, and a porcelain groom who more than resembled Liam, embraced before a bright green palm tree standing on white sand, set against a tropical cardboard sea.

Jessie had wept with happiness.

"Turn it over," Liam had said gently. She did, and as the sand turned the placid scene into a hurricane, she saw the inscription engraved on the bottom of the globe.

Let The World Tilt, it said.

Now, the ceremony that would join them forever was moments away. Their future stretched ahead, brightly shining. There had been some difficult moments as Jessie's friends made peace with the fact that she'd fallen in love with another man on what was to have been her wedding day, but she and Liam were so much in love that no one could fault her, or him, for following the dictates of their hearts. And they were filled with plans, plans that Liam had already put into motion. He was CEO of Flamingo Resorts; she was Chief Financial Officer. They worked together, played together, loved together.

Their lives had taken the shape fate had meant them to take all along.

And it would all be perfect, Jessie thought, as

she stood in the encircling curve of her husband's arm—they'd both agreed that they didn't want to be separated, not even for the hours prior to their wedding. It would be perfect, but for one thing.

"You're thinking about Bill," she said softly.

Liam nodded. It was the first time she'd referred to William by his nickname. Liam knew that, in some subtle way, it marked a passage in their lives.

"Yeah," he said. "I am. I didn't really expect him to come." He ran an index finger under his collar. "I just thought—"

"Liam?"

"I thought, well, maybe he'd realize that our friendship—"

"Liam." Jessie looked up at Liam and smiled. "He's here, darling."

Liam stiffened, then looked across the room. Bill and Carrie were coming toward them. A huge smile broke over his face.

"Bill." He stepped forward. "Man, I'm so happy you—"

"Me, too."

The men stared at each other. Then Liam held out his hand and Bill clasped it.

"Good to see you," Bill said.

"Yeah." Liam grinned. "Same here."

Bill let go of Liam's hand and drew a smiling Carrie forward. "We're engaged, Carrie and I." He looped his arm around her shoulders. "Crazy, isn't it? That so much good came out of this whole thing?"

"I think it's wonderful." Jessie touched her cheek to Carrie's. Then she took Liam's arm and smiled at the others. "Just wonderful."

"So," Bill said briskly, after a moment had gone by, "what's the deal here, huh? Did you manage to bribe some poor slob into standing up for you?"

Liam laughed, though Jessie noticed his green eyes were suspiciously bright.

"Actually, I figured, why go to all that trouble when the best man of my choice was going to show up any minute?"

Bill grinned. "You really sure you want to do this, Malone? Sign your freedom away to one woman?"

"Absolutely." Liam turned to Jessie and took her in his arms. "For all of my life."

Jessie smiled. "Forever," she said, and kissed the only man she had ever, would ever, love.

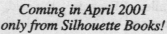

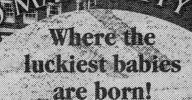

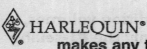

From bestselling
Harlequin American Romance author

CATHY GILLEN THACKER

comes

TEXAS VOWS

A McCABE FAMILY SAGA

Sam McCabe had vowed to always
do right by his five boys—but after
the loss of his wife, he needed the small-town security
of his hometown, Laramie, Texas, to live up to that
commitment. Except, coming home would bring him
back to a woman he'd sworn to stay away from.
It will be one vow that Sam can't keep....

On sale March 2001
Available at your favorite retail outlet.

HARLEQUIN®
Makes any time special ™